"Would you like to
Travis asked, surpri
not that difficult anc
older, well-trained horses that would be perfect for a beginner to learn on."

Tilting her head, Scarlett considered his offer. "And you'd be willing to teach me?"

"Yep." Though doing so would entail them spending more time together, he didn't reckon it would take that long. She just needed to know the basics, not anything fancy.

"I think I'd like that." The mischievous sparkle in her emerald eyes should have warned him. "As long as you promise to be civil."

"Civil?" He frowned. "I've gone out of my way to be—"

"I'm kidding." She cut him off with a wide grin. When she placed her hand on his leg, he knew he was in trouble. "You don't have to take everything so seriously."

Though logistically impossible, her fingers seared his skin through his jeans. He was staring down at her, her lovely face raised to his, laughter curving her sensuous mouth...

* * *

If you're on Twitter, tell us what you think of Harlequin Romantic Suspense! #harlequinromsuspense

Dear Reader,

Imagine growing up without the slightest idea of your father's name. And then, in the midst of grief over losing your mother, she gives you one last gift—his identity. This is what happens to Scarlett Kistler, and when she travels to the small town of Anniversary, Texas, to meet him, she gains so much more than a father.

Travis Warren has been a rancher ever since he could walk. Raised by his stepfather, Hal, he has taken on everything during Hal's illness. With big oil companies wanting to drill on the land and disrupt their way of life, the last thing Travis wants or needs is a Southern belle showing up on their doorstep claiming she's Hal's daughter.

In the days that follow, when it seems like someone is trying to either scare Scarlett off or hurt her, will Travis step up and do what he always does, take someone in need under his wing? Or will the sexual lure she presents be too much for him since he's already had his heart broken by a city girl? The ranch is his life and he'll do whatever he has to in order to preserve that.

Trying to make up for lost years with a dying man, Scarlett, too, tries to resist the pull of attraction Travis presents. But she's never been a quitter and any attempts to scare her off make her more determined to stay. The rewards are greater than she ever could have imagined.

If you like a good mystery, a Texas ranch and a sexy rancher, you'll enjoy this story. I sure enjoyed writing it.

Happy reading!

Karen Whiddon

TEXAS RANCH JUSTICE

Karen Whiddon

HARLEQUIN® ROMANTIC SUSPENSE

Recycling programs for this product may not exist in your area.

ISBN-13: 978-1-335-66195-1

Texas Ranch Justice

This edition published by arrangement with Harlequin Books S.A.

For questions and comments about the quality of this book, please contact us at CustomerService@Harlequin.com.

Printed in U.S.A.

Karen Whiddon started weaving fanciful tales for her younger brothers at the age of eleven. Amid the gorgeous Catskill Mountains, then the majestic Rocky Mountains, she fueled her imagination with the natural beauty surrounding her. Karen now lives in north Texas, writes full-time and volunteers for a boxer dog rescue. She shares her life with her hero of a husband and four to five dogs, depending on if she is fostering. You can email Karen at kwhiddon1@aol.com. Fans can also check out her website, karenwhiddon.com.

Books by Karen Whiddon

Harlequin Romantic Suspense

The CEO's Secret Baby
The Cop's Missing Child
The Millionaire Cowboy's Secret
Texas Secrets, Lovers' Lies
The Rancher's Return
The Texan's Return
Wyoming Undercover
The Texas Soldier's Son
Texas Ranch Justice

The Coltons of Red Ridge

Colton's Christmas Cop

The Coltons of Texas

Runaway Colton

The Coltons of Oklahoma

The Temptation of Dr. Colton

The Coltons: Return to Wyoming

A Secret Colton Baby

Visit the Author Profile page at Harlequin.com for more titles.

To the caregivers. All those nursing a parent,
spouse or child through a serious illness.
I know how hard it is. It's the purest demonstration
of love.

Chapter 1

The next time he heard the words *oil well* mentioned with the same sort of breathless tone used when speaking of "sweet tea" or Jesus, Travis Warren thought he might just lose what little shred of self-control he had left.

It wasn't bad enough that he did the work of three men along with a small, handpicked crew of ranch hands, trying to keep the HG Ranch afloat. Or that he'd given up his privacy and allowed his mother, sister and five-year-old nephew to move in with him in the small foreman's house he previously occupied alone. In addition to that, he had the monumental worry about his stepfather, Hal Gardner, who appeared to be wasting away while not a single doctor could come to a consensus as to what might be wrong with him.

Hal was just as opposed as Travis to allowing an oil

company to take over even one-half acre of his land. In fact, as owner of the HG, he'd insisted he didn't want to hear another word about allowing drilling.

At least that decree shut everyone up. As long as Hal was around. But the rest of the family as well as most of the neighboring townsfolk felt no compulsion to be quiet around Travis. In fact, his own mother, Vivian, continued to act as if making a deal with Wave Oil Company would be their salvation. Quite frankly, the notion made Travis feel sick.

For Travis, working hard and looking after his own was a matter of pride. For over fifty years, his seventy-eight-year-old stepfather, Hal, had managed to keep the HG Ranch going as a profitable cattle operation. Travis planned to do the same, without any help from any oil company or their money. Right now, a company called Wave Oil was pushing hard for the right to drill on Hal's and several of the other ranchers' land. Hal had already said no, privately confiding to Travis that he'd continue to do so until the day he died. Which unfortunately might be sooner than either of them would like.

Wave Oil and their offers of easy money had managed to divide the town. The townsfolk, those without stakes to the land, were all for it. They liked the idea of more jobs and money being spent in downtown Anniversary. As for the ranchers and farmers, almost every single one of them had refused. They'd even banded together in order to present a solid front. Travis just kept hoping the commotion would die down, the oil people would move on to another town and life could return to normal. Or as normal as it could be with Hal so sick.

Ideally Travis preferred to spend most of his time outside, whether working cattle or repairing fences, but these days he made sure to take breakfast, lunch and dinner a couple of times a week at the main house, so he could make sure Hal ate. They'd hired a day nursing-housekeeping aide named Delilah, who helped out between ten and five. She'd turned out to be irreplaceable.

The rest of the time either Travis's mother, Vivian, or his sister, Amber, poked their heads in to check on Hal and keep things running smoothly.

Even though Vivian and Hal had been divorced for five years, they'd remained friendly. Which was helpful, especially since Vivian continued to live on the ranch, staying with Travis in the foreman's house. Travis had just started to get used to having her there when his sister, Amber, had arrived back home a year ago. She'd been sad and angry and a little needy, smarting from her own failed relationship, and Travis couldn't say no. Especially since she'd come with her young son, Will, in tow. Having a five-year-old boy around had been an unexpected bonus, and Travis treasured the relationship he had with his nephew.

These days, the only peace and quiet Travis could find was on horseback, working on the ranch. He had a full house and no one seemed to have the slightest inclination to move out. To be honest, Travis wasn't sure he wanted them to. He'd gotten a little lonely with the place all to himself, especially after his fiancée had broken off the engagement. These days it felt good to have family to spend time with. Between the ranch and his stepfather, Travis considered his life to be mostly full, even if he didn't have a life-mate to share it with.

Pulling up to the main house at the end of a hard day's work, he sat in his truck for a moment and admired it. The stately Victorian farmhouse could use some work, but it still managed to appear inviting. He particularly loved the wide front porch. As a kid, he'd spent plenty of time there, watching while Hal made homemade ice cream, or rocking in one of the big rockers while watching a storm sweep in from the west. If he ever built his own place, he planned to make sure it had a porch just like it.

He entered the main house just as Hal slammed the old-fashioned rotary telephone back in its cradle. The old rancher slumped in his wheelchair, wheezing for air. Immediately, Travis rushed over, kneeling down next to him. "Are you all right? Where's Delilah?"

"I banished her to the kitchen." Straightening, Hal frowned and scratched his head. "I told her to go away and quit treating me like an invalid. That goes for you too, so get up and quit acting like I'm about to keel over at any second."

Hal preferred everyone to pretend he wasn't sick. Travis got it. He figured he'd probably be the same way if he were in Hal's shoes. Pushing to his feet, he squeezed his stepfather's bony shoulder. "She should know better," he said. Hal's breathing seemed better, so Travis relaxed a little. "Who called?"

"Damn oil company again." Grimacing, Hal wheeled himself over to his spot in front of the television, which was currently off. "*Nightly News with Lester Holt* comes on in a few minutes."

Which was his way of saying he wanted to be left alone. Fine. As long as daylight remained, there was work to be done. Travis glanced at his watch, then headed outside to check on the barn. One of his best mares was due to foal at any time, and he'd stationed a couple of teenagers inside the barn, with instructions to fetch him immediately if she showed signs of labor.

Once outside, Travis dragged his hand across his jaw and then strode out toward the barn. He'd been keeping tabs on Hal for years, even before the older man had gotten sick. They were close, in the way of firm-jawed, silent types. Travis admired him and looked up to him. Though not related by blood, he considered the older man his father, and knew Hal felt the same.

Several times over the last few years, Travis had stepped in and kept Hal from getting bilked of what remained of his savings. The older man believed in living simply, much to the dismay of his ex-wife, Travis's mother, Vivian. And since she'd signed a prenup agreement before they'd married, once they divorced, she could do nothing to change that. Still, as Hal aged, he became a frequent target for scammers.

So far, Travis had managed to fend off two religious organizations, one long-lost cousin who'd claimed to have millions in a foreign bank and a few gold-digging women looking for a sugar daddy. It wasn't that Hal was stupid—far from it—but the old man had a heart of gold. He always tried to see the best in everyone. And if he could help, he'd do his damndest to try.

At least this time, he refused to listen to Wave Oil with their false promises of untold riches and undisturbed land. Travis would be eternally grateful for that.

At the barn, he interrupted the teens giggling and playing games on their phones. Though they assured him nothing had changed, Travis checked on the mare anyway. She still wasn't ready, though he had a feeling it would be soon. Maybe even tonight. He reminded the boys of their responsibilities, reiterated that they were to call him at the slightest sign of the horse going into labor and left.

Walking back toward the house, he stopped and stared at the cloud of dust heading his way. A little red car, moving much too fast, barreled down the private road toward the entrance to the ranch.

What now? He cursed. He figured it would head past the main house, toward his place, most likely to visit either his mother or sister. One of them likely had made a new *friend* or something. Though usually they took care to give him advance notice so he could stay far, far away.

But no, the car pulled up in front of the main house instead and parked. He couldn't make out if the visitor was a man or a woman due to the tinted glass.

Until she opened her door. Definitely female. Moving with a long-legged grace that reminded him of a thoroughbred filly, she got out of her little compact car. Huge sunglasses in place, perfectly curled, long black hair swirling around her slender shoulders, everything about her screamed north Dallas. In other words, high society.

A chill snaked up his spine, sweeping over him. He shook it off, still staring, since he was not a man who believed in intuition or omens. Picking up his pace, he beat her to the house and waited, watching as she strode up the sidewalk, her high heels clicking on the cracked cement.

She didn't acknowledge him until only a few feet separated them, and then she pulled off her dark glasses and met his gaze. Her vivid green eyes were both startling and familiar—he knew only one other person with that exact, unusual shade. Hal.

Again, a feeling that everything was about to change swept over him. He squared his shoulders. Not if he could help it. Like everything else in his life, he'd meet this challenge head-on. Head tilted, he crossed his arms, waiting for her to speak first. When she didn't, he shook his head. "No point in wasting time. I don't know how many times we have to tell you people to stay off our property. The answer is still no. Now go on and get back in your car and head back toward town."

With that, he turned and went inside, closing the door behind him with her still standing silently out on the front porch.

And then he waited. Though he doubted it, he really hoped she'd get back into her car and leave, exactly as he'd told her to.

Of course she didn't. A sharp knock on the front door made him curse under his breath. The sound startled Hal awake in his recliner. "Well?" he demanded, his faded green eyes bright as he stared at Travis. "Are you going to answer that?"

Damn. He'd been hoping to keep Hal out of yet another confrontation with someone from Wave Oil. Reluctantly, Travis nodded. Though both he and Hal had told them in no uncertain terms to stay off the property, clearly they'd once again completely ignored his wishes.

Taking a deep breath, he yanked open the door to glare at the dark-haired young woman standing there, coolly composed in her formfitting dress and high heels. Ignoring the instant tug of attraction, he glared at her.

"I thought I asked you to leave," he said. The coldness in his tone should have warned her he wouldn't be amenable to a sales pitch, no matter how much she fluttered her pretty green eyes.

"Well, that's not really up to you, now is it? I'm here to see Mr. Hal Gardner," she drawled, appearing not the least bit put out. He couldn't place her Southern accent, though it definitely wasn't East Texas, that's for sure. Out of state, most likely. Alabama, Tennessee, maybe even Mississippi or Georgia. Another spark of interest, which again he immediately quashed.

"For the one hundredth time, he isn't interested. Stay off our land." He started to close the heavy door, but she slipped one pointy-toed, clearly expensive, patent leather high-heeled shoe inside to prevent him from doing that.

"What do you think you're doing?" He stared at her foot in disbelief.

"So sorry," she drawled. Her clearly false smile lit up her heart-shaped face, making her emerald eyes sparkle. "While I'm not sure why you think I'm here, I can tell you Mr. Gardner isn't even aware of my existence. Therefore, there's no way you can truthfully state he's not interested. Maybe you should give him the chance to meet me and decide for himself. Now if you don't mind fetching him...?"

Fetching? Any other time, any other place, any other man might have fallen for her over-the-top feminine charm, but Travis was immune. He'd learned the hard way that women like her and men like him wouldn't work.

"For Pete's sake, Travis. Let her in," Hal ordered, his cantankerous tone curious. "I want to hear what she has to say."

Though he didn't want to, Travis opened the door wider and stepped aside so she could enter.

"Thank you," she said, confidently moving past him, close enough that he caught a whiff of her scent, something exotic and floral. Heels clicking on the wood floors, she walked with an easy sort of grace, both innocent and confidently sensual. Desire hit him low in the gut, which irritated him, though it didn't come as a surprise. No matter what she wanted, she was a gorgeous, sexy woman. Even men like him couldn't ignore such flawless beauty.

Heartbeat echoing in her eardrums, Scarlett stepped into the old Victorian house, admiring the polished wooden floors. A million times she'd pictured the man who'd sired her, even though her childhood fantasies eventually became replaced with teenaged bitterness and, finally, adult acceptance. She'd never met him and hadn't even known his name. Until she'd found her mother's diary after her death and finally learned his name and address.

Hal Gardner of Anniversary, Texas.

Though at first she'd been frozen in fear, how could she not go meet him? She'd made the trip out west as fast as she could. Finally, here she stood. Hopeful, and trying not to be. Yearning, yet telling herself she'd made it thirty years without him, so it wouldn't hurt at all if he refused to acknowledge her and ordered her to leave as the handsome younger man had.

"In here," the tall, grumpy guy ordered, turning and leading the way. "He's in the living room."

Trailing along after him, she caught her breath at her first glimpse of a man who could only be her father.

Sitting in front of the TV in a wheelchair. He looked frail, old, and she could see that he was ill from the pallor of his skin, the way his green eyes—the exact shade as her own—seemed to burn too brightly in his wan and lined face.

He wore his thinning gray hair combed to one side. His too skinny body appeared almost skeletal, though his smile seemed friendly enough. She caught a hint of skepticism in his expression, as though he also believed she might be here to try to sell him something.

Deliberately, she kept her expression neutral, though her steps faltered for a second before she regained her equilibrium.

"Well, ain't you a pretty one," the old man drawled. "Now tell me you ain't with Wave Oil so I don't have to throw you out."

Suddenly struck dumb, she shook her head. "I'm not," she managed. She'd rehearsed a speech a bunch of times while she'd searched for him. All of that seemed woefully inadequate now.

Cocking his grizzled head, he continued to study her. "You look awfully familiar. Like someone I used to know, many years ago."

Finally, she found her voice. "My name is Scarlett. Scarlett Kistler. People always said I'm the spitting image of my mother, Maggie. Maggie Kistler."

When she said her mama's name, Hal stiffened. Suddenly alert, watchful even as he slid his gaze over her once more. "Maggie," he breathed. "You do look an awful lot like her. Maggie Kistler was the love of my life." He swallowed, his Adam's apple bobbing in his throat. "Now there's a name from the past. I always wondered what became of her."

For the first time she realized her mother's death might come as a shock to him. "She passed away," she said softly. "Not all that long ago."

He stared at her, disbelief and perhaps a brief flash of pain in his expression. "Was she ill? She wasn't very old."

Younger than he, that's what he meant, Scarlett figured.

"She had breast cancer," she said, her voice still going shaky when she said the awful words. She'd think she'd be used to the idea by now. She'd helped her mother fight for the last year and a half, and the word *cancer* had become an integral part of their vocabulary.

A shadow crossed his face. "Cancer. I hate cancer," he said, his voice thick with emotion. He turned his face, giving her his hawklike profile while a muscle worked in his too-thin cheek.

Wondering if he also had some sort of cancer, she waited silently, not sure what to say. Her mother's passing had drained her, made her realize she was now completely and utterly alone in the world. Without family. Until she'd found the diary, buried deep in a box of old photographs and mementos in the back of her mother's closet. She'd realized she wasn't actually alone. She had him. Her father. Whether he wanted to be or not. For the first time she wondered if he'd even been aware of her existence.

Finally, he swiveled his head to look at her again. "Why have you come here?" he rasped. "Surely you didn't travel all this way to bring me news of her death."

"No," she admitted, glancing toward the doorway to see that the other man had remained, standing in a defensive stance just inside the doorway. As if he thought she might attempt bodily harm on the old man and he might have to jump in and perform a rescue. She wished he would leave, but lacked the nerve to ask him to go. Instead, she squared her shoulders and turned back to face the old man in the wheelchair.

"When my mother left you, she was pregnant," she told him, holding her chin high and hoping her voice didn't quiver with nerves. "I'm realizing you might not have been aware of that." Another deep breath. Steady, steady. "That's why I'm here. I wanted to meet you. I'm your daughter."

Hal stared, his mouth working. "No," he said faintly. "She wouldn't have done that to me."

Behind her, she was conscious of the other man moving into the room and toward her. A gesture from Hal's age-spotted hand stopped him.

Scarlett refused to look away from her father, fully expecting him to deny her, demand proof, a DNA test. She wouldn't blame him. Here she was, showing up after thirty years, a grown child he hadn't even known he had.

"Why?" The plaintive question tore at her heart. "Why wouldn't she have at least let me know?"

"I'm not sure. She was a proud woman," she said softly. "She never even told me your name. All she would say was that she'd loved you once."

Pain formed new creases in the loose skin on his face. He swore, looking away and covering his face with his shaking hands.

"You need to go." The younger man grabbed her arm. "Don't be bothering him with your ridiculous claims."

Furious, she jerked away, glaring up at him. "Don't even think you can sum up my life that way. I came here to meet this man—my father. This has nothing to do with you, whoever you are."

Eyes hard, he started to speak.

"Wait," Hal interceded. "She's right, Travis. This is private, between the two of us."

The other man shook his head. He wouldn't go easy, she saw. "Don't let her come in here and try to con you. I'm not sure what she wants, but she wants something. I can see right through her. She's a gold digger, nothing more."

"A gold digger?" She glanced around the room with its threadbare carpet and worn furniture in disbelief.

He snorted, opening his mouth again. Hal's sharp bark of laughter forestalled him.

Her first reaction was hurt, that he found her somehow amusing. Her second, alarm as his laughter segued into a wheeze, then a round of jagged coughing that appeared to steal his breath away, making him gasp for air.

She rushed over, ignoring the other man completely. Once she reached the wheelchair, she wasn't sure what to do. She settled for patting Hal's hunched back as if he was a small child, making soothing sounds while praying he wouldn't choke to death or something.

After a moment, he recovered. Swiping at his eyes with his gnarled fists, he flashed her a wan smile. "I want you to stay and visit awhile."

The other man made a sound of protest, which both Scarlett and Hal ignored.

"You must be hungry," Hal said. "After such a long

trip. Let's go into the kitchen and I'll have my nurse's aide make you something to eat."

Nurse's aide. She wanted to ask out loud if he was ill, though the question seemed so superfluous since he clearly was. With what, she didn't know, though maybe he'd tell her.

Her mother had been much younger than him, so much so that Maggie had written in her diary that the two of them had kept their affair secret. She'd wanted to marry, but Hal had refused, saying it wouldn't be fair in the future, when he'd become an old man and she remained a young woman still.

This had only served to break Maggie's heart. She'd believed their love could easily have survived such a test. Clearly, Hal had felt otherwise.

Scarlett followed the wheelchair into the kitchen, marveling at how easily he controlled it with his stick-thin arms. This room too had clearly seen better times. The faded linoleum had begun to crack and chip, and the wooden cabinets were scratched and dull.

She almost shook her head at the other man's earlier comment. Why would she attempt to take anything from someone who clearly had so little? Her mother had left her wanting for nothing—their little home paid for, along with the proceeds from a nice life insurance policy. She had more than enough to open her own art gallery, a long-term goal of hers.

The nurse appeared, a stout, dusky-skinned, stern-faced woman with a mop of curly black hair. Seeing Scarlett, she smiled, which totally transformed her face. "A visitor!" she exclaimed, sounding delighted. "It's been so long since someone came to see Mr. Hal. Have a seat, let me get you a tall glass of sweet tea."

Smiling back, Scarlett pulled out a chair. "Thank you, I'd like that."

"And something to eat," Hal put in. "Please, Delilah. She's come a long way to get here and I'll bet she's starving."

"Definitely." Delilah glanced toward the other room. "What about Travis? Will he be joining us?"

Travis. So that was the other man's name. Who was he exactly? Did he work for her father or was Travis Hal's son, her half-brother? She watched Hal carefully, curious to hear his answer.

"I think he went out to the barn," Hal finally said. Catching Scarlett's gaze, he grimaced. "Don't mind him. He feels he has to look out for everyone, particularly me."

"Does he work here?" she asked.

Hal smiled. "He's my stepson and, yes, he runs the place."

Stepson. So not related. She only nodded.

"Tell me about yourself," Hal urged, covering her hand with his. The gnarled and age-spotted fingers made her inexplicably feel like crying. "After all, I have thirty years to catch up on."

Delilah placed two plates in front of them. Huge sandwiches, overflowing with chicken and lettuce and tomato, as well as a generous dollop of potato salad, and a pickle. She beamed at Scarlett as she placed tall, sweating glasses of iced tea on the table. "Y'all let me know if you need anything else, okay?"

"This looks fantastic," Scarlett said. "Thank you so much."

Looking from one to the other, Hal nodded. "Yes, thank you, Delilah."

"You're welcome. Now, Scarlett, how long are you staying? Would you like me to make up one of the guest beds for her, Mr. Hal?"

"Please," he rasped, before eyeing Scarlett. "If that's all right with you? I'd really like you to stay as long as you like."

"I'd love that," she responded softly. "And Delilah, I don't want to make extra work for you. If you'll just leave the linens on the dresser, I can make the bed up myself."

"As if," the older woman sniffed. "Not in my lifetime. I'll get everything ready for you myself." She bustled off without a backward glance.

Hal chuckled, but his smile disappeared the instant the nurse was out of sight. Grimacing, he pushed his plate away. "She keeps trying to get me to eat, even though she's a nurse and should know better. It's hard for me to eat much these days."

Scarlett squeezed his hand. "Please try, for me. You've got to keep your strength up so you can get better."

Though a slight frown creased his forehead, as if her comment baffled him, he didn't argue. Instead, he released her fingers and made a show out of lifting up his own sandwich. He took a huge bite, winking at her, and then nearly gagged as he tried to swallow.

Concerned, she jumped out of her chair and went around to pat him on the back. "Are you all right? Should I call Delilah?"

"I'm fine," he rasped, eyes watering as he waved her away. "Just swallowed wrong. Sit down and enjoy your food."

Heart still pounding, she sat back down. Still watching Hal closely, she picked up her sandwich, struggling to keep parts of it from falling out. Her stomach rumbled as she took a big bite. Not wanting to appear ravenous, which she was, she chewed slowly, even though she wanted to wolf the entire thing down.

Some of the tightness in her chest eased as Hal took another, much smaller bite. Maybe this was going to be all right after all.

It appeared she'd be staying. As she walked out to her car to retrieve her bags, she resisted the urge to do a happy jig. Honestly, she'd been hoping her father would invite her to spend some time getting to know him. There was nothing like the death of the person you believed to be your only parent to make one feel rudderless and alone.

Grief slammed into her. She missed her mama. Maggie had been fascinating and lively, a bright light in Scarlett's world. She had also been mercurial, flitting from one thing to another as her interest dictated. But she'd loved Scarlett fiercely, and the two of them had been close. Maggie had supported Scarlett's interest in the arts, even when another parent might have insisted she get her degree in something practical, like business or education.

And now Maggie was gone too soon, though she'd fought long and hard. Scarlett had been forced to bury her terror and sorrow, offering her support as she watched her vivacious flame of a mother burn down to a smoldering ember, and finally ashes.

Learning about her father had pulled Scarlett away from the depths of her grief. Even though she hadn't realized Hal was sick. From the looks of him, whatever ailed him was serious.

Dagnab it, she wasn't sure she had the fortitude to go through this again. Right now, she knew she'd do whatever it took to get Hal well. With or without the taciturn Travis's support.

Chapter 2

After Hal informed him Scarlett would be staying in the main house for as long as she wanted, Travis took himself home. He didn't say a word to Vivian or Amber about Hal's visitor. They'd find out about her soon enough and he didn't feel up to attempting to answer all their questions. Especially since he knew so little himself.

Scarlett Kistler. Gorgeous, sexy and totally out of her league on a working cattle ranch. Was she really Hal's daughter? Her eyes were the same shape and color as his, but otherwise Travis saw little resemblance. Regardless, this woman, with her bright green eyes and her false air of sincerity, had come at the worst possible time, right as Hal appeared to be losing his battle with whatever mysterious illness attacked his body.

To be objective, on the plus side, as Hal neared the

end of his journey, Scarlett's appearance offered him the one thing he'd always craved and never had. Family. Despite the fact that Travis considered Hal his father, and vice versa, Travis would always only be a stepson. He wasn't blood, wasn't true kin. Though Hal had never said so to Travis, he'd told Vivian that the lack of a son or daughter of his own was one of his biggest regrets. Vivian, who never could keep a secret to save her life, had passed this on to Travis without a thought for how this knowledge might make him feel.

Most days, Travis tried not to think about not being Hal's actual son. When he'd been younger, he'd often hoped the rancher would adopt him, but Hal never had. And now, it was too late. He couldn't change anything, and things were what they were. He'd do as he always did—work hard and take care of Hal and the others as best he could. If this dark-haired newcomer brought Hal happiness, Travis wasn't one to begrudge him that.

And if Scarlett had ulterior motives for being there, hopefully she'd look around the decaying Victorian and realize Hal didn't have ready access to huge sums of money. Most of his savings had been depleted trying to find out what was wrong with him.

As for his assets… There was the ranch, of course. And the livestock. Oh, and the fact that oil had been found on neighboring pastures. Once she learned about that moneymaking potential, she'd probably be all over the oil company's offers like a flea on a dog. Vivian and Amber certainly were.

Travis couldn't worry about that. He had enough on his shoulders as it stood. No matter whether Scarlett was the real deal or not, her very presence had the potential to break Hal's heart.

Damned if he'd let it get to that. For now, he'd keep an eye on her. But the second she gave the slightest inclination toward trying to use Hal in any way, Travis would immediately put a stop to it. He'd get rid of her, offer her money, whatever it took. And make sure she told a good, believable story so Hal would be none the wiser.

The next morning, up before sunrise as usual, he chugged down a large cup of strong black coffee and ate his usual breakfast of eggs, bacon and toast. Though he normally stopped by and had breakfast with Hal, he wasn't up for dealing with Scarlett first thing before starting his day.

Like always, he had a long list of chores to take care of. Today, he planned to repair some fence line on one of the remote pastures. Most of those were best accomplished on horseback. Eager to get started, he saddled up his best gelding and headed out.

Riding always soothed away any ill temper or worries. The motion of the horse under his saddle, the connection he shared with the animal, felt better than driving any machine made by man. He checked on some fence line under repair before joining up with a couple of ranch hands bringing in a herd of cattle. By the time they'd gotten them into the new pasture, he was tired and dirty and hungry. And it wasn't even much past noon yet.

He headed back in, figuring he'd stop by and see Hal and have lunch. Might as well check on how things were going between the old rancher and his new daughter.

When he reached the barn, he saw Scarlett perched on a bale of straw. Today, she wore another brightly colored dress and bright red high-heeled shoes. She looked both exotic and completely out of place. And much more beautiful than she had a right to be.

For all intents and purposes, she appeared to be waiting for him. Ignoring the way his heart skipped a beat at the sight of her, he rode past, deliberately ignoring her while he dismounted. He tied the reins to a hook outside the stall and removed his saddle, which he carried over to the saddle rack. Returning, he dipped his chin in a small nod of greeting and began brushing down his mount.

He knew the instant she got up and came around to stand silently behind him, though he pretended not to notice. He hated the way his body hummed with hyperawareness of her presence, as if he'd merely been sleepwalking and only came awake when she was near.

But then again, beautiful women had always been his weakness. A blessing and a curse. Once, when he'd cared enough to actually try to attract them, they'd flocked to him like moths to a flame.

Now he knew better. Beautiful women were nothing but trouble. Trouble and a world of hurt. These days, he managed to avoid them. He'd even stopped dating, having neither the time nor the inclination to have his heart shattered again.

Luckily, he kept an iron grip on his self-control.

Still, having Scarlett watch him without speaking managed to make him feel uncomfortable. He pretended to be entirely focused on his task, refusing to allow her to bother him.

Only once he had the horse taken care of and back in the stall did he turn and face her.

"Hi," she said, offering a friendly smile. "You

seemed so engrossed in brushing your horse that I didn't want to disturb you. I'm guessing you love working with your hands."

Suggestive? Whether intentional or not, when he raised one eyebrow at her comment, she blushed. Strangely enough, this actually made him like her a little better.

He decided to ignore what she'd just said. "Is there something I can help you with?" Direct and to the point. Much better than asking her what the hell she was doing in his barn.

"Yes." She met his gaze dead on. "I came out here to talk to you. Hal said you're his stepson as well as his foreman. I guess that kind of makes us kin."

"Kin?" He shuddered. "Not hardly. Hal and I aren't related at all. Now what did you need to talk to me about?"

When she didn't immediately respond, he braced himself, figuring whatever it was would probably be a doozy.

"I just thought..." She looked down, twisting her hands as she let her words trail away. He almost felt a pang of sympathy—almost—before reminding himself that he needed to be wary around her.

"I just thought we might be friends." When she lifted her face to his, the raw vulnerability in her green eyes had him taking a step toward her before he realized.

"Friends?" he repeated, dazed at how close he'd come to letting down his guard. "Why?"

"Why not?" She smiled, the beauty of which made his mouth go dry. "I'm getting to know my father. I didn't even know about him for most of my life, so he and I have a lot of catching up to do. Hal asked me to stay awhile and I've accepted. Clearly, you care about him. And he you." Still smiling, she shrugged. "I just think it would be easier if we all got along."

"Delilah mentioned that you'd be staying awhile. Let me ask you something. Did Hal ask for a DNA test?"

She recoiled, almost as if he'd slapped her. "No. But if he does, I'll be perfectly willing to have one done."

"Good. I'll be sure to mention it to him." He kept his tone friendly. "After all, that's the only definitive way to know you're actually his daughter."

Though she narrowed her eyes, she still didn't look away. "Why don't you like me? You don't even know me."

"Does it matter?" he asked.

"Yes."

He shrugged. "Look, I don't dislike you. As you pointed out, I don't know you. I just don't trust you."

"Again, I have to ask why?"

He decided to be blunt. "I protect Hal. That's what I do. I might not be able to stop his illness, or even identify it. But I can keep him away from people who want to hurt him or use him. Do you understand?"

"I do." She didn't even blink. "And since I have no intention of doing either, you have nothing to fear from me."

"Fear? Interesting choice of words."

This made her groan, clearly frustrated. "Oh, please. Give me a break."

To his surprise, he realized she'd managed to coax a reluctant smile from him. He immediately turned that into a frown. "I'm guessing you feel I should just take you at your word. I promise, I'll be watching you. So help me, it won't look good for you if you try to take advantage of a dying man."

She froze. "Dying? What do you mean, exactly? I know he seems ill, and he has a nurse, but..."

"We don't know what's wrong with him. We've had every test run and the doctors can't figure it out." He decided to be brutally honest. "We've had him checked out at MD Anderson also. It's definitely not cancer. But whatever it is, it's killing him. We've hired a nurse to be here during the day since he's not yet at the point of needing help 24/7, but he's already been authorized for hospice care."

"Hospice care?" She blanched as she said the words. "But that means..."

"Yes, his doctor has certified that he probably has less than six months to live."

"Damn." Closing her eyes, she swayed. "I went through this with my mother." When she opened them again, he was surprised to see the sheen of unshed tears. "It's horrible," she said, her mouth working. "And hard. So damn painful."

"Yes. It is." At the powerful urge to hold her and comfort her, he clenched his hands into fists, resisting. "Which is why someone—a total stranger—showing up claiming to be his daughter is the last thing he needs."

"I disagree. He's my father," she insisted. "And I might be a stranger right now, but once he gets to know me, things will be different. We're family." She lifted her chin. "You know, everyone needs family, especially in times like these."

He guessed she had no way of knowing that sounded exactly like something Hal might have said.

"I'm not getting through to you," he began.

Crossing her arms, she stared at him, disappointment and confusion warring in her expression. "No, you're not. I don't see your point. If I can bring a little happiness to Hal when he's so ill, then what's the harm?"

"What do you get out of it?"

To his surprise, she considered his question seriously. "Me? Well, I missed out on having a father my entire life. I really want to get to know him while I can."

Still, he couldn't help but notice the way she said nothing about an inheritance. People just didn't show up out of the blue at the very end of a formerly rich man's life without a good reason. And in most, if not all, cases this reason was money.

His only consolation was that Hal was no fool. If anyone could be convinced to see through a shakedown, Travis would convince Hal. He'd done it before. He'd do it again.

"Don't you have your own home to go to?" Another cruel question, another deliberate attempt to get her to reveal the truth. "I know you said your mother had recently died, but surely at your age, you'd long ago moved out."

Rather than annoying her, this made her smile. "Like you have?" she asked. "Or is my impression that you still live on the premises entirely wrong?"

"Touché." He gave a two-finger salute to the brim of his cowboy hat. "But I'm the ranch foreman and I live in the foreman's quarters. Which is where the foreman always lives. In addition, I support my mother and my sister and her son. They moved in with me."

She jerked her head in a nod. "You know, for someone who claims to care about Hal, you appear to be focused on the negatives. I think having me here will be good for him."

"Maybe," he allowed. "I guess we'll just have to wait and see."

"Exactly. Until then, how about we call a truce?"

A truce. "I'll think about it. How long are you planning on staying?"

The tension in her shoulders softened. "I don't know. As long as he'll have me."

He nodded. "A truce it is." He allowed himself a slight smile. "Since you're going to be around here awhile, you'll need to meet the rest of the family."

"The rest of the family?"

Clearly, she hadn't expected there to be others. He nearly laughed out loud. "Yes, there's Hal's ex-wife, my mother, Vivian. And my younger sister, Amber, and her son, Will. He's five. As I mentioned, they all live with me."

Her expression cleared. "That means I have extended family, sort of. I know you find this hard to believe, but I'm delighted."

Delighted?

"You haven't met them yet. Come on." He reached a rapid decision. Maybe once she met the others, she'd realize it wouldn't be so simple to scam the old man.

He held out his arm. "There's no better time than the present."

"Now?" She didn't move. "You want me to meet them right now?"

"Sure, why not?" He gave her a look plainly daring her to chicken out. "You want family, you've got family. My house is on the property. It's not far at all."

Since he hadn't really given her a choice, she took his arm. "I'd rather freshen up first," she said.

"No need. They won't be expecting you and even if they were, we don't put on airs. We're just down-home country people." Sort of. His mother was an avid churchgoer who loved to gossip, drink, smoke and play bingo. His sister was...he didn't know what. A vampire wannabe? And then there was his nephew, Will. Most awesome five-year-old ever. Travis loved that kid.

He took Scarlett over to his truck, opening the passenger side door and helping her climb up before going around to the driver's side. She seemed slightly nervous, twisting her hands over and over in her lap. She didn't speak again as he started the truck and they drove down the bumpy dirt road toward the part of the ranch where he lived.

The foreman's house had once been the main ranch house, sixty some-odd years ago. Hal had been born in the rectangular wood-and-stone house. He had built his own house and moved out. His parents had lived there until their deaths, at which time Hal had decided to use the place for his ranch foreman. Travis was the third foreman to take up residence there. He'd had the place to himself for a couple of years before Hal and Vivian had divorced. These days, Vivian considered the place hers.

A few minutes later, they pulled up in the short gravel drive and he killed the engine. She didn't move, not even to unbuckle her seat belt.

"Are you okay?" he asked quietly, resisting the utterly strange urge to reach out and cup her chin in his hand.

She blinked. "Sure." Shooting him a brilliant smile, she unclipped her seat belt and opened the door.

Shaking his head, he got out after her. She waited at the end of the sidewalk, her shoulders back and her head held high. He got the strangest sense she was putting on an act, playing a role, though he didn't know her well enough to say for sure.

Whatever. She'd need all the help she could get once Vivian got a hold of her.

At the front door, he glanced once more at Scarlett. She flashed him an eager smile, looking as if he was about to give her the best Christmas present in the history of the world.

Inhaling, he squared his shoulders and opened the door.

Once inside, the sound of the television blaring greeted them. *Judge Judy* or one of those other courtroom shows his mother and sister seemed to find so fascinating. But the small living room was empty.

Travis debated calling out, but Vivian hated being called Mom or Mother, so he didn't. "Maybe they're in the kitchen," he said instead. They trooped into the kitchen, where his sister, Amber, sat at the table playing games on her phone. With black lipstick and fingernails, her fondness for heavy eyeliner and mascara, and bright red lipstick, she looked as out of place on the ranch as Scarlett did, though for entirely different reasons.

"Hey," Travis said, resisting the urge to irritate her and ruffle her hair like he used to when they'd been younger.

"Hey," she grunted, without even looking up.

"Where's Will?"

At the sound of his name, the five-year-old dynamo rushed into the room, throwing himself at Travis's legs. "Unca Travis!" he squealed.

Travis picked him up and swung him around. Will giggled, his brown eyes wide and excited. They grew even rounder when he caught sight of Scarlett when Travis set him back on his feet.

"Who are you?" he demanded, tilting his head and studying her. "You're pretty."

"Thank you," she replied, smiling. "My name is Scarlett."

The sound of another female voice must have registered. Amber glanced up from her phone, frowning. "New girlfriend?"

Travis laughed. "No. She's a friend of Hal's."

"A *friend*?" The emphasis Amber put on the word made Travis laugh again.

"Not that kind of friend."

"Good." Amber raked her gaze over Scarlett once more. With her heavy black eyeliner and several layers of mascara, the effect made her appear owlish rather than menacing. "She looks kind of young to be his friend."

"*She* is standing right here," Scarlett put in coolly. She held out her hand. "I'm Scarlett."

After a second's hesitation, Amber shook her hand. "Amber. And this is my son, Will."

"We've met." After ruffling the boy's hair, Scarlett looked around the cluttered kitchen with interest. "I love the color scheme."

Travis managed to suppress a snort. Right. With

green cabinets, orange walls and beige countertops, the kitchen looked like it had been decorated by an insane artist on drugs. For all he knew, it had.

"Where's…?"

"Vivian?" Amber yawned, making her disdain and boredom clear. "She's getting ready for bingo. I'm guessing she didn't know we were having company."

"Oh, you're not," Scarlett put in. "Having company, that is. Don't think of me as company. After all, I'm going to be staying here awhile."

"Here?" Amber's eyes widened in black-smudged horror. "Where are you planning on sleeping?" She cut her gaze to Travis and then back again. "Oh. Sorry. I didn't realize you two were a couple."

Travis couldn't help laughing again as he waited for Scarlett to deny it.

"We're not." Scarlett sounded calm, rather than flustered, which disappointed him. "I'm staying at Hal's place."

"Hal's place?" Amber narrowed her heavily made-up eyes.

"That's right." Scarlett glanced at Travis. "We should probably go. I promised to help Delilah this afternoon."

"But you just got here," Amber said.

"And you haven't met Vivian," Travis put in. "You definitely need to get to know her if you plan on hanging around the ranch. She knows everything and everyone." He raised his voice to be heard over the TV. "Vivian!"

"What?" Vivian came bouncing into the room, the movement graceful despite her recent knee replacement surgery. She stopped short the instant she caught sight of Scarlett. “Who’s this?” she asked, glancing from Travis to Scarlett and back again. “Do you have a new friend?”

Even though *friend* was how she referred to her gentlemen callers, Travis knew Scarlett had no idea. Even so, he shook his head. “She’s here to visit with Hal.”

“Hal?” Vivian’s perfectly arched brows rose even higher. “You can’t be serious.”

Again, Travis found himself laughing out loud. He hadn’t had so much cause to find things humorous in a long time, at least since Hal had gotten sick. “Not like that,” he began.

Scarlett, who still had no idea of the underlying meaning to Vivian of the word *friend*, looked perplexed. “I’m his daughter,” she said.

Travis nearly groaned aloud. Now the *S* was sure to hit the fan.

“His daughter?” Vivian sounded as if she was choking. She glared at Scarlett for a moment before turning her stare on Travis. “Is this your idea of a joke?”

He opened his mouth to respond, but before he could, Scarlett spoke again.

“What is wrong with you people? Why do you all find the idea that Hal could have a daughter—me—so threatening?”

“As if you didn’t know,” Amber drawled, barely looking up from her phone.

“I don’t.” Scarlett crossed her arms. “So please, someone enlighten me.”

“This is ridiculous,” Vivian put in. “Young lady, who do you think you are? How dare you perpetuate a scam like this on a dying man?”

“For the last time,” Scarlett said, a thread of steel

hardening her voice. "I am not scamming anyone. Or joking. Hal Gardner is my father. I just learned about him after my mother died. Now if any of you want to tell me why that's a problem, I'm all ears. If not, I need to get back to the main house."

Despite himself, Travis admired her backbone. His mother could be intimidating to people, especially those she didn't like.

Vivian opened and closed her mouth with a snap. Without saying another word, she spun around and strode back to her room, her huge dangling earrings swinging.

Staring after her, Amber laughed. "I think I like you, Scarlett," she said. "You're the first person I've met who can get Mama to stop talking."

Clearly not sure how to respond to that, Scarlett nodded.

"I like you too," Will declared, coming out from behind Travis and bestowing a quick hug. Scarlett smiled down at the little boy, her expression somewhere between enchanted and uncertain.

"Thank you," she said, once Will had released her and stood staring expectantly up at her. "You're very nice."

Will beamed at the compliment. He went and grabbed one of his favorite toys, a large plastic dump truck, and brought it over to her. "Do you wanna play?"

Scarlett looked at Travis, clearly asking for help. He could venture a quick guess that she didn't have a lot of experience around children.

Finally, Travis took pity on her. "Come on," he said. "I'll take you back. We'll try introductions again later when everyone isn't acting like they've lost their minds."

"Hey," Amber protested. "Just because Mama went off on a tear, don't lump me in that category. Scarlett, there aren't a lot of women our age out here in the country. I think you and I could become friends."

Travis shook his head. "She's probably not going to be here that long," he told his sister, which earned him an angry glare from Scarlett.

"Thanks, Amber," Scarlett said. "And despite what your brother thinks, he has no idea about any of my plans. Hal gave me an open-ended invitation, which means there are no time constraints on my visit. So yes, we should hang out. There's no such thing as too many friends."

Amber's answering snort of laughter made Travis frown, which she ignored. "Good for you, Scarlett. I like that you refuse to let my big brother intimidate you."

"Intimidate?" Travis protested. "Your choice of words wounds me. I'm just trying to help."

"You're just trying to control the situation," Amber shot back, her eyes still sparkling with humor. "Lighten up, Travis. You've been taking care of everyone for so long, you've clearly forgotten how to act toward a guest."

He shouldn't have been surprised when Scarlett nodded. "You're right about that. Your brother hasn't been the slightest bit welcoming."

"He doesn't like change."

Travis rolled his eyes. "Enough already. Scarlett, are you ready to go?"

When her gaze locked on his, again he felt that tingle of awareness. “I guess so,” she said, her voice full of reluctance.

“Don’t worry,” Amber interjected. “Both Mom and I are frequent visitors up at the main house. I’ll see you tomorrow.”

Scarlett immediately brightened. “Okay. That sounds great.” She started for the door, glancing back over her shoulder at Travis. “Are you coming?”

He couldn’t keep from grinning as he followed her out. Best to keep his distance, because if he got too close to her, he’d do something stupid, like kiss her.

Chapter 3

As she trudged outside back to Travis's truck, stunned and a bit shell-shocked, Scarlett had to bite the inside of her mouth to keep from demanding answers from him. She couldn't help but feel like he'd enjoyed himself a bit too much in there.

Kind of like his mother was a piranha and Scarlett newly trapped bait he'd hung dangling above the water for Vivian to snap at.

But since he'd already made it clear he didn't trust her, she kept her thoughts to herself.

At least his sister had been friendly.

Everyone else's reactions were far too weird, with the exception of Delilah and Hal himself. She could understand her presence was a shock and they'd need time to adjust, but still. Why no one could even pretend to be happy that Hal had a long-lost daughter, she didn't understand.

Whatever she had expected, it hadn't been this. She'd entertained dreams of being welcomed into a new family; a bit naive, clearly. Truthfully, she hadn't thought much beyond getting to know her father and, while she'd never expected to find him with a terminal illness, she saw no reason for Travis and his kin to doubt her.

Maybe she should have expected some resistance. After all, to these well-established existing members of Hal's family, she'd just come up out of the woodwork. Clearly, Hal hadn't even known Maggie was pregnant when she'd walked out on him. Though nothing could make up for the years without a father, knowing he hadn't deliberately ignored her all this time felt like salve upon her wounded heart.

Still, Vivian was Hal's ex-wife. Why would she care if Hal had a daughter from a prior relationship? Why would this bother anyone? They all acted like Hal was a multimillionaire whose fortune Scarlett had come to steal. What they didn't seem to understand was, if she'd truly been a gold digger, she'd have taken one look at Hal's worn and battered furnishings and turned around to beat a retreat as quickly as she could.

These people didn't know her, but if they'd take the time to try, they'd realize money was the last thing she cared about. Her mother had left her enough to ensure her comfort. And even before Scarlett had left the art gallery where she worked to care for her mother, she'd been able to save a significant amount with the goal of eventually opening her own gallery someday.

She'd temporarily put that dream on hold. What she wanted more than anything was a relationship with the man who'd sired her.

Bittersweet now too, as his time on this earth was apparently limited. She'd be damned if she'd let anyone take that away from her.

"Wait," Travis said, just as she reached the side of his truck.

She spun around to find him right there, mere feet away from her. Handsome as sin and sexy as hell. She reached up, cupped her hand along the side of his ruggedly chiseled cheek. Desire flared. It must have shown in her eyes or on her face because he muttered her name and then hauled her up against him, covering her mouth with his.

Too stunned to react at first, she froze, heart pounding, blood pumping. As he slanted his lips over hers, a jolt of fire shot through her. In the same way that had compelled her to touch him, he acted as if he couldn't help himself. She could relate. Punishing and angry, true. At first. Opening her mouth to him, she kissed him back with a hunger that surged up from deep within her and surprised the hell out of her.

When he finally lifted his head from hers, her entire body quivered.

"Let's go," he rasped, releasing her so quickly she stumbled backward.

What the actual hell? Yanking open the truck door, she swung up and clicked the seat belt into place without saying a word.

Travis cleared his throat, probably intending to apologize. She ignored him. He turned the key, started the engine and put the vehicle in gear. They headed back to the main house in silence.

Lost in her own thoughts, she couldn't help but wonder if the kiss had affected him as deeply as it had her.

Honestly, his behavior completely baffled her. She alternated between anger with him and annoyance at herself for enjoying the kiss far too much.

The truck had barely stopped rolling when she unhooked the belt and jumped out, striding into the house without a backward glance. Though technically, she and Travis really needed to discuss what had just happened, right now she felt way too frustrated to even attempt to deal with him.

Hal waited in the living room, his wheelchair parked in front of the television. His tired face lit up the instant she walked into the room, which instantly banished her exasperation.

"Hey there," she murmured, crossing the room to crouch near him.

"Delilah said she thought she saw you and Travis go off in the pickup," he said, smiling.

"We did." Travis came inside, his gaze flicking over Scarlett before returning to Hal. "Since she says she's staying awhile, I took her out to meet Vivian, Amber and Will."

"Excellent." Hal chuckled. "Well, Scarlett? What'd you think?"

"They all seemed…nice," she said, aware she sounded lame but aware she had to be careful what she said.

Hal burst out laughing, which quickly turned to a rasping cough. Delilah bustled into the room. "What's going on?"

"Nothing," Hal managed, trying to straighten up. "My daughter is funny."

Behind her, Scarlett swore she could hear Travis grinding his teeth.

"I'm sorry," she ventured. "I wasn't trying to be amusing or anything. I didn't actually spend a lot of time with them, so can't really form an opinion."

For whatever reason, this comment had Hal and Travis exchanging looks.

"It's okay," Hal finally told her. "Vivian can be a handful, but she has a good heart. I'm not sure about her new boyfriend, Frank, but if she likes him, that's okay with me."

"I didn't meet him," Scarlett replied.

"He doesn't live on the premises," Travis interjected. "He just visits."

Despite trying not to, she found she kept sneaking looks at his mouth. The raw sensuality of his kiss had taken her by surprise. Worse, she found herself wanting to kiss him again.

Which made her think she must be losing her mind.

"What's for supper?" Hal asked, eyeing Delilah. Since she was a nurse-type aide, Scarlett wondered why everyone seemed to expect her to cook.

If cooking wasn't supposed to be in her job description, Delilah didn't seem to mind. She simply smiled and told them they'd have to wait and see. When she disappeared into the kitchen, Scarlett jumped up and followed her.

"Let me help," she offered.

"What?" Delilah shook her head. "That wouldn't be right. You're a guest."

"I'm family," Scarlett insisted firmly. "And as far as I can tell, your official capacity here is something like a nurse's aide. Am I right?"

"Sort of. I cook, clean and do whatever I can to help Hal feel comfortable. You might call me a jackof-all-trades." She chuckled at her own joke. "And tonight I'm just making sloppy joes and french fries. It's a simple matter of browning the meat and baking the fries. I bake them so there won't be as much grease. Hal's stomach can't handle a lot of fat."

"Do you use ground beef or ground turkey?"

"Turkey or chicken. It's healthier. But don't tell Hal or Travis. Since they run a cattle ranch, they tend to frown on any meal that doesn't include beef. Now go back in the other room and keep your father company. I've got this handled. I'll let y'all know when it's time to eat."

Scarlett did as she was told. This time, she took a seat on the end of the couch closest to Hal's wheelchair. Travis had lowered his big body into the recliner and both men seemed intent on watching the news.

Half an hour later, Delilah announced it was time to eat. She'd set everything out on the dining room table, along with plates and utensils. She'd also poured four tall glasses of ice water. "Dig in," she said, standing back and beaming.

The simple meal tasted delicious. When Travis went back for seconds, Scarlett gave in to temptation and did the same. When Delilah brought out a fresh pan of brownies for dessert, both Scarlett and Travis groaned.

Naturally, they had to sample the brownies, especially when Delilah offered vanilla ice cream to put on top.

"That was great," Hal said, even though he'd only taken a few bites out of his food. Scarlett noticed the way both Delilah and Travis exchanged worried glances. As soon as possible, she planned to ask Hal more detailed questions and do her own research. She found it hard to believe that not a single doctor could figure out what ailed Hal. There had to be something they were overlooking. She at least had to try to find it.

After taking a nibble of his brownie, Hal wheeled himself into the living room, parking his chair in front of the television. He used the remote to turn the set on, ready to be engrossed in whichever of his favorite shows might be about to come on.

Delilah mentioned she needed to get home, so Scarlett shooed her out of the kitchen and took over washing dishes. A moment later, Delilah said goodbye and left.

When Travis appeared and grabbed a dish towel, Scarlett glanced up at him in surprise, but didn't argue. They worked side by side in silence, she washed and he dried. The simple camaraderie of the chore almost made her think they could be friends. Almost. If she didn't think about the kiss, that is.

The kiss. Handing him the last clean plate, she chanced a sideways glance at his profile. Rugged and masculine, he looked steadfast and strong, like someone you could count on in a storm. She'd never have guessed that firm mouth could also be tender and passionate. But why? He clearly disliked her. So why'd he kiss her like a man dying in the desert getting his first mouthful of rainwater?

He looked up and caught her staring, so she hurriedly busied herself rinsing out the sink. Should she ask? Or would that be making too big of a deal over a single kiss? While she dithered, he hung up the dish towel to dry and left the kitchen, taking the opportunity with him.

When Scarlett went back to the den, she realized Hal had fallen fast asleep in front of the TV. Chin on his chest, he looked fragile, parchment-thin skin stretched too tight over hollows and bones.

Heart aching, she sighed, catching Travis's gaze. "I want more time with him," she murmured.

"I do too," Travis quietly responded as he got to his feet. For one startled second, she thought he might kiss her again. Instead, he grabbed his cowboy hat off the coatrack and dipped his chin in a goodbye nod. Then he slipped out the door to head home. He left without speaking, or even giving her a chance to ask the question that had bothered her ever since he'd kissed her.

Disappointed but not surprised, Scarlett locked the door behind him. Interesting how the instant he left, so did her restless tension. Now that he was gone, maybe she could finally relax. It had been a long day.

Kicking her heels off, she sat and swung her legs up on the couch. Massaging her aching feet, she thought maybe the time had come to invest in a pair of flats or, heaven help her, some boots. Though she adored shoes and had managed to amass quite a collection of heels, what worked in downtown Atlanta seemed foolish out here in the middle of nowhere on a cattle ranch.

Settling into the comfortable sofa cushions, she looked around the room and marveled at how quickly this place had come to feel like home. Despite the weathered furniture and a decorating style that screamed early 1980s, the ranch house gave off a genuine, rustic vibe.

Though most of that was probably due to the man dozing in his wheelchair. Her father. Words she'd never believed she'd be able to utter.

Watching Hal sleep in front of the TV, her throat felt tight. She'd gone thirty years of her life without a father. It didn't seem fair that she'd finally found him, only to learn he was dying from a terrible, apparently incurable and completely unknown disease.

All she could do was make the most of the time he had left. Travis and his family may not want her here, but Hal did. That was what mattered.

Since Delilah had gone, Scarlett wondered if she needed to take Hal back and help get him ready to sleep. Earlier, when Hal had shown her the room that would be hers, Scarlett had seen the hospital bed that had been set up inside the master bedroom. She'd also seen the oxygen tank and IV pole. She wouldn't have any idea what to do.

And, since everyone had gone, Hal must be used to doing it all himself.

But she wasn't sure. As she pondered, Hal opened his eyes and blinked. "Are you still awake?" he asked. "What time is it?"

"Nearly nine," she told him. "Travis went home and I've been sitting here relaxing. I've been wondering—do you need help getting from your chair to your bed?"

"Nope. I'm not there yet, sweetheart." He wiggled his bushy eyebrows at her, making her laugh. Right after that, he yawned, not even covering his mouth with his hand. "I am tired, though. I think I'll turn in. Will you be okay with me leaving you alone?"

Impulsively, she jumped up and gave Hal's weathered cheek a soft kiss. "I'll be fine. Good night," she said softly. "Sleep well."

Beaming, he nodded. "You too."

Once he'd wheeled into his room and closed the door, Scarlett shut off the TV and retreated to her room. Once there, she closed her door and pulled out her laptop. She linked to Hal's Wi-Fi—secretly surprised he had one, and then went in search of his router so she could get the password. Once she'd done that, she accessed the internet so she could research Hal's symptoms.

Cancer seemed most likely, but Travis had said that had been ruled out. The weight loss and lack of appetite, the wasting away, those were all serious symptoms. And she figured the doctors had thoroughly investigated each potential disease.

Things didn't look good for Hal. Travis had tried to tell her, but she didn't want to believe him.

Her throat ached. She'd stay here as long as Hal would let her, no matter what Travis or his family thought. She'd look on the positive side and consider it a blessing she'd get to spend time with Hal at all and that she hadn't located him after it was too late.

And she'd continue looking. Just because there were a thousand possible illnesses, she wouldn't give up easily.

Travis started the morning the same way he'd done for the last ten years. Got up, showered and dressed, and made a single cup of coffee, taking care not to wake anyone in the house. Then he hopped into the cab of the truck and Travis drove himself to Hal's house to have breakfast.

In the old days, Hal would have the meal ready before Travis arrived, but as Hal got sicker, Travis had taken over the duty. He had two specialties—scrambled eggs with onions, peppers and hot sauce, and biscuits and gravy. Both of them were pretty darn good, if he said so himself.

As he made the turn into the drive, he saw Scarlett's

little red car. At least he wouldn't have to deal with her this morning. He doubted she got up before ten.

But when he strolled into the kitchen, he stopped short at the sight of her sitting at the table with Hal, heads bent close over steaming cups of coffee. His traitorous heart skipped a beat. She wore no makeup and she'd pulled her glossy black hair back into a jaunty ponytail, which showcased the delicate lines of her features.

Before he could help himself, he managed to zero in on her kissable mouth, until he quickly dragged his gaze away. She managed to look lovely and sexy and natural, all at once.

And way too damn cozy with Hal.

Suppressing a sharp stab of resentment, Travis worked on manufacturing an easy smile. "Good morning," he said, nodding at her before looking at Hal.

"Mornin'." Hal grinned. "Scarlett here was just fixin' to fry up some eggs."

Though he wondered if she really knew how to cook, Travis nodded. "Sounds great."

His tone mustn't have been too convincing, judging from the narrow-eyed glance Scarlett sent his way. Travis shrugged and poured himself a mug of coffee before taking a seat at the table. "You know you don't have to cook," he said. "That's usually my job, at least for breakfast."

In the act of placing a large skillet on the stove, she turned. "You can cook?"

"Barely," Travis allowed. "Judging from your tone, you don't believe it."

"Show her," Hal said, grinning. "She's our guest and really shouldn't be making her own meals."

"Nonsense." Scarlett stood her ground. Those ridiculously high heels of hers had the effect of making her legs look even longer. "I don't mind helping."

Travis debated getting up and asking her to sit down, but if she really wanted to make breakfast, he truly didn't mind. "Knock yourself out."

Shaking his head, Hal went back to reading the paper. He passed the sports section over to Travis, just like he always did, but Travis barely glanced down at the page. He couldn't seem to tear his gaze away from the woman standing in front of the stove.

With her back to him, she moved with a sensual grace, despite the tall shoes. Today, instead of her usual fancy dress, she wore a pair of formfitting blue jeans. He had to admit, she filled them out a heck of a lot better than he'd imagined.

When she glanced over her shoulder, as if she'd felt his gaze on her, he blinked and hurriedly looked down at his newspaper. He read the cover story three times, not absorbing a single word.

A few minutes later, she set a plate down in front of him. Three perfectly cooked eggs, two slices of bacon and toast. She placed an identical plate in front of Hal, before returning to the stove to fetch her own.

"Did you want some orange juice?" she asked, her direct gaze and her sweet tone daring him to find something wrong with his breakfast.

"No thanks," he replied, changing his mind when Hal asked for some.

Finally, all three were seated, the hot meal in front

of them. "This looks great," Hal enthused, before digging in.

Again, Scarlett glanced at Travis, as though she expected him to make a snide comment. Instead, he nodded. "It does look great. Thank you."

He ate, trying not to be too obvious about the fact that he was also watching Hal. The man had to take nourishment sometime. If he didn't, he'd not only continue wasting away, but he risked having heart and kidney issues.

To Travis's relief, Hal ate most of one egg and an entire piece of toast. He only nibbled on a slice of bacon, but that was definite progress.

When Scarlett caught his eye, he realized she was thinking the same thing. A sudden image of his hands tangled in her hair, pulling it loose from the ponytail, before he placed his mouth over hers and tasted her once more.

What the… Quickly glancing down at his plate, he concentrated on sopping up the rest of his egg with his toast. Why the hell had he given in to impulse and kissed her in the first place? Now he couldn't get her out of his head.

But he would. Immediately.

"What's on the agenda today?" Hal asked. Travis looked up, realizing the older man was addressing him. Relieved, he listed all the chores he had in mind for today. Though they were remarkably similar day to day, Hal knew this all too well. Running a ranch entailed supervising various ranch hands and making sure they did what needed to be done. There was always fence needing repair, cattle needing rounding up or feeding. Though Travis preferred spending his day on horseback, taking care of a ranch this size often entailed using his pickup.

As he wound down, he became aware of Scarlett watching him. The hunger he thought he saw in her gaze rekindled his own desire, simmering flame igniting into an instant inferno.

Look. Away. Mindlessly, he reached for his coffee cup, gulping down the last two swallows. “I’ve got to get going.” He pushed back his chair, scraping it on the linoleum floor.

Trying not to rush, he strode to the coatrack, grabbed his hat and crammed it on his head. He slammed outside without another word.

Though today was one of those days when he probably needed to take the truck, instead he went to the barn and saddled up his favorite gelding. He needed to clear his mind and get himself straight. Not only did he still not trust Scarlett Kistler, but he couldn’t help but be aware of how the lure of a sexy woman had brought stronger men than him to their knees.

And it wasn’t just that he wanted her. He could tell she wasn’t the kind of love ’em and leave ’em woman who could handle a strictly sexual fling. Which was all it could ever be between them. She definitely wasn’t the type who’d thrive on a ranch, with a simple man like him. Angry that his thoughts had even gone down this path, he shook his head. His horse snorted, sensitive to his mood.

Calming himself, he slipped the bridle on and adjusted the bit. Working the familiar motions of saddling his horse helped. Climbing up, swinging his leg over and settling into the saddle helped even more.

When he rode out onto the dirt trail, he felt like himself again. The easy rhythm of hooves hitting the earth, the warm spring breeze and the birdsong from the nearby trees helped to erase his tension.

His cell phone rang, startling him. Caller ID showed the landline from his house, which meant either his mother or his sister needed something. Despite the fact Travis had told both of them numerous times not to call him during the workday unless it was an emergency, they still did.

Since he still had a few more minutes before he reached the area where he knew the men would be working, he went ahead and answered.

"Good morning, son," Vivian chirped. "I tried to catch you before you left, but I overslept."

In all the time she'd been living with him, he'd never once seen her up before sunrise, so he didn't reply.

"Anyway, I wanted to talk to you about that girl."

Of course she did. She'd been out late the night before, so she hadn't gotten the opportunity to bring it up before bedtime.

"What about her?" he asked, unsuccessfully trying to keep from letting his annoyance show.

"Do you think she's for real?"

"What I think isn't important. Hal believes she is, so that's all that matters."

Her expressive sigh told him what she thought of that.

"I'd planned on going over there today to visit with Hal, but now I'm not sure I should," she said. "But I need to try to get to know her. I feel like I should try to keep Hal from getting hurt."

"I feel exactly the same." Inwardly wincing, he went ahead and said it anyway. "It wouldn't hurt for you to get to know her. You and Amber might be able to learn things about her more easily than I would."

Vivian laughed. "Okay, you twisted my arm. It's always best to keep your enemies close."

Poor Scarlett. He almost felt sorry for her, as if he'd unleashed a horde of locusts or something. His mother definitely could be a force to be reckoned with.

"You never know," Vivian continued. "She might be for real. Anyway, I'll keep you posted."

"You do that," he agreed, and ended the call. He fought back the desire to call the main house and warn Scarlett. Where had that notion come from anyway?

He'd just settled back into the saddle, enjoying the natural beauty of the landscape, when his phone rang again. He groaned, especially when he realized it was from the same number.

"What now, Mom?" he asked, by way of greeting.

"It's not Mom, it's Amber," his sister replied. "Did you really just sic Mom on Scarlett?"

"I wouldn't put it quite that way. If Scarlett's planning to be around awhile, which she said she is, she needs to get to know everyone." His answer, while true, sounded weak, even to him.

Amber snorted. "You have a point, but maybe you should have let it happen a bit more gradually instead of having Mom go at her full strength."

Ahead, he could see the group of ranch hands, loading cattle into chutes in preparation for the work they had to do.

"Look, Scarlett's a grown woman. I'm sure she can handle anything Mom throws at her. Now, unless there's anything else you need, I've got to get to work."

"Nope, I'm done. But a word of warning, big brother. Don't be surprised if this backfires on you." She ended the call before he could ask her what she meant.

Chapter 4

"What got into him?" Hal mused, scratching his head as he stared at the door Travis had just slammed.

"I think I annoy him," Scarlett replied, keeping her tone light.

"He'll get used to you," Hal reassured her, reaching across the table to pat the back of her hand. "He might come across as gruff, but he's got a big heart. I promise you."

Though privately she wondered, she nodded.

"What are you planning to do today?" Hal asked, his expression curious.

"Just hanging out with you, I think."

"Vivian will be over here around ten. She's taking me to a doctor's appointment. Delilah will be here, but I think you should get out and explore. Do you know how to ride?"

"Ride?" she repeated, then realized what he meant. "Horses?"

He snorted. "I'm guessing from your response that the answer is no."

"You would be correct." She thought for a moment. "I would like to go into the nearest town, though, if you could point me in the right direction. I've got a little shopping I'd like to do."

"Why don't you ride with us?" Suddenly animated, Hal eyed her as if she'd already agreed. "You can do your shopping while I'm at my doctor's appointment and then we can all have lunch together."

With Vivian? The woman who'd all but called her a liar and a cheat two minutes after meeting her? Carefully, she kept her expression neutral while she considered. Surely the woman wouldn't be that obnoxious in front of Hal, would she?

Either way, Scarlett knew she couldn't avoid Hal's ex-wife forever. "Sure, I'd like that," she said. "I'd better go shower and get ready. Is there anything I can do for you before I go?"

"Nope." He wheeled himself around with a deft motion, displaying more energy than she'd seen from him. "I've got to clean myself up too. My bathroom's all rigged up for me. See you in a few."

After a hot shower, as Scarlett blow-dried her hair, she told herself she'd probably made too big of a deal out of Vivian's behavior the day before. After all, her sudden appearance had to have been a shock.

Still, she took pains with her makeup and dressed with extra care, choosing her favorite red dress to match her lipstick. Luckily, she'd had a gel manicure done before leaving Atlanta, so her nails still looked perfect. Silver-and-black dangling earrings, bracelet bangles and a large ring with a black stone completed her outfit.

As she surveyed herself in the mirror, she smiled. Red was her favorite color. When she wore it, she felt confident, able to do anything. If any outfit could help her deal with Vivian Gardner, this one could.

When she emerged from her room, she saw Hal had finished before her. He wore a freshly pressed button-down shirt, which hung on his too-thin frame. At the sound of her heels on the wood floor, he looked up.

"Wow," he exclaimed. "You sure look beautiful, darlin'."

"Thank you." Beaming, she glanced at her watch. Five 'til. She wondered if Vivian was usually punctual. If the other woman planned to start out unpleasant, she wanted to get it over with.

A moment later, the sound of a car door slamming told her she was about to get her wish.

"She has her own key," Hal told her, making her wonder.

Vivian breezed into the house, stopping short when she caught sight of Scarlett. "You look…really pretty," she said, her tone stating the opposite.

"I invited Scarlett here to come to lunch with us," Hal told her. "I understand you two have already met."

"We have." Vivian frowned. "And I'm looking forward to getting to know her. But, sugar, we're just having lunch at the local café."

"Are you saying I'm overdressed?" Scarlett kept her tone light, amazed the other woman had put her claws out right away.

"I think what Vivi is trying to say," Hal began.

"I can speak for myself," Vivian interrupted him sharply. "And all I'm saying is that Anniversary is a small town. The locals are mostly farmers and ranchers, or small business owners." She shrugged. "I just thought you might be more comfortable in jeans and boots, that's all."

Chin up, Scarlett met her gaze and held it. "I'm perfectly comfortable in what I'm wearing. This is one of my favorite dresses. And I don't own a pair of boots."

"We'll have to rectify that, for sure. My treat. There's a great boot shop in town." Hal wheeled himself toward the foyer. "Let's get going. I can't be late to see Dr. Dugan."

Vivian sighed and strode past him. She held the door open for him, leaving Scarlett to bring up the rear.

The SUV Vivian drove had been outfitted with a lift and a ramp. Scarlett watched while Vivian helped Hal get situated. Once he'd been strapped in, the older woman turned and eyed Scarlett.

"You can ride shotgun if you like," she said. "There's not a whole lot of room in the back with Hal's chair."

"Sounds good." Determined not to let Vivian intimidate her, Scarlett climbed into the passenger seat.

Vivian did a double check of Hal, making sure everything had been secured, before going around and getting in the driver's side. She started the engine and they were off.

"How far is it to town?" Scarlett asked, trying for polite conversation.

"About twenty-five minutes," Vivian answered. "While we're on the road, why don't you tell me a little about yourself? What's the story with your mother and Hal?"

"Vivian!" Hal's sharp rebuke made Vivian shrug.

"Sorry," she said. "But I'm curious. I really want to know."

"Maggie was my girlfriend," Hal interjected. "Long before I met you. We discussed getting married, but she was so much younger and I refused. I didn't think it would be fair to her. When she ran off, I took that as confirmation that I'd been right, even though she broke my heart."

"You never mentioned her to me." Vivian sounded peeved. "Not once."

"Did you tell me about every single relationship you had?"

"Of course not." Vivian sighed. "Point made. But I'm more interested in hearing from Scarlett here. Why'd you wait until now to contact Hal?"

Once again Scarlett relayed her story, glossing over the pain and the horror of her mother's illness and death. She described finding her mother's papers and finally learning the name of the man who'd sired her. She omitted mentioning the diary, not comfortable with sharing that with anyone else.

"Wow," Vivian commented, once Scarlett had finished. "I wonder why she never told you."

"Me too." Hoping her smile hid most of the pain retelling everything brought back, Scarlett looked out the window. There were a lot of thick patches of trees with the occasional grassy pasture. So far she'd seen cattle and horses and even goats, but only one other house.

"My story is completely different," Vivian offered, surprising Scarlett. "Hal was my second marriage. He came along when Travis and Amber were toddlers. We have a fifteen-year gap in our ages too, but after we married, he was a great husband and stepfather to my kids."

"Tell her why we got divorced," Hal said from the back seat. "She's way too polite to ask."

Since he was right, Scarlett simply waited.

Finally, Vivian shook her head. "I don't think that's any of her business."

Hal snorted. "You're all up in hers, though, aren't you?"

Afraid they might start bickering, Scarlett decided to try to change the subject. "Amber's son is adorable, isn't he? It must be nice to have your grandson live so close."

Both Vivian and Hal gave her identical looks of disbelief. Then they both laughed.

"It is," Vivian conceded. "Nice change of subject."

Hal only shook his head.

"Thank you." Scarlett smiled. "I really didn't want to know your personal business either."

As they pulled up to a stop sign, Vivian reached over and squeezed Scarlett's shoulder, surprising her. "You know what? I like you. I think you and I might just get along fine."

"I'd like that," Scarlett answered. Oddly enough, she found herself thinking of Travis. She wanted to ask Vivian about him, but feared if she did, the other woman would assume more of an interest than Scarlett would be comfortable with.

Once again moving forward, Scarlett realized the countryside appeared to be becoming more urban. Instead of pastures and livestock, more houses appeared. Set back from the road on large lots or acreage, these properties seemed more urban. Instead of livestock, they had decorative water fountains or large garages.

"We're almost to town," Vivian said, noticing Scarlett's interest in the surroundings. "We don't really have suburbs or anything—Anniversary's not big enough for that—but after these ranchettes, you'll see a few subdivisions before we get to town proper."

"This reminds me of an area of Georgia that's southeast of Atlanta. Newnan. I worked at a small art gallery on the square there."

"Art gallery?" Vivian asked. "Is that what you do for a living? My special friend Frank is an artist."

"I have a business degree with a minor in the arts," Scarlett replied. "And yes, I started out working at the small gallery in Newnan to learn. After a couple of years there, I moved to a larger gallery in Atlanta." She kept to herself the fact that her dream was to someday open her own gallery. "I'm hoping to check out the local art gallery, if there is one."

"In Anniversary?" Both Hal and Vivian spoke at once. "There isn't one."

Disappointed, Scarlett nodded. "That's a shame."

"If you want to see art, I can take you over to Frank's house one of these days," Vivian offered. "He's really good."

Hal made a face. "That's a matter of opinion."

Vivian ignored him. "You know, Anniversary really could use an art gallery. It's about time we got a bit of culture around here."

No way did she plan to touch that comment with a ten-foot pole. While she'd thought about opening her own art gallery, since she wasn't even sure she planned on staying in Anniversary, she didn't want to give Hal false hope. "I'm sure you'll get one someday. Is there a bookstore?"

"Now *that* we do have," Vivian replied.

"Good." Which meant she could get some reading material, and maybe a book on art.

Finally, they reached the subdivisions Vivian had mentioned. As subdivisions went, these were small, but well-maintained.

"Next up, Anniversary," Vivian announced. Her entire posture had relaxed and she seemed much less intimidating than when Scarlett had first met her.

Sure enough, they rounded a curve in the road and a Dairy Queen came into view. Various other businesses lined both sides of the street.

"We're going through downtown to get to Hal's doctor's office," Vivian said. "Would you like me to drop you off in the square? We can meet you at the café for lunch since it's right there."

"Sounds like a plan." Growing excited, Scarlett watched for her first sight of the town square. Though she'd grown up in suburban Atlanta, she harbored a fondness for small towns. She'd loved the two years she'd spent living in Newnan.

Catching sight of downtown Anniversary, she wasn't disappointed. With its variety of brick buildings that appeared to have been built in the 1800s and then restored, the lively downtown scene actually reminded her of Newnan.

Vivian pulled up in front of a coffee shop and parked. "Here you go. The bookstore is a few doors down."

"I'll call you when I'm finished at the doctor's," Hal said. "I have to get blood work done too, so it might be a little bit. The café is on the other side of the street, right there on the corner." He pointed.

"Perfect." Scarlett started to get out of the SUV, but

then realized she hadn't given Hal her number. As she read it out loud, she realized Vivian was adding her as a contact also. "Can both of you text me your numbers?" she asked.

Vivian agreed, promising to help Hal since apparently the older man didn't text.

Once they'd settled that, Scarlett set out to explore Anniversary.

As soon as Vivian and Hal drove off, she decided to grab a cup of coffee inside the coffee shop. Several people eyed her as she entered. Despite the fact that everyone else seemed to be dressed casually, Scarlett was glad she'd taken extra time with her appearance. When she dressed her best, she felt more confident and happier.

"One medium cappuccino, please." After giving her order and paying, she stepped over to the side to wait. Whenever anyone looked her way, she smiled at them.

After getting her drink, she carried her cup outside, planning to sit at one of the numerous tables. She'd barely sat down when another woman approached her. About her same age, the curvy blonde wore her hair in a sleek bob. Instead of jeans, she wore fitted slacks and a stylish blouse. She had stunning designer earrings swinging from her ears, which Scarlett instantly coveted.

"Excuse me, but did I see you getting out of Vivian and Hal Gardner's van?"

"You did." Still smiling, Scarlett looked up. "I love your earrings."

"Thanks. If you don't mind me asking, how do you know them?"

Rather than risk opening a huge can of worms—Scarlett knew all too well how quickly gossip could fly in small towns—she simply answered that she was staying with them.

"Oh." Without being invited, the other woman pulled out a chair and sat. "I'm Kendra. Maybe you can tell me how Travis is doing?" she asked. "I've been hoping to run into him, but he doesn't come to town all that often."

"Travis?" Surprised, Scarlett wasn't sure how to answer. "I just met him, but he seems okay. Are you and he friends?"

"Not hardly," Kendra grimaced. "We were engaged once. I broke it off and moved to Dallas. Now that I'm back, I thought I'd touch base and maybe reconnect." She grinned. "There is one thing he and I were really good at, if you know what I mean."

Jealously mingled with shock as Scarlett struggled to find a response. Her silence didn't appear to faze Kendra, who leaned forward and touched Scarlett's arm. "Look, he still has my number, I'm sure. Will you pass along to him that I'm in town, in case he wants to get together?"

Scarlett nodded, relieved when the other woman thanked her and left. Now that she'd talked to Travis's ex-fiancée, she felt like she needed to rethink everything she'd decided about Travis.

Worse, should she mention this to him? To anyone? It sure felt weird, to say the least.

Even though he knew Hal had a doctor's appointment, Travis stopped by the house around noon. If Scarlett was there, the two of them could have lunch and talk. He really needed to put more of an effort into finding out what exactly made her tick.

To protect Hal, of course. Not because he wanted to get to know her better or anything.

But when he got there, the house was empty. Since Scarlett's car still sat in the drive, that meant she'd gone into town with Vivian and Hal. He would have liked to have been a fly on the wall for that car ride. No doubt Vivian had pestered Scarlett with questions, Hal had protested and the two had gotten into one of their signature brawls.

Travis, Amber and even Delilah were all used to them. Scarlett, not so much.

Feeling oddly left out, he made himself a couple of sandwiches and grabbed a Dr Pepper. He ate at the kitchen table, checking his email on his phone. For the last several months, he'd been talking to a couple of new potential buyers for his cattle, hoping to work out a better price per head.

His phone rang. Frank, his mother's *friend*.

"Hey, Travis." Though it was early afternoon, the wobble in Frank's voice made Travis wonder if the older man had already started sipping whiskey. Hope fully that didn't mean Frank and Vivian were fighting again.

"What's up, Frank? I'm just finishing up my lunch and about to get back to work."

"Can you settle something for me?" Frank asked.

"Not if it's something you and my mother are arguing about. I'm not getting in the middle of that."

"No, nothing like that. But Vivian tells me some girl showed up claiming to be Hal's daughter. Is she for real?"

Strangely reluctant to say anything negative about

Scarlett to anyone else, Travis sighed. "Hal thinks she is. And that's all that matters."

"Is he going to ask her to take a DNA test?" Frank pressed. "I mean, that would seem to be common sense."

"I don't know. That's really up to him."

"Well, maybe you can talk sense into him," Frank pressed, to Travis's surprise. "He trusts you."

"Maybe," Travis allowed, his tone neutral. "Now I really need to be getting back to work, so..."

"But you will talk to Hal, right?"

"What's it to you, Frank?" Travis let his annoyance show in his voice. "I know my mother didn't put you up to this, because she wouldn't hesitate to ask me herself."

"She did not. I care about Vivian and since Hal is important to her, he's important to me too." Frank took an audible deep breath. "In fact, I'm hurt that you would even ask such a thing. You know that Hal and I get along just fine. If I wasn't dating your mother, I daresay the two of us would become great friends."

Rubbing the back of his neck, Travis murmured what he hoped sounded like assent and managed to end the call.

The rest of the day passed uneventfully. He took comfort in the familiar routine. And every time Scarlett's long-lashed emerald eyes and thick black hair entered his mind, he forced himself to think of something else.

By the time six o'clock had come, he felt good. Pleasantly exhausted and once again in control of his thoughts.

Back at the barn, he removed his saddle and brushed

down his horse. Briefly, he considered stopping by the main house to check on Hal, but decided to head home instead. Since Vivian had taken Hal into town, Travis hoped maybe she'd decided to continue her visit afterward. He really just wanted to grab a beer, heat up a frozen pizza for dinner, put his feet up in his recliner and watch mindless television until it was time to go to bed.

To his relief, his house was empty. Even Amber and Will had taken off somewhere. Since he had no idea how long this would last, he planned to make the most of it.

Pizza in the oven, cold beer in hand, he turned on the TV and went into his room to grab a quick shower. Once he'd washed away the day's dirt, he put on a pair of comfortable sweatpants, a faded old T-shirt and flip-flops before making his way back to the kitchen.

He'd just finished enjoying his pizza when his phone rang. Glancing at the screen, he stared in disbelief at the caller's name.

Kendra Stewart, his former fiancée. Long ago, he should have deleted and blocked her number, but hadn't as he'd considered it a point of pride to never call her.

Now she was calling him. The fifty-thousand-dollar question was would he answer?

Curiosity won and he did. She'd long ago lost the power to hurt him anyway.

"Hi, Travis," Kendra sounded determinedly cheerful, which meant she was nervous. "I wasn't sure you'd pick up the call."

"What can I do for you?" he asked, making his voice carefully blank. "I honestly can't imagine why you'd be calling me after all this time."

"I know, right? I can't believe it's been two whole years! I spoke to that woman who's staying with Hal and asked her to pass along a message to you. Did she?"

"Scarlett?" Puzzled, he scratched his head. "I haven't seen her today, so no. How did you happen to run into her?"

"Downtown at the coffee shop. I saw her getting out of Vivian's van and approached her. She's very pretty, isn't she?"

When he didn't respond, she gave a little laugh and continued. "Anyway, I'm in town on business and I thought you might want to get together for dinner and catch up."

He stared at the television in disbelief. "You thought wrong. I have nothing to talk to you about."

Silence. When she spoke again, a note of determination colored her voice. "I want to speak to you about a business opportunity."

Instantly suspicious, he waited.

"You could make a lot of money," she continued, apparently emboldened by the fact that he didn't immediately hang up on her.

"Who do you work for?" he asked, even though he figured he already knew.

"Let's talk over a meal first," she replied. "My treat."

"You're in the oil industry these days?"

"Umm. Yes. How did you know?" Still overly sweet, she gave a little laugh. "I recently took a job with Wave Oil. Since you and I had a prior…relationship, I thought I might be of assistance in helping make a deal."

"Did you?" This time, he didn't keep the steely anger from his tone. "I would have thought you might have considered this a liability rather than a benefit."

"Oh, come on now, Travis," she purred. "You know we can still be friends, maybe even with certain... benefits. Meet me for dinner. Name the time and the place and I'll be there. You can't tell me you haven't missed me."

"Yes, I can. I haven't missed you. Don't call me again." He ended the call.

Though his throat felt tight, it wasn't from pain at hearing Kendra's voice. No, he'd gotten over her a long time ago. The anger filling him was the idea of how low the damn oil company was willing to go to get what they wanted—Hal's consent to let them drill on his land.

Again, he had to wonder about Scarlett's motives. They'd brought in Travis's former fiancée and he wouldn't have put it above them to go searching for Maggie Kistler. Once they'd found out she'd died, why not bring in her daughter? It certainly wasn't out of the realm of possibility, especially now that he'd heard from Kendra.

Draining the rest of his beer in a couple of swallows, he paced, trying to release his pent-up frustration. Though working out after having a beer and pizza wasn't optimal, he decided to change into his workout clothes, drive into town and hit the gym anyway. Thirty minutes with weights and time on the treadmill would definitely help him feel a lot better.

His phone chimed, indicating a text message. One of the guys he played baseball with had seen Scarlett in town and wanted to know her story since he'd heard she was staying with Hal. He referred to her as a "babe" and wanted to know if Travis had any claim on her.

Before he could even think about answering, he got

two more texts, both from different friends, both with similar inquiries. Apparently, Scarlett had caused quite a stir around Anniversary. All the single men who'd seen her had been intrigued. Travis couldn't actually blame them.

Right now, he was in no mood to deal with answering the texts, so he decided to ignore them.

As he drove, he turned the radio to the classic rock station and cranked it up. Singing along to old Aerosmith, AC/DC and The Eagles, he felt his mood lighten with every familiar song.

When he pulled up in the parking lot of the only gym in town, he realized he'd arrived during peak hour—the time right after everyone got off from their jobs and went to work out. He decided right then and there he wouldn't stick to one of his usual workout routines, he'd simply grab whatever machine happened to be available.

He got in his thirty minutes, then spent a few on the treadmill. As he stepped down and made a stop at the water fountain, he became aware of a change in the noise level. As in almost all sound ceased, with the exception of the music they played on a continuous loop.

Every single person working out near the front door stared at a woman who'd just walked in. Her lithe, toned body on display in tiny shorts and a bright pink sports bra, she appeared oblivious to the attention. Instead, she glanced around the room, clearly trying to locate someone.

Furious, Travis suspected that someone was him. Kendra Stewart never did anything by half measure.

The instant her gaze locked on his, she smiled and

waved. "Hi, Travis!" Her greeting rang out loud and clear in the unnaturally quiet gym.

Travis glared at everyone, his expression hopefully plain enough in telling them to mind their own business. One by one, each person resumed their workout. Since most of them knew Travis by name, he figured he'd be the subject of much gossip in the next week.

He realized there were two ways he could handle Kendra's unwanted intrusion into his life. He could storm out without saying another word, which would no doubt give rise to a lot of speculation over whether this meant he still harbored deep feelings for her. Or, he could act surprised and greet her the way anyone else would an old friend with whom they'd lost touch.

Since the second would also throw Kendra off balance, he decided to go with that.

"Kendra?" Voice full of surprise, he started toward her. "Long time, no see. How are you? When did you get into town?"

Only a momentary flash of confusion in her bright blue eyes. She wore a pink-and-black headband, pushing her platinum blond hair away from her face. "Oh my gosh, if it isn't Travis Gardner? Who would have ever believed I'd run into you here? I'm doing great. How about you?"

Though he'd bet fifty dollars she'd come to the gym trolling for him, he flashed a completely insincere smile. "I'm doing well." Checking his watch, he kept the smile going. "Well, it's been great seeing you, but I've got to get going. You take care now."

She let him almost make it to the exit before calling out his name. "Wait, Travis?"

Pretending surprise, he turned, raising a brow in question.

"Don't forget, I'll be at your place at ten tonight. I can't wait."

Damn. Seriously? Now she'd left him no choice but to put her in her place.

"Kendra, not only do I have no idea what you're talking about, but I made it perfectly plain when you called me. Just in case you didn't get it then, I'll repeat it here, out loud and in front of everyone. I have nothing to discuss with you, especially regarding your oil company employer wanting to drill on my stepfather's land."

That said, he strode out of the gym, furious.

Chapter 5

Scarlett had thoroughly enjoyed her time perusing the Anniversary town square. Everyone had seemed friendly, even if a few looked askance at her dress and heels. Scarlett didn't care. She'd always enjoyed dressing up. Though maybe, she'd thought as she'd stopped in front of a cute little boutique right on the square, it wouldn't hurt to purchase a few more casual outfits. She could still wear jeans and be fashionable.

By the time she'd backtracked to the bookstore, she'd gotten loaded down with shopping bags. In addition to several pairs of jeans and cute tops, she'd stopped in a Western boot store and purchased a pair of intricately tooled red-and-black boots with a slight heel. Before leaving, she'd spotted a red cowboy hat, which she'd also bought.

Struggling with all her loot, she'd truly wished Vivian and Hal would pull up, so she could stow everything in the SUV.

For her final purchase, she'd managed to buy the newest bestseller by her favorite romance author before deciding to make her way to the café and wait. Luckily, she'd just gotten settled on the bench outside the front door when they'd pulled up.

They'd enjoyed a delicious lunch, with Vivian telling amusing stories about her past, before heading back to the ranch. Once there, Scarlett carried her purchases to her room before attempting to rejoin the others.

Delilah asked if anyone would be wanting supper. Still full from lunch, everyone declined.

After watching the early news, Hal, claiming exhaustion, had gone off to his room to go to bed. As soon as Scarlett reappeared, Vivian explained she had to meet her friend Frank at his place and took off also, leaving Scarlett alone.

Once she'd left, Scarlett went to check with Delilah, just in case she needed any help. She found her hiding in the kitchen, clearly trying to avoid Vivian.

"She just left," Scarlett told her.

"Thank goodness." Delilah breathed a sigh of relief. "She leaned in the door and told me she'd be back in the morning to bring the next couple of days of Hal's vitamin smoothies."

"She brings them instead of just giving you the ingredients to make them here?"

"Yes. I think she feels this is her way of doing her part. She and Frank have been into healthy supplements for a while and they came up with some green-looking smoothie to help Hal. She always makes a batch at home and has Hal drink eight ounces every morning. He says it doesn't taste too bad."

"That's nice, I guess."

Delilah eyed her. "You look tired. How was your day in town?"

"I shopped." Scarlett grinned. "That's one of my favorite activities. And Vivian was pleasant. She has a lot of interesting stories. No one else could get a word in, but I actually enjoyed myself just listening. I think Hal did too, even if he'd already heard the stories a thousand times."

"Vivian can be fun sometimes," Delilah allowed. "As long as the focus is all on her."

"I'll remember that." Stifling a yawn with her hand, Scarlett shrugged. "You know, I think I might turn in early myself, after watching a little TV to help me relax. All that shopping can wear a girl out."

"I imagine so." Delilah grinned. "I'm just going to do some food prep for tomorrow morning and then I'll be taking off."

"Do you need any help?"

"Nope. You go on and get your rest. I'll see you in the morning."

Any other time, Scarlett might have insisted on helping. But she really was tired and Hal had been kind enough to put a decent size TV in her room.

Changing into her comfy pajamas, she scrubbed off her makeup and brushed her teeth. Before climbing into bed, she hung up her new outfits.

She barely watched a two-hour crime drama before dozing off. She slept deeply and well, waking shortly after sunrise feeling restored and refreshed.

In the morning, after her shower, she dried her hair and expertly applied her makeup. Then she put on another one of her favorite dresses, a lovely bright yellow color that always made her feel cheerful. This time for shoes she chose a comfy pair of wedge heels.

After heading into the kitchen, she made a pot of coffee and checked the fridge to see what Delilah had prepped for breakfast. Scarlett got a kick out of making Hal's morning fare.

Inside the refrigerator, she found baggies of chopped tomatoes, onion and shredded cheese next to a package of corn tortillas. Delilah had left a note—*Scramble some eggs and make breakfast tacos. Hal loves them.*

"So do I," Scarlett said out loud. Maybe making one of Hal's favorite foods might entice him to eat. She fixed herself a cup of strong coffee and got busy scrambling eggs to fry later.

Hal wheeled himself into the kitchen just as she was setting up the cast-iron skillet on the stove. "Good morning," he said, eyeing the coffee with bleary eyes.

"Let me get you a cup," Scarlett said. "There's nothing better in the morning."

Once she had him situated at the table, cup of coffee at his right, newspaper in front of him, she got busy making their breakfast. She went ahead and made him a plate, ladling scrambled eggs and sausage onto two corn tortillas. She placed this in front of him, along with the cut-up tomatoes and onion, picante sauce and shredded cheese.

"Wow," Hal said, making no move to touch his food. "I can't remember the last time I had this."

After making her own plate, she sat down across from him. "It's not exactly a breakfast staple in Georgia either. But it smells great, so let's dig in." She stared at him until he finally dropped a bit of cheese on one of his tacos and picked it up to take a bite.

When he took another, she relaxed enough to doctor up hers.

They were delicious. Keeping an eye on Hal, who chewed slowly but continued to take small bites out of his first taco, she devoured her two and considered making herself another. Only the possibility that someone else might stop by for breakfast kept her from doing that.

Hal put his taco down before finishing it. He looked across the table at Scarlett and shook his head. "I'm sorry," he said. "I tried. But that's all my stomach can handle."

No wonder he appeared to be wasting away. He barely ate anything.

"Are you sure?" she asked, letting her worry color her voice. "Could you at least try to finish one?"

"I'll get sick. I already feel queasy." He slid his plate toward her. "You go ahead and take the other one. I didn't even touch it." Taking one final sip of his coffee, he wheeled himself into the living room and turned on the TV.

Feeling defeated, Scarlett cleaned up the table, refrigerating the remaining scrambled eggs along with everything else, just in case someone else showed up.

Someone else. Who was she kidding? Travis. She kept hoping he'd come by before starting his workday. She really wanted to ask him about the kiss.

When Delilah arrived, Hal had fallen asleep in front of the TV and Scarlett was nursing her second cup of coffee.

"Did he eat?" Delilah asked.

Shaking her head, Scarlett admitted defeat. "I honestly tried. There are leftovers in the fridge if you want to heat them up."

"Thanks." Looking over at Hal, Delilah frowned. "I swear he's getting weaker by the day. He's got to eat. Did Vivian bring his vitamin smoothie yet?"

"No, not yet."

"She'll be along sooner or later." Delilah glanced at her watch. "This is still early for her."

Scarlett grimaced. "I'll make sure to stay out of her way. In the meantime, is there anything I can do to help you? I'm at a bit of a loss to keep myself busy. I'm not used to sitting around doing nothing."

"Well…" Delilah thought for a moment. "Would you mind grabbing the mail for me?" she asked. "I didn't get it yesterday and completely forgot to stop at the mailbox when I drove in this morning. If not, I can ask Vivian to bring it when she comes."

"I can do it. Where's the mailbox?"

"At the end of the driveway. It's a bit of a walk and my knee is bothering me."

"No problem at all." Relieved to have something to do, even something so minor, Scarlett glanced down at her cute wedge heels and grimaced. "Though I think I'll put on something more suited for walking. I brought my favorite pair of Asics, plus yesterday I purchased a pair of boots."

In her room, she switched out her heels for the sneakers and then headed down the drive with a jaunty step. Once, she'd used to jog for exercise. Maybe she'd take it up again. Out here in the country would be the perfect place.

Outside, the air felt clean and fresh. With the sun shining, birds singing, and the trees and grass so green, she felt like singing. Instead, she walked at a brisk pace down the long drive.

The mailbox was crammed full of mail, making her wonder how long it had been since anyone bothered to empty it. As she pulled envelopes and advertisements out, a large, white envelope caught her eye.

Scrawled on the front in black Sharpie was her name. Just Scarlett. Nothing else, no stamps or address.

Trepidation running through her, she glanced around, almost expecting some shadowy figure to magically appear. But other than the cows grazing in the nearby pasture, she remained alone.

She stuffed the envelope in with the rest of the mail and headed back toward the house.

Once there, she took everything into the kitchen and dumped it on the counter. Then she withdrew the white envelope and stared at it.

Delilah came over. "What's wrong? You look like you saw a rattlesnake or something."

"This was in with the mail." Scarlett held up the envelope. "I have no idea who it's from."

Shaking her head, Delilah sighed. "Why assume it's something bad? Maybe some folks just want to welcome you to Anniversary."

"I don't know..."

"Well, open it then. You won't know until you do." Opening one of the cabinet drawers, Delilah slid a letter opener across the counter.

Unable to explain or rationalize her sense of foreboding, Scarlett realized the other woman was right. She used the letter opener to slit under the seal.

Inside, she found one single sheet of paper. As she withdrew it, she realized her trepidation had been well-founded. Four words, formed of a mishmash of letters that had been cut and pasted from magazines.

GO HOME! OR ELSE!

"Or else what?" Delilah made a tsk-tsk sound. "What kind of fool would do something like that?"

Shocked, all Scarlett could do was shake her head.

"Not only that," Delilah continued. "Why not just use a printer? Why go through all the trouble of trying to make this look like an old-school type of threat?"

Again, Scarlett had no answer. "I just don't understand. Ever since I arrived, people have been acting weird. Starting with Travis, who treats me like I'm out to hurt Hal. And Vivian's initial reaction was similar, though she seemed to warm up quite a bit yesterday. The thing is, I have no idea why?"

"Well…" Glancing around as if to make sure no one else was listening, Delilah leaned in. "Apparently, Wave Oil Company believes there's oil on this land. They've been making more and more outrageous offers, trying to get Mr. Hal to let them drill. Both Hal and Travis are against it. Vivian, her boyfriend, Frank, and Amber are all for it."

"Okay, that's interesting. But what does that have to do with me?"

Instead of answering, Delilah gave her a minute to think about the answer.

"They believe I'm working with the oil company?" Scarlett guessed. "Or at least Travis might."

"Exactly. I think that's part of it, I'm sure. I'd also venture a guess that Travis and Vivian both worry that you got wind of possible oil money and that's why you showed up here."

Scarlett let her mouth drop open. "Are you serious?"

"Well, it's only a guess. No one has come out and actually said that, at least to me. But it's the only explanation that makes sense."

Scarlett studied the letter again. "What about this? Surely you don't think Travis or Vivian sent it?"

"No. Neither of them would do something like that. Travis is an honest man. He'd sooner speak his thoughts out loud to your face than do something crazy like send a vague threat made up out of cutout letters."

"What about Vivian?" Scarlett frowned. "She really seemed to warm up to me yesterday."

"Vivian would also have no problem with saying her feelings directly to you. She's not the type to send a threatening letter."

"I met someone named Kendra in town. She said she was Travis's ex. She wanted me to give him a message to call her, which I haven't since I haven't seen him. Is she the jealous type?"

"Kendra?" Delilah made a face. "She was before my time, so I've never met her. But from what I hear, she wouldn't have any reason to be jealous of anyone. Plus, since she found you, I think if she had something hateful to say, she'd say it in person."

"Then who?"

They both stared at each other.

"I don't know," Delilah finally said. "Show it to Travis the next time you see him. But for pity's sake, don't let Mr. Hal find out about it."

Scarlett agreed. She slid the paper back into the envelope. "I'm going to put this in my room. And then, I think I'll change into my jeans and go for a walk. Getting some fresh air might help clear my head."

Even though she preferred to wash new clothes before wearing them, this time Scarlett decided to make an exception. The new jeans were soft and fit like a glove. Though the boots had a slight heel, it was nothing like her stilettos, so would be much more suited for a walk on the ranch roads.

She debated wearing the new cowboy hat, but decided to wear her old favorite Atlanta Braves baseball cap instead. Pulling her hair back into a ponytail, she surveyed herself in the mirror. Much better suited to the HG Ranch lifestyle. In fact, she knew she would have fit in better walking around Anniversary if she'd worn something like this instead of what her mother used to call her Sunday best.

Grabbing a bottle of water from the fridge, she told Delilah goodbye and set off. The odd letter had her amped up.

Out in front of the old Victorian house, she stepped off the front porch and tried to decide which way to go. Of course, she'd have to walk down the long driveway to the mailbox again, but once there she had her choice of directions.

When she reached the mailbox, she refused to allow that stupid letter to make her afraid. After all, it hadn't actually contained a specific threat. And, since very few people knew she was here, she figured maybe it might be possible Vivian was playing some sort of prank. Despite what Delilah had said, Scarlett could see Vivian enjoying the drama something like the letter would cause.

Which was why Scarlett knew she'd be keeping it

quiet. Sure, she'd probably mention it to Travis, but only him. And even then, she figured she'd ask him not to say anything about it to anyone else.

Where the driveway met the dirt road, she chose to go right. Even though she remembered that was the way toward the ranch foreman's house—Travis, Vivian, Amber and Will—she also recalled seeing another road branching off between two fenced pastures. She'd take that way. Maybe she'd even see some horses or cows or goats. Any kind of cute animal would do.

After a solitary breakfast, Travis went to the barn and saddled up his horse. He'd felt a bit weird, skipping out on Hal, but now that Scarlett was there, he'd wanted to give them a bit of privacy. And truth be told, he needed some distance from her as well. The constant pull of attraction warring with distrust made him uneasy.

The early morning sunshine and warm air felt more reminiscent of spring rather than early fall, but considering sometimes October had a heat wave, he'd take it. Here in East Texas, the leaves were still green and wouldn't even begin to turn until they'd had at least one good cold snap. Travis loved this time of the year. No longer the smoldering heat of July, August and September, the more comfortable temperatures made working outside much more pleasant.

Today he planned to ride the perimeter of the pastures closest to the barns. Every fall before winter, they brought the cattle in from the more remote locations. He needed to personally inspect miles of fence and make note of any needed repairs.

He took care of the western pastures first. Tedious

work, but he got it done in only a few hours. Even his horse appeared to be enjoying the day. Next, he would ride the eastern acreage. Hopefully he would finish before lunch.

When he reached the crossroads, he turned right. Ahead, he saw someone walking alone and frowned. As he drew closer, he realized it was Scarlett. Her long, dark hair had been pulled back in a ponytail and she wore an Atlanta Braves baseball cap. Even more astonishing, instead of a dress and heels, she wore jeans and…boots?

This area just happened to be where the oil company wanted to put their first well. Coincidence? He had to wonder.

She must have been lost in pretty deep thought because he got pretty close before the sound of his horse's hooves registered. Spinning around, she eyed him in silence before finally reluctantly smiling.

"Naturally," she said, her gaze sweeping over him. "You look like you were born to be in the saddle."

Though she probably didn't realize it, she'd just given him one of the highest compliments possible. "Thank you," he replied, touching the brim of his hat. "Are you feeling faint or something?"

"Of course not," she scoffed. "Back home, I try to hit the gym at least three or four times a week. Since I didn't see a gym in Anniversary, I figured I could at least start walking. Though," she said, glancing down at her feet, "I'd have done better leaving my sneakers on instead of wearing a brand-new pair of boots. I think I'm getting heel blisters."

"We have a gym," he said. "It's not on Main Street, though. I was just there last night."

"You work out?"

"Yep." Tilting his head, he eyed her. "As a matter of fact, last night I talked to someone I used to know. She said she asked you to pass a message along to me. Did you forget?"

"Kendra?" She said the name as if it tasted bad in her mouth. "No, I didn't forget. I just didn't see you. I figured I'd tell you when I did. But since you apparently already hooked up, I guess there's no need."

"We most certainly did not *hook up*," he drawled, deciding his non-relationship with Kendra wasn't anything he needed to elaborate on. "You're kind of far from the house. You're not lost, are you?"

"No. I needed to walk." She took a deep breath, looking around as if she expected someone else to show up out of thin air. "I'm a little upset. Someone hand delivered a threatening letter. They put it in the mailbox with the mail."

Instantly alert, he kept his gaze locked on her while getting his restless horse settled. "Threatening how?"

"It was vague, not a specific threat, so I'm not too frightened." Her calm, matter-of-fact tone contrasted the worry in her eyes.

"Maybe not, but tell me what it said."

"Go home. Or else."

"That's all?" He relaxed slightly.

"Yes. I told you it wasn't specific. But the fact that they—whoever they are—took the time to cut out letters from magazines and paste them, instead of simply printing out something, has me a bit concerned."

She had a point there. His first thought was of Hal. "You didn't tell Hal about this, did you?"

"No. Only Delilah. And I hid the letter in my bedroom so Hal won't see it. I just can't figure out why anyone would want to do such a thing."

Impatient with the delay, Travis's horse shifted his weight and stomped his feet. While getting the animal back under control Travis used the distraction to remind himself he really didn't need to be thinking about her lips. "From what you've said, that letter sounds more like a prank than a threat."

"Maybe so." She gave a graceful shrug. "But if it was, again I have to wonder why? And who? As far as I know, there are only a handful of people who even know who I am. You, Hal, Delilah, Vivian and Amber."

"That's probably where you're wrong. Anniversary is a small town and gossip travels fast. Especially since you walked around the square yesterday. I've already gotten a few text messages from my guy friends asking about you."

"Really?" Hands on her shapely hips, she peered up at him. "What were they wanting to know?"

Belatedly realizing his ambivalence about all that, he decided to tell her anyway. "They saw you in town yesterday and wanted to know if you're single."

Her face colored. "Oh. That's nice, I suppose."

"Are you?" he pressed. "Single, that is?"

She lifted her chin, once again appearing cool and collected. "Why do you want to know?"

Since he didn't have an answer for that, he said nothing. He supposed he could have offered to fix her up with one of his friends, but the thought of another man putting his hands on her had him clenching his teeth.

She took a step closer, which intrigued his mount.

Since the horse seemed more curious rather than startled, Travis simply kept an eye on him.

"Travis?" She stopped and gazed up at him. "Why did you kiss me?"

Damned if he knew how to respond to that, especially since he had no idea. Even worse, he wanted to kiss her again. He went with the truth. "I don't know." Aware he revealed his frustration in his tone, he took a deep breath before continuing. "I apologize."

"No need. I was into it, actually." The lightness of her tone contrasted the determined glint in her green eyes. "But it doesn't seem like us taking that any further would be a good idea. I'm thinking maybe we should make sure it doesn't happen again."

Though he managed a nod, he didn't want to make a promise he wasn't sure he could keep. Especially since she'd admitted she'd been into it. Now all he could think about right now was how badly he wanted to dismount and sweep her into his arms.

"Is that what you want?" he finally managed to ask. Maybe if she told him directly that she wouldn't welcome his kiss or that she found him repulsive, that would help him get past this absurd attraction to her.

"I'm not sure," she answered, surprising him. "To be completely honest, you're a pretty good kisser."

Elation and desire surged through him, which he quickly throttled. He might want her, true, but he needed to be more than careful. Until he learned exactly what her true purpose was here, he'd try to keep his distance.

Though he suspected that might be easier said than done.

"You've been walking a lot lately, haven't you?" Changing the subject to something safe.

"I have." Her smile let him know she understood exactly what he was doing. "I've been enjoying the countryside, plus getting some exercise. Walking is a great way to see the ranch. It's much more up close and personal than driving around in my car."

"Would you like to learn how to ride?" he asked, surprising himself. "It's not that difficult and I have a couple of older, well-trained horses that would be perfect for a beginner to learn on."

Tilting her head, she considered his offer. "And you'd be willing to teach me?"

"Yep." Though doing so would entail them spending more time together, he didn't reckon it would take that long. She just needed to know the basics, not anything fancy.

"I think I'd like that." The mischievous sparkle in her emerald eyes should have warned him. "As long as you promise to be civil."

"Civil?" He frowned. "I've gone out of my way to be—"

"I'm kidding." She cut him off with a wide grin. When she placed her hand on his leg, he knew he was in trouble. "You don't have to take everything so seriously."

Though logistically impossible, her fingers seared his skin through his jeans. Staring down at her, her lovely face raised to his, laughter curving her sensuous mouth, he couldn't breathe, never mind think.

"When?" Scarlett asked.

"When what?" he managed to reply.

"When do you want to teach me how to ride?"

"Soon." Nudging his horse with his leg, he moved away from her. "I'll let you know."

Then he rode off, refusing to look over his shoulder, aware he'd be seeing her face in his mind the rest of the day.

Chapter 6

A hint of crispness had begun to creep into the air, signaling the possibility that summer might be ready to relinquish her grip on East Texas and allow autumn to visit awhile. Back in Atlanta, Scarlett knew decorated pumpkins and scarecrows would be appearing on people's front porches. In the South, the leaves might have begun to turn—nothing dramatic, just a few spots of bright red or yellow here and there. So far, she hadn't seen any leaf changes here, though Delilah assured her it would eventually happen.

Since they were so far out in the country and so isolated, there wouldn't be any trick-or-treaters, so there was no need for any decorations. Though Scarlett didn't comment, inside she felt disappointed. Halloween had always been one of her favorite holidays. She'd amassed quite a collection of ghoulish decorations. They were all in storage now.

As she walked into the kitchen, something caught her eyes. An invite sat on the Formica counter. A bright orange jack-o'-lantern on a jet-black background. A yellow crescent moon decorated one corner and the words *You're Invited* were spelled out in silver glitter.

"What's this?" Scarlett asked, picking it up.

"An invitation to the annual Anniversary Halloween Harvest Fair and Costume Ball," Delilah said. "It's quite a big deal around here. Hal is usually involved in the planning committee."

"Not this year," Hal said grumpily. "Been too damn sick. Who knows what it'll be like without me?"

"I'm sure it will be fine." Delilah's brisk tone warred with her watchful expression as she met Scarlett's gaze. "I'm hoping we can talk Hal into attending, even if it's only for a little while. Vivian already said she'd take him."

"Not gonna do it." Hal shook his head. "I don't want people staring and pointing and telling me how much weight I've lost. As if I didn't already know."

"It won't be like that." Stubbornly persisting, Delilah glared at him, her hands on her ample hips. "And it would do you a world of good to get out of this house once in a while."

"I'd love for you to show me around," Scarlett interjected.

"I'm sorry." Hal's gaze softened. "But maybe you and Travis can go instead."

Though Scarlett nodded, she couldn't help but frown.

"What's wrong?" Hal asked, clearly noticing.

While she didn't want to say anything bad about

Travis, Hal also needed to understand that everything wasn't roses and sunshine between them.

"I'd rather go with you," she settled on.

"Oh, horse-pucky," Hal countered. "Travis could do a much better of job of making sure you have a good time. Me, I'd get exhausted within thirty minutes and need to be taken home. You go with Travis."

"Travis is a difficult man to get to know," she said, quietly.

Her comment made Hal hoot with laughter. "Tactful as your mother was, aren't you?"

Reluctantly, she nodded. "I just don't know what I've done, but Travis doesn't like me very much." Or trust her, but she'd leave that unsaid. And she also wouldn't mention the tiny fact that he'd kissed her.

"Though he did offer to teach you how to horseback ride," Delilah put in helpfully, making Scarlett regret telling her.

"He did?" Hal raised both his bushy eyebrows. "That's promising. See, he likes you. He wouldn't have offered to show you the ropes around his beloved horses if he didn't."

Thankful she hadn't said anything to anyone about the kiss, Scarlett reluctantly nodded.

"I worry about him," Hal confided. "Even as a young boy, Travis had a serious nature. He works hard, too hard if you ask me. Never makes time for fun. Ever since Kendra..."

"I met her in town," she confessed. "She asked me to pass a message on to Travis."

"She's back?" Hal frowned. "That can't be good,"

"What happened between her and Travis?"

Hal looked down. "Now I feel like I'm gossiping.

But maybe if I tell you, it'll help you understand why Travis acts the way he does."

Intrigued, she waited.

With a sigh, Hal leaned forward in his wheelchair. "Kendra was Travis's high school sweetheart. After they graduated, they'd planned to get married but she decided to go away to college. She chose the University of Texas, down in Austin. She wanted Travis to go with her, but he'd never wanted to do anything but run the farm. He was happy for her, though. He said he'd never begrudge her getting an education."

"I can guess what happened," Scarlett interjected. "She got to college, met other boys and broke off the engagement."

"Not exactly." Hal's morose expression had her reaching out to cover the back of his hand with hers. "They stayed engaged the entire four years she was at school. She came home on breaks and during the summer and he tried to get down to Austin at least once a month. It was tough on both of them, but they did it."

"Wow. I'm impressed. That's some dedication."

"It is." Grimacing, Hal shrugged. "She came back with a business degree. She stuck around, sent out résumés, but she wanted to work in Houston or Dallas for a big company. When she landed her dream job, she kept it a secret for two weeks."

Scarlett winced. Clearly hearing this story for the first time, Delilah did the same.

"She wanted them to try to make it work. A long-distance thing, like they'd done while she was in college," Hal continued. "Travis put his foot down. He wasn't moving to Houston and she wasn't staying in

Anniversary. When he told her she had to choose, I suspect he knew that the choice had already been made."

"How long ago did all this happen?" Scarlett asked.

"Right about two years. Travis was a wreck for a long while, but he dealt with it by throwing himself into work. I swear, he did more around the ranch than five men the first months after she up and moved to Houston."

Two years. "I'm guessing he's over it now."

"As far as I know," Hal agreed. "Anyway, the reason I told you this story is I wanted you to understand why he might be a little uncomfortable around you."

"Because I'm a woman?" Incredulous, she shook her head.

"No. Because you're a lot like Kendra. You're also college-educated and you clearly prefer big city life to that in the country. You wear designer clothes and high heels. And you're beautiful."

"I have a fine arts degree," she protested. "Not business. There's a huge difference."

Hal shrugged. "Maybe so, but not to him. Why does it bother you so much?"

Now she squirmed, not wanting to admit how attractive she found Travis. "I don't know," she finally said. "I just couldn't figure out why he didn't like me. I go out of my way to be pleasant to him…"

Eyeing her, Hal nodded. "I see."

Though she suspected she hadn't fooled him, she kept her expression bland. "Thank you for telling me. That explains a lot."

"You're welcome. But you can't say anything to Travis."

"I won't," she promised.

Hal gripped her hand. "Will you help him?"

This confused her. "Help him how?"

"He needs a friend," Hal said.

"I'm sure he has plenty of those." She hastened to assure the older man. "He told me about some of his friends texting him."

"Yes, he has a couple of guys he plays ball or poker with or goes drinking with. They watch football occasionally. All but two of them are married with kids." Hal shifted in his chair, his frustration evident. "I'm not really sure what I'm asking of you. Maybe just be there for him, in case he wants to open up. He's got a lot on his plate right now. He runs the ranch, worries about me and takes care of his mother and sister and nephew."

Touched, she nodded. "I'll do the best I can. But honestly, I'm pretty sure he's not going to want to be friends with me." Friends. When all she could think about was the intensity in the way Travis had kissed her. She knew if they were to take things any further, smoldering embers would ignite into a blazing inferno.

Not only was she not sure she could handle anything that deep, she suspected Travis definitely couldn't. And since the last thing she'd ever want to do was hurt him, or get hurt herself, it'd be best for both of them if they kept their distance. She didn't see friendship as a possibility at all.

None of that could she say to Hal, who continued to eye her hopefully. "You're a good man, Hal Gardner."

Delilah snorted. "I wouldn't go that far." She and Hal grinned at each other. "I see what you're doing there, Mr. Hal."

"Innocent until proven guilty." He held up both hands in mock protest.

"Don't let him play matchmaker on you," Delilah told Scarlett. "That kind of thing rarely works out for the best. There. I've said my piece." And she turned and stomped away.

Not sure what to make of this, Scarlett stared after her.

"She's not really mad," Hal claimed. "She's actually tickled pink at the possibility of getting Travis to come out of his shell."

"I'm not sure I'm the right person to do that," she protested. "Seriously."

"But you'll at least think about going to the Halloween ball, right?"

"Yes." With Vivian and Amber, if they invited her. No way was she going to try to force Travis to endure her company at a Halloween ball. He definitely didn't seem like the type to feel comfortable wearing a costume whereas she quite naturally would revel in it.

For lunch, Delilah fixed an assortment of sandwiches. "Travis called and said he'd be stopping by," she informed Hal and Scarlett. "You know how hungry he gets after working all morning."

Just the mention of Travis's name made Scarlett's entire body perk up, though she took care not to show it.

He arrived a few minutes later, striding through the door, his sheer size filling the room. Scarlett almost lost her words as she let her eyes drink him in, but she managed a casual greeting.

They ate at the kitchen table. Surprisingly, Scarlett managed to finish her sandwich. She hadn't realized it would be such a struggle to keep herself from staring at him. So she did what she always did when she got nervous—chattered about inconsequential things like the monarch butterfly migration. She caught both Hal and Delilah giving her odd looks, but Travis pretty much ignored her.

When they'd finished eating, Delilah gathered up the plates and began washing up the dishes. Though she knew she was rambling at this point, Scarlett continued her discourse on butterflies.

"I need a word with you," Travis said, interrupting her as she'd just about finished describing the time she'd been right in the middle of thousands of the beautiful creatures. "In private."

Though both Hal and Delilah stared, neither commented. Delilah shot Scarlett a look of warning, while a small smile played around Hal's mouth.

Heart pounding and curious, Scarlett stood and followed Travis outside.

As they stood on the front porch, he shifted his weight from one foot to the other, making her realize he was uncomfortable.

"What's wrong?" she asked, genuinely concerned. "Is it about Hal?"

"No, nothing like that." He cleared his throat. "I need to ask you for a favor." The reluctance coloring his tone revealed how much doing so pained him.

"Okay."

"As you know, my ex is in town—long story—and I need a date for the Halloween ball. Every year, Anniversary does this big Halloween festival, culminated by a costume ball on the weekend before October 31. Since I represent the HG Ranch, I always go."

Her first reaction was suspicion. "Did Hal put you up to this?" she asked.

"Hal?" He frowned. "Not at all. He doesn't even know Kendra's in town."

"He does now," she replied. "I just mentioned her in passing."

Travis shrugged. "He never liked her anyway. About the ball. Will you go with me?"

"You're honestly telling me you can't find a date from among the women in town?" she asked, crossing her arms.

"I could," he replied, again surprising her. "But I need someone spectacular. Someone like you."

For a few seconds she allowed herself to bask in the glow of hearing that Travis found her spectacular, but then reality crept in just like it always did.

"So you're still hung up on your ex? So much so that you want to try to make her jealous?" That stung, yes it did, though she sure as heck didn't want Travis to know.

"Not at all." Grim-faced, he shook his head. "She's already stalking me. Apparently, she works for Wave Oil Company now. I just want her to leave me alone. If she thinks I'm in love with someone else, she will."

"In love with..." Her knees felt weak. "Have you lost your mind?"

"No. I just hadn't worked my way around telling you the rest of the favor I need from you. I need you to not only be my date for the night, but to pretend to be madly in love with me and vice versa."

"And vice versa," she echoed, dazed. "What makes you think I'd be any good at acting?"

"Because of the way you kiss." Though his skin reddened slightly, he held her gaze and didn't back down. "Here." He handed her a slip of paper. "My phone number. You don't have to answer right now. Call me when you decide."

"Oh," she squeaked, accepting the paper. She wondered if he realized that with a request like that, there was no way she could turn him down. "I don't need to think about it. It's okay, I'll go with you." And then she turned and went back inside the house, telling herself she wasn't retreating. The last thing she needed to do, though sorely tempted, would be to kiss him again.

Jaw clenched, Travis didn't follow Scarlett back into the house. Damned if he knew how or why he'd managed to make an even bigger fool of himself than he'd thought he would. All he'd planned to do was to invite her to the ball, letting her know the actual reason why and simply leaving it there.

Instead, he'd not only managed to tell her he found her spectacular—and where had he come up with that word?—but to also admit he'd enjoyed kissing her. And then, to top it off, he'd asked her to pretend to be in love with him. He certainly hadn't planned *that*.

What the actual hell? But then, she had agreed to go with him, so his mission had been accomplished. She'd let him off the hook too. Most women would have taken his comment about kissing as an invitation to kiss him again. He wasn't sure if he should be relieved or disappointed.

The Halloween ball. Arguably one of the most important events in Anniversary. If he could have managed to skip out on it, he would have, but the HG Ranch had to have representation.

Years ago, the ball had been known as the Harvest Ball. Tradition decreed that all the area farms and ranches send representatives. Even after the ball had been changed to the Halloween Harvest Fair and Costume Ball, the long-established custom had continued.

Until his mysterious illness took away his strength, Hal had always made attending a priority. Who he'd choose as his escort had been anyone's guess. Sometimes he'd have a woman he'd been dating on his arm, other times he'd let Vivian or even Amber fill in. Travis just knew if Hal had been well enough, he'd have insisted his newfound daughter accompany him this year.

Instead, she'd be going with Travis. He hoped Hal would approve. Travis figured he would. Next, he'd need to work with Scarlett on choosing their costumes. He suspected if he left it up to her, he'd end up wearing a clown costume or something.

Back at work, this time driving one of the big trucks pulling a trailer to bring in hay for the winter, he found he couldn't stop thinking about her reaction to his comment about the way she kissed. For one heart-stopping moment, he'd thought she might kiss him again. Luckily for both of them, she'd fled.

When he reached the meadow where the hay was being made into huge round bales, he backed his trailer up and got out to watch as a loader placed his hay, bale by bale, until he had two huge stacks covering the entire length of the trailer. Another one of his ranch hands had pulled up with a second truck and trailer and had parked, waiting his turn.

Travis waved to him as he drove past, heading back to the huge hay storage barn. They kept this filled over the winter, just in case. Though East Texas generally enjoyed mild temperatures during the winter months, some years brought ice storms and snow. Once the grass died, the cattle depended on the hay as a major source of food.

His cell phone rang just as he'd pulled up to the barn. Amber. "You are not going to believe who showed up at the house a few minutes ago."

His heart sank. "Please don't say Kendra."

"How'd you know?"

"Because she not only called me yesterday, but showed up at my gym. She's back in town working for Wave Oil and trying to get me to sign that oil lease."

Amber swore. "Seriously? I mean, you know I'm in favor of the oil drilling, but not if it benefits her in any way."

"Is she still there?" Escorting Kendra off his property was the last thing he felt like dealing with.

"No," Amber replied. "I sent her packing."

"Thank you," he said, meaning it. "I'm about to supervise having a bunch of hay unloaded, so can we talk later?"

"Definitely." A note of mischief had crept back into his sister's voice. "I really want to talk about what you and Scarlett are going to dress as for the ball." She hung up before he could reply.

He could only imagine how his inviting Scarlett had started everyone talking. Since, he couldn't tell them the truth, he had no choice but to let them believe what they chose.

For the first time, he wondered if Kendra would be tactless enough to attend. But he already knew the answer to that. Brazen and shameless, Kendra would enjoy trying to make him or Scarlett squirm in front of the entire town. He'd have to make sure that didn't happen.

Part of him couldn't help but wonder how it had come to this. Kendra wasn't a bad person, she'd just chosen a different lifestyle and they'd gone their separate ways. Sure, there'd been pain on both sides, and bitterness. But time had helped him heal and he'd always supposed it'd been the same for her.

So why was she acting like this? Skirting the edges of outright stalking him. And for what? No matter how badly she wanted to be successful at her job, she had to know such behavior wouldn't make him more inclined to sign on the dotted line.

For the first time, he wondered about the timing of Kendra's arrival in town and the strangely vague note someone had sent to Scarlett. But that made absolutely no sense.

After he finished working for the day, instead of going home, he texted his friend Mike to meet him for a beer in town.

When he arrived, Mike had already claimed a barstool and ordered them both a tall glass of draft beer.

Sliding onto a stool, Travis greeted his friend and thanked him for the beer.

"How's Hal doing?" Mike asked. "Lots of people are praying for him."

"He's about the same." Though it pained him to say those words, he managed to keep his tone light. "My mother is looking into getting him into some specialty diagnostic place in Dallas. Not a single doctor has been able to pinpoint what's ailing him. One guy even went so far as to suggest it was all in Hal's head."

"That's ridiculous."

"I agree." Travis shook his head. "But some of those doctors get pretty defensive when you question them."

"Speaking of questioning..." Mike nudged him with an elbow. "Why didn't you just tell me you'd staked a claim on that woman from Georgia when I asked for her number?"

Which meant the gossip about him taking Scarlett to the ball had traveled with lightning speed and had already reached town.

"I didn't know if she'd agree to go," Travis replied, wanting to stick as close to the truth as possible, without bringing up Kendra. "If she'd said no, then I might have introduced the two of you. Now, there's not a chance in hell of that happening."

Taking a swig of his beer, the other man laughed. "Can't say I blame you. She's a pretty one, that's for sure. I've also heard that someone has been threatening her, trying to get her to leave. Are you on top of that?"

Instantly alert, Travis wondered if Mike meant that vague note Scarlett had received or if something else had happened. "What exactly have you heard?" he asked, cautiously. "Clearly, I don't have access to the steady stream of gossip like you apparently do."

Mike shrugged. "Hell, I've just been talking to Amber. I'm taking her to the ball."

"My sister?" Travis wasn't sure how he felt about that. But Amber was a grown woman recovering from an ugly divorce, so he figured she knew what she was doing.

"Yep. Amber loves gossip. But I'd heard stuff even before Amber told me. Nothing serious. Just rumors. But you know how it is. Anniversary is a small town and people like to talk. Some of them ain't got much else to do. Everyone's fascinated by Scarlett. Her being so damn gorgeous doesn't help. Women are jealous and the men can't take their eyes off her. Some people think she might be a scammer, pretending to be related to old man Gardner just so she can take over the ranch."

To Travis's surprise, hearing this from someone else made him feel oddly protective of Scarlett. Despite initially wondering the same thing himself, he realized he didn't like outsiders thinking or speaking ill of her.

"Eh." Waving away Mike's concern, Travis sipped his beer and tried for nonchalance. "She seems genuine. You used the word *threat*, though. Is someone making threats against her? If so, I need to know about it."

Mike mentioned the note and when Travis commented on the vagueness of it, the other man agreed. He hadn't heard anything specific, he said. Just a lot of speculation on who might want her gone. By the end of the conversation, Travis got the impression that other people tended to take the note more seriously than he did.

Should he be worried? While he pondered the question, Mike got up went over to chat with the blue-eyed blonde who'd been eyeing him. Her friend had been trying to flirt with Travis, but he ignored her. He already had his hands full dealing with Kendra and Scarlett. The last thing he needed was to bring another female into the mix.

Plus, truth be told, no one could hold a candle to Scarlett. Mike had been right—she was gorgeous. And kind and funny and compassionate. No. He cut off his thoughts. If he kept on like this, he'd be inventing excuses to be near her.

Finishing his beer, he waved a quick goodbye to Mike, who still stood next to the blonde woman, and climbed into his truck.

His phone rang as he drove home. Kendra. Perfect. Time to put a stop to this once and for all.

"Why didn't you tell me you were involved with someone?" The pique in Kendra's voice made her sound shrill. "All I'm hearing about from everyone in town is this Scarlett person."

"I didn't mention it to you because it's none of your business," Travis replied. "And please, stop calling me. I have nothing to say to you." With that, he ended the call. If Kendra kept on calling him, he'd block the number.

On the way to his house, he decided to stop in and check on Hal. The possibility of seeing Scarlett might have been a secondary factor.

When he pulled up, he saw her sitting in one of the large wooden rocking chairs on the front porch. He sat in his truck awhile and watched her. She'd seen him pull up and had straightened, clearly waiting for him to get out.

Apparently, he moved too slowly for her. She pushed to her feet and took the porch steps two at a time, before hurrying over toward him.

He had an instant fantasy flash of him opening his door, climbing out and crushing her to him for a deep, soul-searching kiss.

This foolishness only confirmed his suspicion that being around her any more than he had to would only cause trouble.

"I've been waiting for you," Scarlett declared, skidding to a stop mere inches from him, sending his heart rate into overdrive.

"Have you?" he drawled. "Why?"

"Because I just had the strangest phone call." Scarlett glanced up at him, through impossibly long lashes. "From your ex-fiancée, Kendra, though I have no idea how she got my number."

He swore. "I'm sorry. She called me a few minutes ago as well. I'll speak to her and tell her to stop harassing you."

"Oh, it wasn't like that." A hint of a grin teased the edge of her lips. "She wants to meet me for a drink. So we can be friends. And she can fill me in about you."

Staring, he wasn't sure how to respond.

"Don't worry," Scarlett continued. "I declined. And then I blocked her number so she can't call me again."

This made him laugh. "You know what? I think I like you." He spoke impulsively, but meant every word.

She smiled back, a slow, sexy smile that made her eyes sparkle. "I like you too," she replied, meeting his gaze.

Just like that, electricity crackled between them. He actually took a step toward her, every nerve ending alive, before realizing if he kissed her right here, right now, he'd never stop.

Chapter 7

Breathless with anticipation, Scarlett just knew Travis was about to kiss her. Even though they'd both kind of agreed there could be none of that kind of thing between them, she didn't care. She wanted him, needed him—okay, *craved* him.

Behind her, the front door opened with a crash and Delilah rushed out. "Come quickly," she hollered. "Something's wrong with Mr. Hal."

Travis sprinted for the house, with Scarlett right on his heels.

Though still in his wheelchair, Hal appeared to be convulsing.

"He's having a seizure," Delilah stated. "He's never done this before."

"Did you call 911?" Travis demanded.

"I did," Delilah answered, clearly on the verge of

tears. "They're sending an ambulance, but because we're so far out, it's going to be a while."

Scarlett knelt down next to Hal. She had no medical training, so stroking his arm softly and murmuring reassurances were the only things she knew to do. Somehow, that must have worked, because Hal grunted, before slumping back in his chair with his eyes closed. She had the random, panicked thought that she needed to do a DNA test before something happened, so no one would have the slightest doubt that Hal was her father.

After the paramedics arrived and ran through his vitals, they wanted to transport him to the hospital so more in-depth tests could be done. Hal, who'd regained consciousness and appeared both flustered and angry, refused. When Scarlett and Delilah both protested, the EMT informed them he couldn't take an adult against his will.

Travis, who'd remained silent, walked over and knelt down by Hal. "We need to find out what this is," he said softly. "Especially since this is something new. Let them take you to the ER. Maybe this time, the doctors will be able to figure out what's wrong."

Hal sagged in his chair. "I'm tired of being poked and prodded. Those fools don't have a clue. What makes you think it will be any different this time?"

"You won't know unless you try." Travis clapped his large hand on the other man's frail shoulder. "I'll go with you and I'll stay until they say you're okay to go home."

"I'll go too." Scarlett moved closer. "I can be there in case Travis has to attend to something here at the ranch."

Heaving an exhausted sigh, Hal looked from one to

the other. "Neither of you are going to let me get any rest unless I agree, are you?"

They both shook their heads.

"Fine." Hal gestured at the paramedic. "Load me up and we'll go."

Once at the hospital, Travis handled the paperwork while Scarlett told the triage nurse what had happened. An orderly immediately came out and wheeled Hal back.

"Stay with him," Travis ordered. "I'll be right there as soon as I finish this."

Once they had Hal inside a small ER room, the orderly transferred him from the stretcher to the bed. Eyes closed, Hal didn't resist. Another nurse came in and began peppering him with questions, to which he gave monosyllabic answers, mostly yes or no. She hooked him up to a blood pressure machine and put something on his finger to monitor his heart rate.

By now Travis had joined them, crossing over to stand next to Scarlett. When he took her hand, wrapping his larger one around hers, she nearly sagged against him. Struggling to hide her worry and fear, she managed a small hopeful smile.

"The doctor will be in soon," the nurse finally said briskly.

Once she'd gone, Hal opened his eyes. "I told you this was a waste of time," he grumbled. "I guarantee they're going to say they have no idea what's wrong with me and send me home."

"But you had a seizure," Scarlett said. "Surely they'll at least order a CT scan or an MRI or something."

"I've already had both of those." Hal sighed. "Inconclusive. They won't order another. Medicare won't pay for it."

"Is it possible he might have confused his medicines?" The doctor, an older man with steel-gray hair and a no-nonsense manner, stepped into the room and peered at them through his glasses. "Maybe taken too many, or even someone else's?"

Scarlett and Travis exchanged looks. "That's doubtful," Travis answered. "We have an in-home aide who oversees all of that. Why?"

"We've ordered several tests and a urinalysis. Some of these have to be sent off-site and we won't have the results for a few days."

Arms crossed, Travis nodded. "No offense, but we've heard this before. His health has been steadily going downhill and not one single doctor or clinic has been able to tell us why."

"I'm sorry." The doctor consulted his notes. "Do you know if Mr. Gardner has a history of drug or alcohol abuse?"

"He does not."

Scarlett laid her hand on Travis's shoulder. Judging from the tension in his jaw, his frustration levels were climbing. He glanced at her when she touched him, his gaze shuttered, but she swore she could feel him release some of his exasperation.

"Does he use any supplements, herbal remedies, medicines that aren't regulated by the FDA?"

Again, Travis shook his head no.

"I see. We've seen a few patients who ordered powdered caffeine over the internet. One of them had seizures."

"As far as I know, Hal doesn't take anything unusual. He rarely even uses a computer, never mind order things online."

"Okay. Anyway, we'd like to keep him here under observation overnight," the doctor continued.

"No." Hal protested loudly from in his room. Clearly, he'd been listening in. "I feel fine. I want to go home."

"There's nothing wrong with his hearing," Scarlett said, smiling.

The doctor consulted his notes and didn't smile back. "I'll let you discuss this with him," he said, and hurried off.

When Scarlett and Travis entered the small ER room, Hal glared at them. "Find my clothes," he ordered. "I want to go home."

"Maybe you should let them observe you," Scarlett suggested gently. "That seizure seemed pretty rough."

Hal snorted. "Travis, tell her how many times they've kept me for observation. And while you're at it, tell her what they've found."

"I think she knows." Travis exhaled. "Let me get you dressed and I'll take you home."

About to protest, Scarlett closed her mouth when Travis shook his head at her. "I'll wait in the hall," she said instead.

As soon as Travis had gotten Hal ready, they sent Scarlett in search of a wheelchair, a nurse, or both. She located an empty wheelchair near the deserted nurses' station, and commandeered it.

Rushing with the chair toward Hal's room, she felt a jolt of adrenaline. No one stopped her—the nurses were apparently all busy with other patients.

As soon as she got the chair into the room, Travis

lifted Hal up as if he weighed nothing, and carried him to the chair. Once he'd gotten the older man settled, he straightened and smiled at Scarlett. "Are you ready?"

She glanced around. "Don't we need to get discharge papers signed or something?"

"Nope," Hal answered. "We're doing this against doctor's orders. They'll be mad, but they'll get over it. Believe me, I know. This ain't my first rodeo."

She shrugged. "Okay, then. Let's go."

Travis commandeered the chair, leaving Scarlett to trail along behind them. Sure enough, they'd just made it past the nurse's station when one of the nurses noticed them.

Travis explained what they were doing. With a quick nod, she asked them to wait while she went to get the doctor. She hurried off. As soon as she'd disappeared around the corner, Travis pushed Hal toward the double doors that led to the triage area. When they were through, he asked Scarlett to wait with Hal and went to get his truck.

Standing by Hal and the wheelchair, Scarlett kept glancing over her shoulder, certain at any moment several nurses and the doctor would descend on them.

Instead, Travis pulled his truck up and parked. He got out, picked Hal up out of the chair and placed him in the back seat of his club cab. "While I make sure he's buckled in, would you mind returning that wheelchair to the ER?" he asked.

Though mildly uncomfortable, she did exactly that, pushing the chair up to the triage nurse and letting her know it was there. The busy nurse nodded but didn't ask any questions.

Relieved, Scarlett hurried outside and got in the truck.

When they arrived back at the main house, Vivian and Amber rushed out and waited on the front porch. After he parked, Travis asked his sister to bring out Hal's wheelchair. Even though Hal rarely went outside, Travis had built a ramp on one side of the house. Amber pushed the chair down this and over to them.

Travis got Hal settled once again. Though the constant jostling seemed to bother the older man, he didn't complain.

Inside the house, Will sat on the couch, engrossed in a game on a tablet. He looked up and brightened when he saw Travis and Hal, but continued to play.

"Well?" Vivian demanded. "Delilah told us what happened. What did the doctors have to say?"

Instead of answering, Hal sagged back in his chair and closed his eyes. Travis sighed and filled everyone in.

"I can't believe that," Vivian protested. "Why on earth can't anyone figure out what's going on with him?"

"I'd like to go to bed," Hal interjected, loudly. "Y'all feel free to talk about me once I'm gone. Travis, I'm going to need some help."

Hearing this, Delilah's brown eyes filled with tears. She waited until Travis had wheeled Hal into his room before speaking. "I've always felt as long as he could still lift himself in and out of that chair, he was going to be okay. Now, it seems as if he's taken a turn for the worst."

Vivian narrowed her eyes. "No. Don't even say such

a thing. He might still get better. We don't need negativity if we're going to win this battle."

Though Delilah nodded, when she turned away Scarlett saw the tears flowing down her cheeks.

Feeling a bit weepy herself, Scarlett thought of the doctor's questions and began rummaging through the cabinets to see if there were any strange supplements. Hal kept his medications in a plastic tray tucked inside the pantry, so she started there.

Most of the medication appeared to be prescription. She did find some vitamin E, some D3 and B12. All from reputable manufacturers.

"What are you doing?" Amber asked, coming over to stand next to Scarlett.

After repeating the doctor's query about unsafe supplements, especially from overseas, Scarlett continued looking. The oddest thing she found was a box of Matcha tea bags that were Lipton brand.

"Nothing here," she muttered. Amber, who'd gotten to work digging through another cupboard, shook her head. "Not here either. I don't really think Hal's the type to take supplements."

"He's not," Vivian drawled. "Believe me, I know. I've been trying for years to get him to try some of my herbal remedies."

"Mom's really big into all that," Amber explained. "Holistic medicine, alternative treatments, you name it."

Suddenly Scarlett couldn't help but regard Vivian with suspicion, though she tried not to let her thoughts show. "Have you given him anything, anything at all, that might have caused the seizure today?"

Vivian drew herself up tall, her lips pursed. "Certainly not. The only thing he gets from me are his green smoothies, which I drink as well."

"What's in them?" Scarlett persisted.

"Kale, spinach, banana, protein powder, Greek yogurt and some vitamin powder. He's been drinking them for years. So have I. Even Amber's tried them."

"True," Amber said, making a face. "I'm not fond of them, but they do seem to provide a pick-me-up when I need one."

Vivian went to the refrigerator and opened the door. "He has some left if you want to try it," she said. "I can pour you just a small bit so you can get a taste."

Unsure, Scarlett swallowed hard. "To be honest, it sounds pretty nasty to me."

"It is," Amber laughed. "But you should at least try it, just this once."

"Maybe only a sip," Scarlett allowed, bracing herself as Vivian located a juice glass and poured a few fingers of what looked like green sludge into it.

"Here you go." Grinning broadly, Vivian handed her the glass. "I promise you, you're going to be surprised. It's very healthy, as well as delicious."

"I wouldn't go so far as to say delicious," Amber teased. "Drink up, Scarlett."

Gamely raising the glass to her mouth, Scarlett decided to drink it the way one did a shot of strong alcohol. All at once, thus minimizing the taste.

Somehow, she managed to do this, trying not to gag as the taste lingered on her tongue. "Not bad," she managed, lying through her teeth.

"See?" Vivian crowed. "I told you so. I can make extra if you want to start drinking it every day."

Trying to think of a suitably polite way to refuse,

Scarlett decided to simply be honest. "No thank you," she said.

Wide-eyed, Amber laughed. Wiping at her eyes with the back of her hand, Delilah did too. Eventually, Vivian joined in. Even Scarlett found her lips curling in amusement.

By the time Travis walked into the room, all four of the women were doubled over in laughter.

Not sure what to think, Travis simply stood in the doorway to the kitchen, wondering if they'd all lost their minds. While he understood that everyone dealt with stress in different ways, Scarlett, Vivian, Amber and Delilah all appeared to be on the verge of hysteria.

Heck, Delilah leaned back against the counter, arms wrapped around her middle, laughing while tears streamed down her face.

He caught sight of Scarlett holding a small glass with some of Vivian's nasty green smoothie still in it and grimaced. "Did y'all really make Scarlett drink that stuff?"

Vivian stopped laughing. "We didn't force it down her, if that's what you're implying," she managed, still chuckling.

He shuddered. "What did you think?" he asked Scarlett. "New favorite smoothie?"

"I'm sure it's healthy," she managed. "But not my thing. How's Hal?"

At her question, everyone went quiet, their merriment instantly silenced.

"Exhausted. He could barely keep his eyes open."

Delilah grabbed a paper towel and wiped at her still-streaming eyes. "This is ridiculous. There has to be a way to find out what's wrong with him."

"I agree," Travis replied. "The hospital did a lot of blood work today. Since the doctor didn't comment on it, I'm assuming he thought it was normal. But I'm going to have Hal call tomorrow with me listening in, so I can get the results."

"That sounds like a plan." Vivian made a show out of checking her watch. "I'd better skedaddle. Are you coming, Amber?"

Amber nodded. "I suppose so. Let me pry Will away from the tablet." She left the kitchen. A moment later, they heard Will protesting.

"I'd better get going too." Delilah dabbed once more at her eyes with the paper towel. "If Hal wakes up hungry, there's some cold fried chicken in the fridge. You two help yourself as well."

Once everyone had gone, Travis knew he should also take himself off for home, but Scarlett looked so lost and vulnerable, he didn't want to leave her just yet.

Though he didn't want to touch her either, he gave in to the urge to pull her in for a hug. Clearly, she needed comfort and to be honest, so did he.

They stood still for a moment. It felt right, her nestled in his arms. He wondered if she could feel his heartbeat, steady against her ear. She smelled good, like vanilla, he thought, slightly dazed. The softness of her curves pressed against him made him ache to caress them with his hands. Damned if he knew how she managed to affect him so strongly, without even trying. He wanted her more than he'd ever wanted a woman.

But this wasn't about him, or the way he craved her. Not lust or desire, just simple human kindness. As long as he told himself this and made himself believe it, he stood a prayer of not doing anything stupid.

When he finally released her, he instantly turned to the refrigerator and busied himself removing the meal Delilah had made for them. In addition to the fried chicken, she'd made a potato salad and a broccoli salad.

"That looks wonderful," Scarlett exclaimed, her color high. If she realized he was using the food as a distraction, she apparently didn't care.

"Let's eat."

"I'm not sure I'm hungry," she replied, though he caught her eyeing the chicken.

"Well then, just have a small piece. One of these wings, or a leg. Just something to tide you over until breakfast."

"Maybe," she allowed, rummaging in the cabinet and returning with two plates. "It'd be wrong to let all this food go to waste."

"Right." Grinning at her, he went and got silverware and a couple of paper towels. "Though Delilah made enough to feed a small army. This will be lunch tomorrow too."

She pulled out a chair and sat. He did the same. Odd how comfortable he felt around her, passing bowls back and forth. If not for the ever-present simmering attraction, he might have thought they'd become friends. But he knew even he didn't have that much self-control.

After they'd eaten, she put up the leftovers and he rinsed off the dishes and put them in the dishwasher. She turned to him, almost shyly, and asked him if he wanted to stay and watch a movie or something.

He did. Feeling surprisingly relieved that he didn't

have to leave her just yet, he told her to go ahead and choose something.

Once she'd selected a movie, she took the couch, leaving him Hal's old recliner. He didn't mind. Ever since Hal had gotten confined to a wheelchair, Travis often sat there.

Though the movie she'd picked appeared to be a romantic comedy, aka chick flick, he actually enjoyed it. As the ending credit rolled across the screen, he turned to look at Scarlett. "That was pretty good. I don't usually watch that kind of thing, but I'm glad I did."

She smiled back. "Maybe you just need to broaden your horizons."

He felt the impact of that smile all the way to his bones.

The evening news came on and neither one moved. About halfway through it, Travis caught himself sneaking glances at Scarlett, snuggled under a throw blanket. He couldn't help but wish he could join her.

Reluctantly, he knew he needed to get up and take himself home. But he could have stayed all night there with Scarlett.

"My mother always watched the evening news," she commented, her expression pensive. "I miss her."

"What was she like?" he asked, genuinely curious. "I remember Hal said you look just like her."

"I do." His words had coaxed another smile from her, making him glad. "But I don't have her energy. Gosh, that woman seemed to have an unlimited supply of it. She was a dynamo," Scarlett said. "One of those people who made others happy just to breathe the same air. She could be loud—which embarrassed me no end when I was a teenager—but she had such a good heart, no one minded. Everyone who met her loved her."

Her misty smile moved him, but he forced himself to remain in his chair even though he wanted to touch her with every fiber of his being.

"She taught me so much. To laugh, to see beauty in everyone and everything, and that the best way to deal with people who don't like you is to hug them and smile. When I think Southern belle, my mom comes to mind." She looked down, evidently gathering up her memories and emotions. "I miss her so much."

"I wonder why she never told you about your father," he commented. While he still wasn't 100 percent sure he truly believed she was Hal's daughter, Scarlett clearly did and right now, that was all that mattered.

"I don't know." Scarlett shrugged. "I found her diaries, you know. She called them journals. She made a habit of writing in them every single morning, until she became too ill to hold a pen. I was forbidden to read them, and I honored that until after she was gone."

"The cancer—" He would have given anything if he could erase the stark pain in her emerald eyes.

She nodded. "She fought a hard battle, but in the end, the disease won. I helped her as much as I could, because I couldn't have asked for a better mother." Her voice broke and she looked down, valiantly struggling to regain emotional control.

Travis could no more have remained in his chair than he could have stopped breathing. He took a few steps and dropped down beside her, gathering her in his arms and holding her.

Like before, his body instantly responded to her softness. And like before, he kept his desire under control. "I'm sorry," he murmured, allowing himself the pleasure of caressing her back and shoulders. "I can only imagine how much that hurts."

"And now I'm facing losing Hal before I even get to know him," she continued. "Worse, we have no idea what we're battling, so it's difficult to get together a cohesive defense."

He managed something that he hoped sounded like assent. She wiggled slightly, nestling closer to him. Desire zinged through his veins, and he had to shift his body so she wouldn't recognize his growing arousal.

How could this tiny woman make him desire her without even trying?

"Travis?" She tilted her face to look up at him, her lips parted. "Would you do me a favor?"

At that moment, he would have promised her the moon. "I'll try," he answered. "What is it?"

"Would you kiss me again?" she breathed.

Just like that, she managed to rip away every shred of the armor he'd attempted to build around him. With a groan, he lowered his mouth to her, claiming her lips with a hunger that tore through and gutted him.

Wrapping her arms around him, she kissed him back with equal fervor. This time, he let his hand explore—her soft skin, the curve of her waist and hips, the swell of her breasts. And she, she touched him as though she'd been as starved for him as he'd been for her. She skimmed her fingertips over his torso, sliding them around the waistband of his jeans, hesitating while his aroused body swelled even more.

Rock hard, he could barely move, never mind think. While he wasn't entirely sure she knew what she was doing to him, he knew if she kept it up, he'd lose the last shred of what little self-control he'd managed to hang on to.

"Scarlett," he growled.

She must have heard the warning in his voice, because her hands stilled. Though she didn't move away from him, not yet. And she had to, because right now the only movement he felt capable of making would be ripping off their clothes and pushing himself up inside of her.

"We need to stop," he made himself say.

"Do we?" Pushing slightly back, she gazed up at him, her lips swollen from his kisses and her eyes dark with desire.

Unbidden, his body surged against her, the movement involuntary, though she certainly had to feel it.

Judging by the way her lips curved in a sexy, suggestive smile, she did.

"Are you saying..." He could barely get the words out through clenched teeth. Holding himself back took every ounce of energy.

"Yes." With both hands, she pulled him down to her for a deep, drugging kiss that left him reeling. "Make love to me, Travis. Right here, right now."

He groaned, but retained enough presence of mind to urge her down the hall to her bedroom. Then, once he'd kicked the door closed, he turned and began feverishly undressing her. She did the same for him, her trembling fingers fumbling with his belt. When she finally removed that, she struggled with his zipper, straining over his arousal.

Somehow, he managed to get her clothes off her without tearing anything. Then, he yanked his own shirt over his head and stepped out of his jeans, taking a moment to slip on a condom.

"Come here," he said, drinking in the sight of her naked.

Instead, as she let her gaze roam over him, she crawled up onto her bed and held out both arms. "No, Travis. Come here instead."

Chapter 8

Heaven help her, Scarlett thought she'd never seen a more perfect male body. Muscular in all the right places, from his washboard abs to his narrow waist and broad shoulders.

And his arousal… Her entire body clenched in anticipation.

At her invitation, he crossed the distance between them, the desire blazing from his gaze setting her on fire before he reached her.

He kissed her again, as he lowered his body over hers. She arched herself up to meet him halfway, eager to feel the swollen length of him inside her. Already more than ready, she gasped as he entered her and then, with one swift move, filled her completely.

This, she thought dazedly, this was what she'd been missing her entire life.

When he began to move, slowly, she raised herself up to meet every thrust, trying to make him go faster, harder.

But he only laughed, his expression dark with passion. Finally, he gave in to her unspoken request. She fairly vibrated with the force of him, passion pounding through her with every thrust. The world shifted, and the first starbursts morphed into an explosion that went on and on and on.

Then, as her body clenched around him while waves of release shook her, he cried out and found his own shuddering release.

After, he held her for a few minutes, both of them silent. She wondered if their lovemaking had rocked his world the way it had hers.

Sated, she must have fallen asleep. She woke up to find herself alone in her bed, wrapped up in tangled sheets. The digital clock on her nightstand read 12:03 a.m.

Had he really sneaked out and gone home once she'd fallen asleep? Without even a kiss or a goodbye?

But then her bedroom door snicked open and Travis returned. Apparently, he'd been to the bathroom across the hall and now, not realizing she was awake, he got dressed, using the flashlight on his phone to find his clothes.

Finally, he'd finished. He crossed the room and stood by the edge of the bed, staring down at her. Though she really wanted to see what he'd do, she refused to play games and feign sleep, so she smiled up at him. "Hey there," she murmured.

"I've got to go." He leaned in and breathed a kiss on her forehead.

Slowly, she nodded. "Good idea. Everyone would know if you spent the night. Imagine the gossip." Though she was only half joking, she was also right. While she might not mind if Vivian, Amber and even Delilah suspected she and Travis had been intimate, she sure as heck didn't want Hal to hear about it.

"Exactly," he drawled. He turned around and left, closing her door quietly behind him.

She lay absolutely still, listening for the sound of his truck starting. Only once she'd heard it drive away did she roll back over and try to go back to sleep.

The next morning, she woke up feeling unsettled. What had she been thinking, giving in to that sizzling attraction she had for Travis? Even worse, what was *he* thinking? She'd pretty much thrown herself at him.

Argh. Usually, Scarlett considered herself a self-confident person. She'd never been prone to second-guessing her decisions or questioning her judgment. Nor would she start that kind of craziness now. She and Travis were adults and they'd both been consenting.

Plus, the entire experience had been absolutely, freaking amazing. In fact, she could think of only one small problem. Instead of satisfying her curiosity and desire, making love with him only made her want him again.

Restless, she showered and dressed and then made her way to the kitchen. Hal still slept, which made her slightly worried. The seizure must have taken a greater toll on him than she'd realized. She debated checking on him and finally decided she had to. If something were wrong, she'd need to get him help right away. She didn't have the luxury of waiting for Delilah to arrive.

Taking care to move quietly, she opened the door to Hal's room and crept to his bedside. As far as she could tell, he seemed to be deeply asleep. His chest rose and fell as he breathed. Since she didn't want to wake him, she went back to the kitchen. If he wasn't up and moving around by the time Delilah got there, she'd ask the other woman to check on him.

Fortified by two strong cups of coffee and a plate of scrambled eggs, she stepped out on the back porch and breathed deeply. The unusually warm air actually contained a hint of crispness, hinting of fall. She remembered hearing on the weather report that a cold front was on the way. The kind of perfect weather to do something outside.

But what? Since Travis hadn't yet gotten around to giving her those riding lessons, she couldn't stroll out to the barn, saddle up one of the horses and go for a ride. Or could she? For a brief moment, she actually considered trying, but since she had no idea how to even saddle one of those huge beasts, she discarded that idea.

What did it mean, that she and Travis had made love? How would this change their relationship, for the better or worse? Would they try to pretend nothing had happened? Putting her hands to her flushed cheeks, she hoped not. But then again, she wasn't sure how Hal would react if he were to find out. And what about the others—Vivian and Amber? She could only imagine how quickly the gossip would spread.

And…she'd gotten ahead of herself. Again. Deep breaths. She and Travis had gotten together and had one night of amazing sex. So what? They were both adults. What they chose to do or not do wasn't anyone else's business but theirs.

Despite her pep talk to herself, she still felt on edge. Since she couldn't ride yet, she decided to take a walk. She could use the exercise and getting outdoors would help clear her head.

She went inside and changed into her sneakers. While the boots were more comfortable than she'd expected, she needed the running shoes to cover long distances comfortably.

Back outside, she power walked down the long driveway. When she got to the end, the sight of the mailbox reminded her of the odd, mildly threatening letter, which gave her a moment of unease. She'd even caught herself wondering if Travis's ex-fiancée had written it in a bit of pique once learning another woman resided in Hal's house. Either way, no one else seemed worried about it, so Scarlett wouldn't either. She'd enjoy her walk and just keep her eyes out for anything unusual.

Now that she'd decided, she turned left and then right. The same dirt road traveled east to west. This time, instead of going the way she'd gone on her last walk, she chose the opposite direction. As far as she could tell, the HG Ranch land went on for farther than she could possibly go on foot. It'd be nice to take in some different scenery, even if they were only pastures.

She walked until the trees obscured the main house. As she'd suspected, there were more pastures, some of them occupied by horses rather than cattle.

Step by step, she felt the tension leave her body. While she certainly hadn't expected to, she actually liked this part of the country. East Texas had turned out to be more like her beloved Georgia than she'd expected.

The road curved around a thicket of trees. When she came out on the other side, a small lake spread out before her, the blue water sparkling in the sunshine. She found the unexpected sight so beautiful she paused to take a long look at it. For the first time she could actually see the appeal of exploring the ranch on horseback.

Briefly she considered going closer, though doing so would involve going under or over the fence and trudging through pasture where she might possibly encounter livestock, so she decided against it. Instead, she decided to continue to follow the road and see what else she might see.

On the other side of the lake, she saw a plume of smoke or dust. A fire? Squinting, she realized it was a vehicle, traveling fast. Had something happened to Hal? Since she knew she was in the middle of ranch land, the vehicle had to be heading toward the main house.

Worried, she checked her phone. No messages from Delilah or Travis. That helped her relax somewhat, since she knew they'd have reached out to her. And—she looked again—the absence of flashing lights meant it wasn't an ambulance. Assuming they used such things here in the middle of nowhere.

As the vehicle drew closer, she saw it was a white pickup truck barreling down the dirt road. Shading her eyes with her hand, Scarlett wondered if it was one of the ranch vehicles. For whatever reason, it was traveling way too fast for the bumpy dirt road. The truck bounced and fishtailed, yet each time the driver managed to get it under control.

Teenagers out for a joyride? Or one of the neighboring ranchers with a pressing emergency? Either way, she stepped to the side of the road, and then moved several feet closer to the pasture, right up against the fence, just to be safe. While so far the driver appeared to have great control of the truck, she didn't want to take any chances.

Since she wore a bright red shirt and stood in plain view, she figured they had to have seen her. As the truck approached, still going far too fast, she waved, just to be safe. Due to the tinted windows, she couldn't tell if the driver waved back.

Only one curve and a few hundred feet separated them.

Yet instead of racing past, the truck hit a huge rut and skidded off the road, sliding sideways directly toward her.

She didn't have time to think, just react. She jumped up, hitting the fence seconds before the truck did. Barbed wire tore at her clothing and her skin, but she made it in time to avoid the vehicle.

Somehow the driver managed to regain control, spinning the truck back toward the road. Bleeding, Scarlett climbed to her feet, waiting for the vehicle to stop, but instead, the pickup swerved toward the gravel road and then back around. For one heart-stopping moment, she thought the driver meant to gun it toward her and mow her down, but instead it made another rotation. Once the tires regained traction on the road, it sped off, back in the direction it had come.

Stunned, in shock, Scarlett looked down at her bleeding arms and torn shirt. Had that been on purpose or some kind of crazy accident? The fact that the driver hadn't bothered to stop pointed more toward deliberate. But why? No one even knew she was out here.

Where had the truck been going before it had nearly killed her? And why had it turned around and gone back the way it had come?

Slightly dizzy, Scarlett took stock of her injuries. Nothing serious, though some of the cuts looked deep and hurt like crazy. She reached in her back jeans pocket for her phone, but it wasn't there. It must have fallen out when she'd taken that dive over the fence.

Slowly, she retraced her steps. As she did, she realized her jeans were also ripped and she'd gotten a deep cut in one leg. Part of the fence was down, which meant the truck would have scratches too, making it easier to identify.

Praying one of the tires hadn't crushed her phone, she finally located it in a clump of tall grass. Luckily, it appeared unharmed. She scrolled through her phone until she located Travis's number and called.

"It's Scarlett," she managed, glad he'd answered.

"What is it?" he asked. "Did you change your mind about going to the ball with me?"

"No." She swallowed, willing her voice to remain steady. "I need your help."

"What's wrong?" The teasing note vanished from his voice. "Is Hal all right?"

"As far as I know, he's fine." She took a deep breath, hating the slight hitch in her tone. Quickly, she explained what had happened.

"Where are you?"

"That's just it, I don't know. Near the lake?"

"Lake?" Clearly perplexed, he went silent for a second or two. "The nearest lake is at least half an hour away. Did you drive there?"

She glanced back at the shining body of water. "No, I'm still on ranch land. Maybe it's a pond, I don't know. It's water. I turned left at the end of the main house driveway and kept walking. The road curves and there's a large pond or something. The fence is down too."

"That's one of the stock tanks," he told her. "That one has a nice underground spring that keeps it filled. Stay put. I'm on my way to get you." And he ended the call.

Staring down at the phone, she slipped it into her back pocket and struggled not to cry. She didn't want to be a mess when Travis got there—she had to be strong.

Travis told one of his hands he had to go, and put the younger man in charge for the rest of the day. After hopping into his truck, he drove as fast as he could. The area where Scarlett waited was clear on the opposite side of the ranch from where he'd been working, so would take some time to get to her. While he might have been able to shave off some time by going cross-country through the fields, the moments where he'd have to stop and open gates would negate that completely, so he stuck to the road.

He saw her long before he reached her. At first, he feared the bright red of her shirt might be blood, which nearly stopped his heart. But as he drew closer, he realized she seemed mainly unharmed, except for gashes on her arms and a particularly bad one on her leg.

Skidding to a stop on the edge of the road, he jumped out and ran toward her. Though he ached to gather her in his arms and hold her, he didn't want to hurt her, so instead he settled for taking her hand. "Are you all right?"

She nodded, clearly blinking back tears. Seeing that, he decided the hell with it, and carefully folded her into his arms.

Shoulders shaking, she cried silently while he, a man who hated feeling helpless, felt exactly that. Turning her gently, he steered her toward his truck. The sooner he could get her inside and cleaned up, the better she'd feel.

Once he got her settled in the passenger seat, he made a quick phone call to some of his crew, directing them to send a couple of guys to fix the fence. Then he climbed up in the truck and started the ignition.

"I'm thinking we should get you checked out at the hospital," he said. "That cut on your leg might need stitches. How long has it been since you had a tetanus shot?"

"I don't know. Not since I was a kid, I'm thinking. But I'm not sure I need a hospital. What about one of those quick-care places? Do you have them around here?"

He thought for a moment. "As a matter of fact, I think one just opened up off Main Street. We'll go check it out."

"Okay." Wiping at her eyes, she stared out the window. "I'd like to file a police report after that."

"We can call and get an officer to come while you're getting checked out at the clinic. Did you happen to get the license plate of the truck that hit you?"

"No." She shook her head. "I was too busy trying to stay alive. All I know was it was a white pickup truck."

"Chevy, Ford, or Dodge?"

"I don't know. I'm sorry." Swallowing hard, she looked down at her leg. "The bleeding has stopped, so I don't think this is deep enough for stitches."

He patted her shoulder. "We'll let the doctor decide, all right?"

"Sure." Now she appeared disinterested. "I just don't understand why someone just tried to kill me."

"Are you sure it wasn't an accident?"

"Obviously not," she shot back. "If they'd lost control and nearly mowed me down by mistake, why would they have left the scene?"

"I can think of several reasons. Maybe they'd been drinking. Or it was a teenager who doesn't have their license yet, or was driving the truck without permission."

"Maybe." She didn't sound convinced. "Or it could have been the same person who sent me the note."

Interesting that she linked the two. He'd forgotten about the note, mainly because it seemed so innocuous.

Once he'd located the quick clinic, he helped her inside. The nurse practitioner cleaned up the scratches and cuts on her arms and hands, before moving on to her leg. "You're going to need to take those jeans off," the woman said. "Do you have something else you can wear home? Something loose, like a skirt? I have a feeling we're going to have to bandage that."

Scarlett shook her head.

"I'll go buy something," Travis said.

She nodded. "I'll need a new shirt too. There's a cute little shop called Annie's near the bookstore. If you could, get me a maxi skirt so it will cover the bandage. Size small on everything."

Since she clearly wanted him to go before removing her jeans, he nodded and took off. He knew exactly what store she'd referenced, as he'd bought his sister gifts from there.

On his way, he called the sheriff's office and told the detective on duty what had happened.

"Is she sure it was deliberate?" the detective asked.

"She seems pretty sure." Travis scratched his head and decided to be honest. "Me, I don't know. It could have been a drunk, or some kid out joyriding. But since she got that note telling her to leave or she'd be sorry, she thinks the two are tied together."

To give the detective credit, he didn't completely discount the idea.

"Would you mind swinging by the new clinic on Main and taking her statement? She's there getting patched up."

"She was *injured*?" the detective's tone changed. "Why didn't you say that up front? How seriously was she hurt?"

"Just a few cuts and scratches. One probably will need stitches. Nothing serious."

"Good." The detective breathed a clear sigh of relief. "I'll run over there right now and talk to her."

"Thank you." Parking in front of Annie's, he went inside. To his relief, he didn't know the woman working behind the counter. He told her what he needed, hoping she would have what Scarlett had requested.

"A maxi skirt?" The older woman smiled. "I just put a bunch of those on clearance. They're popular in the summer, not so much in the fall. Any particular color?"

He frowned, but then remembered what his sister always said. "Black goes with everything, so a small one in black would be great."

"I'm pretty sure I have one." She went to the back of the store. A minute later, she returned carrying a long black skirt. "Here you go. Did you want to buy your wife a shirt to go with it?"

He didn't correct her since he saw no need to explain the entire situation. "I think so, yes." He took a quick panicked look around the store. "I have no idea what to choose. Can you recommend something?"

By the time he was done, he'd ended up purchasing the skirt and two shirts, as well as some sort of long sweater thing that the salesclerk had assured him would "complete the outfit."

Back at the clinic, he carried them inside and found Scarlett sitting up and wearing a hospital gown, talking to the detective. She had a large white bandage on her leg.

They both looked up as he entered.

"You were right," she said, pointing to her bandage. "It needed stitches."

"Then I'm glad we came here. Looks like they've got you all fixed up."

"They did. And now I'm giving this nice police officer my report."

"I've just finished taking the info I needed," the detective said, his measured, professional tone seeming to indicate he took Scarlett seriously.

"Thank you." Scarlett smiled at the man and his face instantly reddened. He mumbled his goodbyes and hurried out the door.

Amused, Travis held out the shopping bags. "Here you go. A complete outfit. The saleslady was overjoyed to put it together for you."

"Perfect." When she turned that smile on him, he

understood how the detective must have felt. Because he didn't want to stand there grinning back at her like an idiot, he simply managed to jerk his head in a nod and turned away.

"I'll wait for you out here," he told her.

Five minutes later, she opened the door to her room and grinned at him. "You did a great job. I love this outfit! It's something I'll actually wear again."

He stared. The long black skirt swirled around her legs and somehow managed to look sexy. And the red top clung to her curves, lovingly outlining her shape as if it had been custom made for her."

"Wow," he said. "I can't believe how well that fits you."

"I know, right? Me neither. And the sweater that ties it all together is perfect. I saw the receipt in the bag, so I also know you got a great bargain. I'll pay you back once we get to the house since I don't have my purse with me."

"No need." He shook his head. "Consider it a gift. You deserve one, after all you've been through today."

His comment made her laugh. Enchanted, he smiled back. Damn, he really had it bad where she was concerned.

"I'm going to have to bring them my insurance card," she continued. "And payment. Luckily, they knew Hal and are letting me go and get it. I have to say, that's the nice thing about living in a small town."

He agreed.

By the time they got back to Hal's, both Vivian and Amber had texted Travis and he had missed calls from both of them. He'd put his phone on silent at the clinic and had forgotten to change it back.

"Wow," he said, shaking his head as he scrolled. "They've already heard about the truck nearly running you down and are trying to pump me for info."

"Are you serious?" Scarlett dug out her own phone from her back pocket. "Nothing here. I wonder why they're asking you instead of me."

"Probably because they know I was with you, since I called the sheriff's office." He grimaced. "I sure hope they haven't said anything to Hal. He doesn't need something else to worry about."

"I agree. Look—" she pointed. "Your mother is here, that's her SUV. And Delilah is still here. I wonder if your sister came too."

"I don't know. Amber might have come with Mom, but I know Will gets out of school soon, so probably not."

Scarlett sighed. Though normally, she was the first one out of the vehicle, this time she waited for him to come around to the passenger side and help her down from the truck. Her color was high, making him wonder if she might be in pain.

"No, not pain," she replied once he asked her. "They gave me something for that. I'm dreading all the questions. I think I'm going to say I'm not feeling well and go straight to my room. That might be cowardly, but it's true."

"I don't blame you." He squeezed her hand. "I'll deal with them. You just go to your room and rest."

"I want to check on Hal first. I've been worried about him ever since that incident."

"We all were." They'd reached the front door. Next to him, he noticed how Scarlett stiffened. "Are you sure you're all right?"

"I'm bracing myself." Her attempt at a grimace turned into a grin. "I promise you, I'm not usually such a chicken."

He found himself grinning back. And when the front door abruptly opened, that's how Vivian saw them, grinning at each other like a pair of besotted fools.

"It's about time," Vivian scolded, ushering Scarlett inside. "We were all so worried, especially when Travis didn't respond to my texts or calls."

"I..." Scarlett could barely get a word out before Vivian continued.

"You look really nice." The older woman looked Scarlett up and down. "Not at all like someone who was nearly run over by a drunk driver."

Travis held up the bag with Scarlett's torn clothes. "She had to get a new outfit. Her other one was destroyed."

Behind Vivian, Hal barked Scarlett's name. "Why didn't you call me?" he demanded.

Though Scarlett stiffened, she somehow managed to resist shooting Vivian an accusatory glare. Travis did for both of them.

"I didn't want you to worry." Scarlett moved past Vivian, taking a seat on the couch near Hal's wheelchair. Leaning over, she took his hand in both of hers. Naturally, this drew his gaze to her bandaged arms.

"How badly were you hurt?" he rasped. "I was given to believe it was nothing major, but..."

"I'm okay. I had to get a few stitches in my leg and a tetanus shot, but my arms just needed antibiotic ointment."

"And I've got a team repairing the fence," Travis interjected.

"I don't care about the fence," Hal snapped. "My daughter was almost killed. Tell me the sheriff's department is looking into this."

"They are," Travis hastened to reassure him. "The truck has got to have some damage. Hopefully, someone will notice and report it."

For the first time, he found himself wondering what kind of vehicle Kendra drove these days.

Chapter 9

For the next thirty minutes, Scarlett gamely battled her exhaustion while everyone, including Vivian, made a huge fuss over her. Part of her reveled in the knowledge that someone cared, but mostly she just wanted to crawl beneath her covers and sleep.

Several times she caught Travis watching her, the calm confidence of his expression letting her know he'd catch her if she fell. Something about this touched her deeply, making her eyes sting.

Delilah brought out a platter of meat, cheese, crackers and fruit for everyone to munch on. Just the sight of food made Scarlett feel nauseous. She figured it must have been due to the drugs they'd given her at the clinic.

When the room started spinning, she knew she had to get to her bed. Hoping to slip out unobtrusively, she stood, but swayed from dizziness. Travis immediately came to her and offered his arm, which she gratefully took.

Everyone went quiet as he escorted her down the hall. She could only imagine what they'd be thinking, but right now didn't care.

Travis helped her to her bed and then, once she was seated, bent down and removed her poor running shoes. Though they'd been almost new when she'd originally put them on, they were dirty, stained and torn. She winced. "Those will have to go in the trash along with that bag of my clothes." Then she remembered her cell phone and asked him to get it out of the bag, which he'd put on her dresser.

Once he did, he handed it to her. She pressed the button to mute the sound and placed it on the nightstand next to her bed. "Thank you," she told him.

"Do you need help getting undressed?" he murmured. The slight curve of his mouth told her he was most likely joking.

"You know, I'm too tired to take you up on that offer," she managed to tease, her voice husky. "I'll take a rain check."

"Sounds good." Soothing back her hair from her face, he gave her a gentle kiss on the forehead. "Get some rest. I'll see you tomorrow."

Staring after him as he left, she wasn't sure whether to be elated or worried. She decided not to worry about it and closed her eyes instead.

When she woke up in the morning, still in her new outfit, everything hurt. She removed all her bandages and took a hot shower, wincing as the hot water made her cuts and scratches sting. The gash with stitches looked angry and swollen, but they'd given her antibiotics so she wasn't worried.

Since she'd slept later than usual, Delilah was already busy in the kitchen when she went downstairs.

"Sit, please. I'll get your coffee and something for you to eat."

Grateful, Scarlett thanked her and took a seat at the table. "Where's Hal? Is he all right?"

"He seems to be. Travis took him into town." Delilah glanced sideways at her. "Mr. Hal wanted to have a word with the sheriff."

"About what happened to me? Why?"

"He's pretty upset." Delilah placed a mug of steaming coffee in front of her, fixed exactly the way Scarlett liked it. "He says it happened on his property and he wants whoever did it caught."

While Scarlett sipped her coffee, Delilah fixed her a plate of biscuits and gravy. "This is what Hal had earlier. I kept the gravy warm on the stove for you."

"Oh wow. Thank you." Though Scarlett rarely indulged in this kind of food, after the day she'd had yesterday, she felt she deserved it. She dug in with gusto, polishing off her entire plate. "That was absolutely wonderful," she said.

"I'm glad you enjoyed it." The older woman seemed strangely hesitant. After carrying the plate to the sink, she returned and pulled out the chair next to Scarlett. "I hope you don't mind me asking, but what's going on with you and Travis?"

A little surprised, Scarlett shrugged. She liked and respected Delilah, so she figured she'd be honest. "I'm not sure. We are definitely attracted to each other, but I have no idea where it might go."

"He's a good man. He'd give you the shirt off his back. He works hard and everyone in town knows they can count on him in an emergency. There aren't an awful lot like him."

Touched, Scarlett nodded. "He's easy on the eyes too," she quipped.

But Delilah didn't laugh. "That man has had his heart broken once. I wasn't working here then, but I've heard stories. Mr. Hal said he didn't think Travis would recover."

Now Scarlett understood. "You're telling me this because you want to make sure I don't hurt him."

"Yes." Delilah placed her hand on Scarlett's arm. "I'm not sure what your plans are, whether you're staying or leaving. And you seem like a kindhearted woman, so please consider all this before you get too involved with him. I'm not sure he'd survive having that sort of thing happen to him again."

"I—" Scarlett opened her mouth to reply, but before she could get anything else out, the front door slammed open and Vivian and Amber breezed into the house. They headed directly for the kitchen.

Delilah jumped to her feet and moved away from the table. Scarlett remained seated, managing to summon up a smile. "Good morning," she said. "What brings you two here so early?" Heaven help her, if they wanted to talk to her about not breaking Travis's heart, she might cry. While she had no intention of ever hurting him, things were still too new between them to even think about a future.

"We're here to talk to you about your costumes for

the ball," Vivian stated, a determined glint in her eyes. She wore bright orange slacks with sparkly silver shoes. Her long-sleeved, multicolored silky green blouse had stripes of orange and red. Her long, colorful earrings swung as she shook her head. They appeared to be parrots, or maybe cha-cha dancers—Scarlett couldn't tell.

Amber noticed her looking and grinned.

"We haven't decided yet," Scarlett replied, tearing her gaze away from Vivian's vivid attire. "In fact, Travis and I haven't even had time to discuss it."

Vivian grimaced. "Discuss? I realize you don't know my son very well, but men don't generally like to talk about stuff like costumes for Halloween balls. It's better if you just make the choice for them, and simply fill them in."

Behind her, Amber's grin widened. The polar opposite of her mother, she wore her usual all black, from jeans to tight long-sleeved T-shirt emblazoned with the name of a heavy metal band. Her jet-colored hair had that spiky, just-got-out-of-bed look, though Scarlett knew that hairstyle took time to achieve.

Delilah offered coffee but the two women asked for ice water instead. Once Delilah had brought them each a tall glass with a lemon wedge, she excused herself and disappeared.

"I thought it might be fun if we all coordinated something similar," Amber volunteered.

"Are you going?" Scarlett asked, a bit perplexed but overall happy that they'd thought to include her.

"Of course." Vivian carried a large plastic shopping bag, which she placed on the kitchen table. "I'm going with Frank, and Amber is going with Mike, who is a friend of Travis's."

"That sounds wonderful," Scarlett said, meaning it. "It'll be great to have other people I know there. I was a bit worried about sticking out like a sore thumb."

The other two women exchanged glances, making Scarlett wonder what they were up to. Finally, Vivian shrugged. "I think you should play up to your strengths."

"I agree," Amber said.

Once they were all seated around the table with their drinks, she looked from one to the other. "I'm not sure I understand what you mean, playing to my strengths."

"You're beautiful." Amber took a long drink. "I'd give anything to look like you."

Touched, Scarlett thanked her.

"What she means—" Vivian said, reaching into her bag and pulling out a stack of what appeared to be pages cut out from magazines "—is that you need to choose a costume that enhances or accentuates your beauty, not hides it. Do you follow?"

Heaven help her, but Scarlett thought of Kendra, the reason Travis had asked her to go with him in the first place. The woman who'd broken his heart. Suddenly, she knew she wanted to look her very best in front of her. "Sounds good," she agreed.

Amber clapped her hands in excitement. "I can't wait," she said.

"For the costumes, do you usually order them online or rent them or what?"

"I'm a pretty accomplished seamstress," Vivian answered, drawing herself up proudly. "But even I don't think I can make what we have in mind for everyone in the two weeks we have. Amber volunteered to look online, but if she can't find anything suitable, we've heard great things about a costume rental shop in Dallas. We have to move quickly, though, because if we wait until the last minute, they'll be sold out."

For the first time, Scarlett understood how seriously everyone apparently took this costume ball. "What are you thinking as far as theme?" she asked.

Vivian passed over a sheaf of papers. "I've made several mock-ups. We've thought of a few with a large enough cast of characters for all of us."

The first page showed the crew of *Peter Pan*. While Scarlett would have loved playing Tinker Bell, she couldn't see Travis agreeing to be Peter or even Captain Hook. The second and third pages were both popular fairy tales. "What kind of thing does Travis usually prefer?" she asked.

Again Vivian and Amber exchanged looks. "He's been a cowboy, a police officer and once we even talked him into going as Frankenstein."

"Maybe we should discuss this with him?"

Vivian laughed. "We thought once we decided, we'd let you tell him."

Immediately, Amber protested. "Mom, that's not really fair. You know how stubborn Travis can be."

"True, but you know he'd take it better coming from her," Vivian shot back. She reached her long, coral-colored nails into her oversize purse and withdrew a stick of gum, which she popped into her mouth.

"Ignore her," Amber said, grinning at Scarlett. "Keep looking. My ideas are coming up."

Which meant the first few pages had been Vivian's.

Predictably, the next page was a family of vampires, sort of a knockoff of Anne Rice's popular book and movie. Scarlett paused, trying to imagine Travis as a vampire, but she couldn't.

She continued on, stopping at the next page to consider. For this one, it appeared Amber had drawn her own characters, some symbolizing good, others bad. There were angels, glorious and regal, dressed in elaborate white with wings that rivaled those worn by Victoria's Secret models. And there were fallen angels or maybe demons, all in black.

"This has possibilities," Scarlett mused, tapping the page.

"There are more." Amber grinned, clearly pleased. "We wanted to give you lots to choose from, this being your first Halloween ball and all."

She'd had several more ideas, all of them good, but when Scarlett got to the next to last page, she stopped. "Wow," she breathed. "Now this might actually work."

Vivian leaned across the table to see. "Oh," she commented. "Don't you think that might have been overdone?"

"Not at all," Scarlett replied, eyeing the antebellum costumes, especially that of her namesake. "*Gone with the Wind* is classic." And she could actually picture Travis dressed as Rhett. "My only concern would be the possibility of even obtaining such elaborate dresses."

"I agree." Vivian blew a bubble and popped it. "We only have two weeks. Your average costume shop isn't going to have an abundance of antebellum gowns."

"There's one more," Amber said. "Medieval, kind of like King Arthur and the Round Table."

As Scarlett eyed the pictures, she realized she could see Travis as either the king or as Lancelot, not as Merlin. "But then who would be Lady Guinevere?"

"You, silly," Amber replied. "I'd want to be Morgana."

"Then who would that leave for me? Not anyone fun," Vivian protested, clearly not loving the idea.

"Igraine," both Scarlett and Amber said at once.

"You'd make a fabulous queen," Scarlett reassured her.

Vivian preened. "Yes, I think I would. But again, those are pretty elaborate costumes. Would we be able to get them in time?"

"Actually, I've got that covered," Amber put in. "One of my friends belongs to a group who puts on an annual Renaissance Faire in Longview. They have a huge store of costumes, both for sale and for rent. I could touch base with her if you'd like."

"Or do you need to check with Travis?" Vivian asked, her eyes narrowed.

"I'm...not sure. Though what possible objection could he have to being King Arthur or Lancelot?" Scarlett mused.

"I think you should let him choose. Once he's selected who he wants to be, we'll just assign Frank and Mike their characters." Vivian began restacking the papers, this time putting the medieval page on top.

Again, the front door opened. This time, Travis pushed Hal inside. The older man appeared a bit surprised to see everyone, but he wheeled himself right up to Scarlett.

"How are you feeling this morning?" he asked, peering at her face, his green eyes full of worry.

"I'm okay. How about you?" She thought he looked tired. The circles under his eyes appeared darker, the lines and puffiness more pronounced.

"I'm good." He waved away her concern. Lifting

his head, he eyed Vivian and Amber. "Why are y'all here? What's going on?"

"We came to discuss costumes for the ball," Amber drawled.

Travis looked at Scarlett. A shiver of awareness zinged through her as their gazes locked.

"I was thinking we'd do a Camelot type thing," she said, confident he'd like this. "I could be Guinevere and you could be Lancelot."

Immediately, he shook his head. "No. I'm sorry, but I could never be Lancelot. Not in a million years."

Stunned silence followed his pronouncement. In retrospect, Travis figured he might have been a bit harsh, but if Scarlett couldn't understand his reasoning, it was because she didn't know him well enough.

As for his mother and sister, he supposed they'd never understand.

Hal, though, got it immediately. "It's okay," he told Scarlett. "You have to realize, the one thing Travis values above all others is honor and loyalty. He could never even pretend to be someone who'd betray his king."

Though Scarlett's eyes had widened at his declaration, the instant Hal explained, she nodded. "I get it. How about you be King Arthur instead?"

Again, he had to shake his head. It went without saying that he didn't want to portray a man whose own knight had cuckolded him. Plus, Kendra had always wanted to be Guinevere during their time together.

"Maybe you're taking this all a tad bit too seriously?" Vivian suggested, her tone dry. "It's just a costume ball."

"Maybe so," he allowed. "Let me know what else y'all come up with. I can give you a hint. I make a pretty damn good cowboy."

Everyone laughed. On that note, he left them and headed home. He had a long day tomorrow and wanted to get cleaned up and turn in early.

The next morning, he got up before dawn and was out in the fields alongside his men to watch the sunrise. With the too-short Texas autumn already upon them, it wouldn't be long before winter rode in on her heels.

Winter in Texas could be many things, depending on her mood. From ice storms, snow and below freezing temperatures, to mild weather with flooding rain and decimating winds, winter could be the most dangerous time for livestock. To be safe, the HG Ranch moved all of their herds from the remote pastures to the closer ones. They hauled off many to auction, but the remaining cattle they kept where they could more easily watch over them.

The day passed quickly, as busy days tended to do. By the time the sun reached the edge of the horizon, Travis ached. Tired, but a good kind of tired, and dirty, he enjoyed the pleasant knowledge that he'd completed a good day's work.

Since he'd spent most of the day on horseback, moving cattle and occasionally stopping to pitch in to repair fences, nothing sounded better than a hot shower and a cold beer. Despite that, Travis found himself driving past his place and heading for the main house. Though he told himself he wanted to check on Hal, he knew the real reason was because of Scarlett. He wanted to see her again.

Somehow, without even trying, she'd gotten into his blood. He couldn't stop thinking about her, even while working himself harder than he had in a long while in an effort to distract himself.

Making love with her had actually had the opposite effect than he'd hoped for. Instead of getting her out of his system, she wiggled deeper inside.

When he pulled up at the main house, due to the lateness of the hour, no one else was there. Even Delilah had gone home for the day. He hoped he could grab a bite to eat, but if not, he figured Vivian would have made something and left it in the fridge for him at home.

He let himself in the front door, marveling at how quiet the place seemed lately. Before Scarlett had arrived, Hal had mostly entertained himself by watching hours of television. The TV had been on 24/7, it seemed.

These days, Hal seemed more engaged. Even as his physical body grew weaker, the arrival of his daughter had sharpened his mind and lightened his spirit. That alone made Travis disposed to like her. Even if she hadn't been beautiful and sexy as well.

The low murmur of voices seemed to be coming from Hal's office. Strange, since the older man rarely ventured in there anymore. Bypassing the kitchen and heading down the hallway, his spirit lightened with anticipation. Travis froze when he heard Hal say *oil leases*.

Scarlett asked a question, but Travis couldn't make out the words. All his initial suspicion came rushing back. Had Scarlett's arrival been a front all along? Was she working with Wave Oil Company, maybe even working with Kendra? Or was he just being paranoid?

While he hesitated to eavesdrop, how could he not? Moving as silently as possible, he tried to get closer so he could hear the conversation.

"But why?" Scarlett asked. "What's the objection to letting them drill on part of your land? It sounds to me like it would bring a much-needed infusion of cash. And as long as it wouldn't disrupt your cattle operation, I can't see the harm."

She sounded just like one of the oil company representatives. With his hands clenched into fists, Travis waited to hear how Hal would respond.

As predicted, Hal began talking about the environment, damage to the land, the equipment and trucks and people invading the ranch, though he didn't sound as convinced or impassioned as he usually did.

He sounded weary and old.

Though Travis would have liked to have stayed hidden and determined how hard Scarlett tried to convince her so-called father, his primary concern had to be for Hal. He couldn't let anyone badger the old man.

Travis pasted a false smile onto his face and stepped into the room. "Hey," he said softly, resisting the urge to look at her and locking his gaze on Hal. "What are you two talking about?"

"Nothing," Scarlett immediately replied, which made Travis clench his jaw.

"I was showing her the offers from the oil company," Hal interjected, his tone defensive. "I've been thinking about the future, and what will happen to this ranch once I'm gone."

Talk about a punch in the gut. Not only at the prospect of Hal leaving too soon, but that he even questioned the well-being of the ranch.

"Nothing will happen." Trying to keep it light, Travis moved into the room and squeezed the older man's shoulder. Too thin, too frail, as if Hal's bones would snap if Travis were to squeeze too hard.

"Everything will continue to run just as it always has," Travis continued. "Like we've always discussed."

Conscious of Scarlett watching him, shock and dismay on her beautiful, treacherous face, Travis kept all of his focus on Hal. As it should be, where it always should have been, if he hadn't allowed himself to become distracted.

"I know, I know." Hal covered Travis's hand with his own. "I've always been able to rely on you. But it's only natural to worry now that I have a daughter. I want to make sure she's taken care of."

And so does she, Hal thought, tamping down on his anger. Once again, he felt like a fool. He'd made love to her, invited her to be his date for the ball. He'd thought he liked her—hell, more than liked her. He'd let his guard down and now he felt as if he'd been sucker punched in the gut.

"I see from the expression on your face that you believe I'm trying to convince Hal to go with the oil company's offer so I can make money," Scarlett said.

"Aren't you?" The rancor in his tone made Hal frown.

"Not at all. I was asking questions to understand. Nothing more. I don't need Hal's money. After my mother died, she made sure I'd be taken care of. Believe me when I say that I want for nothing. She was careful with her investments and money. The last thing you need to do is worry about me. I have no need of money whatsoever."

Whatever Travis had been expecting her to say, it wasn't this. Trying to remain skeptical, he finally allowed himself to glance at her, steeling himself for the familiar sizzle of attraction.

Yep, still there. Damn it.

"Nice to know you're so well-off," he drawled.

"Travis, that's enough." Hal's mild rebuke immediately made Travis ashamed. "I'd think you'd be happy to hear that Scarlett is self-sufficient. One less thing for you to have to worry about once I'm gone."

"First off, you're not going anywhere just yet," Scarlett interjected. "And second, there's no reason why Travis would ever have to worry about me. None whatsoever."

Hal raised one bushy eyebrow but didn't say anything, for which Travis was grateful. The last thing he needed was for Hal to comment on a potential relationship between the two of them. Especially since that potential didn't exist. Not now, not ever.

Even if he couldn't stop wanting her. Physical attraction was one thing. A lifelong commitment, another.

"Travis," Scarlett asked softly. "Could we have a word in private?"

His voice stuck in his throat, so he managed a nod. Ignoring Hal's knowing look, he followed Scarlett from Hal's office. Instead of heading toward the kitchen as he'd expected, she led the way toward her room.

He hesitated, but finally followed her inside. When she closed the door and turned to face him, he froze. "Scarlett…"

Her expression had gone all soft, her eyes full of

tenderness. He wanted to back her up against the wall and make love to her, right then, right there. Again and again and again, until he purged his system of her.

"I really don't think we should be in here alone," he managed to rasp. "So why don't we—"

She grabbed him before he could finish, and yanked him to her. Standing on tiptoe, she pressed her mouth to his and kissed him.

Lust jolted through him like an electric shock, frying his brain and all rational capability of reason.

"I want you," she murmured, mouth against his, right before their tongues mated the way his body wanted to.

He wanted her too, hell how he wanted her, but damned if he'd allow her to make him a slave of his own needs and desires. Holding himself back, he allowed her to kiss him, though he kept himself as restrained as he could.

Finally, his lack of enthusiasm got through to her.

"Travis?" She moved back, her expression troubled. "What is it? What's wrong?"

Maybe the time had come to give her the brutal truth, no matter how harsh. "I don't want Hal thinking we're a couple, getting his hopes up that I'll take care of you once he's..." He couldn't bring himself to finish the sentence.

At first, she simply stared at him, attempting to process his words. "Take care of me?" she asked. "What on earth are you talking about?"

"Hal feels horrible that you grew up without him being part of your life. He told me so. I know he worries about what will happen to you in the future." Again, he found he couldn't articulate the rest. Speaking out loud about a time when Hal wasn't alive felt like sacrilege.

"Interesting. Especially since he's never mentioned that to me."

Was she hurt? Or angry? He wasn't sure. While channeling his desire into an all-out brawl might be exactly what he needed, with Hal in the other room, he couldn't chance it. "I apologize," he said. "I didn't mean to offend you."

Though she dipped her chin in a curt nod of acknowledgment, there wasn't the slightest hint of forgiveness in her expression. "Let me make something clear. I don't need anyone to take care of me. Like I tried to tell you earlier, my mother made careful investments and she left me well-off enough that I've been considering opening my own art gallery. I made this detour here so I could get to know my father. I didn't know he was ill."

"Then why are you asking about the oil company's offers?" he shot back. "I couldn't help but overhear what you and Hal were discussing before I walked up."

He could have sworn hurt rather than chagrin flashed in her emerald eyes, so like Hal's. "Travis, I know you manage the ranch, so I'm sure you're aware Hal has financial troubles. All his medical tests and treatments are expensive. He's not just worried about what will happen to me once he's gone. He's concerned about you, Travis. If he doesn't come up with additional funds to pay his bill, there's a very real problem he will lose the ranch."

Chapter 10

He hadn't known. Scarlett saw the shock and disbelief on Travis's face clear as day. She couldn't help but wonder why Hal hadn't discussed it with him, but now she'd gone and gotten herself right where she'd never wanted to be—in the middle between the two men.

"Hal wouldn't keep that from me," Travis said. "And I know for a fact he'd never consider signing an agreement with Wave Oil. He's told me so himself. They'd ruin our land, take away our peace and spook our livestock."

No way did she plan to touch that. "Maybe you should ask him yourself," she pointed out. "Believe me, I've got no stake in this."

"You're from back East," he replied. She suspected that to him that was some kind of insult. "You don't love this land like I do. You've never ridden for miles, knowing you were nowhere near the boundary."

Ridden. She seized the word, welcoming a distraction. "I've never ridden, period. You'd said you would teach me. Believe me, I'd like nothing more than to explore the ranch on horseback."

He stared at her as if she'd suddenly grown two heads.

"You did offer," she repeated. "I know you remember." And, since everyone said Travis was a man of his word, she knew he wouldn't refuse.

They locked gazes. Again, that shiver of awareness, which she quickly throttled.

Though he looked none-too-happy, he finally nodded. "Tomorrow," he said. "Meet me at the big barn at 7:00 a.m. sharp."

And then he spun on his heel and left. Not only her room, but the house. A few seconds later, she heard his truck start up and drive off.

When she returned to the main part of the house, she saw Hal had wheeled himself into the living room and turned on the TV. He turned the volume down when he saw her.

"What got into him?" he asked, gesturing toward the front door. "He took off like the hounds of hell were fast on his heels."

"He's worried about the oil leases," she replied, determined to tell him the truth. "I think he still believes I'm after your money."

"What money?" Hal chuckled. "See, I can still make a joke."

Though she smiled in response, she was determined to stay on track. "Why haven't you told Travis about your financial issues?"

"Boy's got enough on his plate. I don't need to give

him one more thing to worry about. Plus, if his mother gets wind of that, she'll bring that awful boyfriend of hers over with his moneymaking schemes. Between his horrible sculptures and awful paintings, he's always trying to come up with ways to get rich quick. He's already tried to get me to invest once, in those awful green health shakes of his. He sells them locally, but he wanted me to help fund a larger manufacturing plant with statewide distribution. I told him no and also that I never wanted him to discuss his schemes with me again. He hasn't been back to the ranch since."

"Frank?" Scarlett remembered the name. "You know what? I haven't met him either."

Hal shrugged. "Who knows? Maybe he and Vivian are on the outs. She can do better."

"You don't find it odd, living so close to your ex-wife and getting to know her boyfriend?" she asked, genuinely curious. She'd never been married or divorced, but from what she'd seen of her friends, the situation with Hal and Vivian seemed unusual.

"Not really. But then Vivian and I weren't a great love match. We parted ways amicably." Hal's faded gaze sharpened. "What's going on with you and Travis?"

Startled, Scarlett felt her face heat. "He's teaching me to ride horses tomorrow."

"Is he?" Hal laughed. "That's great, but you know that's not what I meant. Are you and Travis a couple?"

"No." Swallowing hard, she decided to give him an amended version of the truth. After all, her physical relationship with Travis was none of his business.

"He doesn't want to be a couple," she elaborated.

"Neither do I. We both have our own plans for our future and they don't include each other."

The sparkle faded from Hal's eyes. "That's too bad," he said heavily. "I had my hopes that the two of you would hit it off."

"Oh, we do." If only he knew. "But it's just not the kind of thing that's going anywhere."

"You sound kind of sad about that," Hal said.

About to respond, she considered. He was right. Odd how quickly this man, the father she'd never known, intuitively understood her. Even more than she understood herself.

Because she suddenly realized she did want a future with Travis. Her heart ached, and with a lump in her throat, the knowledge stunned her. Right now, she couldn't examine her feelings—that would have to come later. The only thing she knew for certain was that Travis—and Hal—could never find out.

"I'm not," she managed, interjecting a bit of what she hoped sounded like carefree confidence into her voice. "It is what it is. Travis is a good man. I'm sure he'll find the right woman."

Never mind that the thought of him with another woman made her clench her teeth.

"You're going to the Halloween ball with him," Hal pointed out. "He hasn't asked a woman to accompany him since he broke up with Kendra."

"And he only asked me because Kendra will be there." She patted Hal's too-thin arm. "Don't make more of this than it is."

Though he appeared disappointed, he nodded and mumbled agreement before picking up the remote and unmuting the TV, clearly dismissing her.

Shaking her head, she wandered into the kitchen and grabbed one of the brownies Delilah had made for dessert. She'd never realized it at the time, but before her mother's illness, Scarlett had enjoyed a carefree, uncomplicated life. She'd been happy, if unfulfilled, with vague dreams of owning her own art gallery someday.

Now, her emotions were on the verge of becoming irrevocably tangled up in a man who felt she wasn't a match for him. The sad part was that she wasn't sure if he was right or wrong.

She liked it here, true. But she also liked Newnan, Georgia. Except now that her mother was gone, Georgia held no family, just a few dozen friends who'd barely even taken note of her absence.

Here, she had family. Not just Hal, but the people living on the HG Ranch. Vivian and Amber, Will and, of course, Travis. The close-knit community of Anniversary had enchanted her also and she looked forward to getting to know it better. She could actually envision herself making this place her permanent home.

Just like she'd begun to see the possibility of making Travis her man.

Shaking off thoughts that were too deep for a comfortable autumn evening, she went to bed early.

The next morning, she woke with a sense of excited anticipation and the tiniest bit of trepidation. She hurried through her morning preparations, got dressed in jeans and her boots, and rushed through breakfast. Again, Travis apparently had decided to sleep in, so she ate alone.

She made it to the barn shortly before seven. Travis was already waiting, polishing up a western saddle. Silently, she walked up behind him and watched, enjoying the play of the muscles in his arms as he worked. When he finally turned, he fixed his smoky gaze on her and nodded a hello.

"We're going to start with saddling the horse," he said. "I got this saddle out and cleaned it up. It belongs to my mother, though she rarely rides anymore. I think it'll suit you."

"Sounds good." She glanced around the barn, not even trying to contain her eagerness. "Which horse will I be riding?"

Her excited tone coaxed a smile from him. "My mother's old gelding. He's eleven years old and has carried Will safely. He'll be perfect for you. Let me go get him and show you how to get this saddle on him."

She nodded. Torn between following him and waiting, she decided to stay put. He stopped at a stall midway down the aisle, grabbed a halter and went inside. A moment later he emerged with the most beautiful gray horse she'd ever seen. A quick glance revealed the animal to be male.

"He's not a stallion, is he?" she asked, a bit nervous.

"No. He's a gelding," Travis explained. "They're different from stallions, which are mostly used for breeding. We also don't ride stallions much around here. Too dangerous."

"Oh." Relieved, she followed Travis's instructions, putting a colorful saddle blanket on first, and then lifting the surprisingly heavy saddle onto the horse's back. He showed her how to secure the cinch strap, not too loose but not too tight either.

When they'd finished that, he grabbed a bridle and showed her how a bit worked, putting pressure on the inside of the horse's mouth. "For that reason, we don't ever jerk on the reins or pull too hard. A gentle touch is all that's needed and Bob is trained to understand the reins on his neck and the pressure from your legs."

"Bob?" she asked, enchanted again. "His name is Bob?"

"Yep." Eyeing her, he held out his hand. "Are you ready to get on?"

"Now? Aren't you going to saddle up your horse first?"

"No. I'm going to work with you from the ground, in the outdoor arena. I'm not riding until I feel confident that you understand the basics."

Pleased and grateful, she smiled. When he cupped his hands for her to step into, she wondered how on earth she could do such a thing gracefully. Since she probably couldn't, she took a deep breath and tried anyway.

"Swing your other leg over his back," Travis ordered and he shoved her up.

She did. To her surprise, she now sat astride Bob's broad back. "Wow." Gripping the saddle horn, she looked down at Travis. "This seems a lot higher than I thought."

"You're fine." He handed her the reins. "Remember, use them gently. Mostly, Bob will respond to pressure from your legs and shifts in your weight. To get him to back up, gather the reins until they're tight, and squeeze both his sides using your legs."

Eager to try, she nodded and cautiously did as he'd said. When Bob took a couple of steps backward, she laughed out loud. "He did it!"

"And he'll do it again. Keep going, until you've gotten him to back a bit more so you can turn him around."

Leading the way on foot, she and Bob followed Travis at a safe distance. A group of cattle had been moved to a large pen nearby and she tensed, worried they might spook her horse. But like Travis had said, the gelding had apparently been around awhile as he barely even noticed them.

The outdoor riding arena was separated from the pen by an open graveled area. As the cattle milled about, they lowed and mooed, shaking their massive heads and stomping their hooves. But since neither Travis nor Bob paid them any mind, Scarlett was determined to ignore them as well.

They spent the rest of the morning in the outdoor arena, with Travis teaching her horseback riding basics. She learned the difference between walk and jog, and once he even had her urge Bob into what he called a lope, which seemed to be a kind of controlled run.

All in all, she didn't want the ride to end. But after about ninety minutes he signaled her over. Proud of herself, she directed Bob to move in Travis's direction and reined to a halt.

"Well?" she asked. "How'd I do?"

"Pretty well." His answering smile heated her insides. "You have a natural seat. You're still a little heavy on the reins, but that's something we can work on."

"Okay. When can we do this again?" She smiled back. "I'd like to go trail riding."

Considering, he glanced at her watch. "Bob's tired. Maybe next time. Let's get him back inside and get that saddle off. Next you'll need to learn how to brush him down."

He opened the gate to the arena and she rode

through. When she reached the area between the cattle pen and the barn, she glanced over at the cows, fascinated despite herself.

A loud crack sounded, then another. Like firecrackers going off. Bob, despite his placidity, reacted instinctively, skittering sideways and half rearing. Gasping, Scarlett tried to grab for the saddle horn, but the horse's sudden movements unseated her and she tumbled off.

She hit the gravel hard, rolling just as one of Bob's hooves narrowly missed her head. Travis caught up, grabbing the reins. The horse instantly quieted.

Scarlett scrambled to her knees, trying to assess how badly she'd been hurt.

Travis's first concern was getting Bob away from Scarlett. He led the still tense horse away from where she lay on the ground. "Are you okay?" he asked.

Before she could answer, there came another volley of pop-pop-pop. Before, he'd thought gunshots, but now he'd bet on fireworks. When he found the idiot who was foolish enough to shoot them off near livestock, he'd give them a stern talking to.

Another sound, the crash and creak of a fence giving way. Bob whinnied and tried to rear up again. Swiftly, Travis brought the horse under control, turning to look at the cattle.

Clearly spooked, they milled about, pushing against the fence, the entire herd all snorting and trying to run.

His heart skipped a second before the fence gave way. He yelled, shouting at Scarlett to get up, to get moving, to get out of the way. Using Bob as a barrier, he tried to get to her. By some miracle he did, grabbing her up by the arm and hauling her against him.

The cattle thundered around them, splitting in waves but missing the even-more-nervous horse. Bob's nostrils flared and the whites of his eyes showed. Trying to calm him and hold Scarlett close and safe, he couldn't breathe until the last of the cattle galloped past.

When he looked down at a clearly shaken Scarlett, Travis noticed that her jeans had been torn. A ruby slash of blood showed on one leg, and both her bloody elbows were raw.

"You okay?" he demanded. The instant she jerked her head yes, he glanced past her. Still running full-out, the herd was heading for the ranch road. Hopefully, the cattle guard midway up the drive would stop them. If not, there'd be a hell of a roundup. At least he had the manpower to do it.

Scarlett wiggled against him. "Let me see if I can stand on my own," she demanded.

Gently, he released enough of his hold so that she was standing on her own two feet.

She swayed, but waved him away. "I'm good. It doesn't feel like anything is broken."

Sheltering her with one arm, he somehow managed to get both her and a still nervous Bob inside the barn. After he deposited her on a bale of hay, he tied up the horse first and then quickly checked Scarlett over.

"Torn clothes, bloody elbows and a couple of cuts. You were damn lucky you weren't seriously injured."

She nodded. "Are you going to do anything about those cows fleeing down the road?"

"That's next," he replied, grabbing his cell and making a quick call. Once he'd sent a crew to retrieve the cattle, he took Bob back to his stall, leaving the saddle on for now, and went back to double-check on Scarlett.

To his relief, she appeared to have recovered from her shock. She pushed to her feet, testing first one leg, and then the other. “Nothing broken,” she mused out loud. “At least that I can tell. My hip hurts, but I think it’s just bruised. And yes, I do have a few cuts and scrapes, but you’re right. I was lucky.” She met his gaze, dipping her chin. “Thank you for saving me. I’ve never been bucked off a horse before and I know you should get right back on, but I think I’m going to wait a bit.”

“That’s understandable.” He couldn’t keep from reaching out and caressing her shoulder. “Will you be all right for a moment while I go take care of Bob?” he asked. “I need to get his saddle and bridle off and brush him down. It isn’t good to let the sweat dry on him.”

“Sure.”

As he removed the horse’s saddle and replaced the bridle with a halter, he willed his heartbeat to slow. The cattle would be fine, he knew. After all, there wasn’t really anywhere they could go that wasn’t part of the ranch. His crew would round them up and get them contained in another small pasture while the fence was repaired.

But as long as he lived he thought he’d never get over the horror of watching as Scarlett had been bucked off the steadiest horse he had and then nearly been trampled to death by a panicked herd of spooked cattle.

He brushed Bob down, removed the halter and left the horse in his stall. Scarlett still waited where he’d left her, perched on a bale of hay. She looked fragile, suddenly. Maybe because he was used to her confident, carefree attitude and now she was shaken.

“It’s going to be all right,” he said, sitting down next

to her. "You're safe and Bob's okay. The cattle will be rounded up and brought back."

"I'm glad." She lifted her chin, meeting his gaze. "That was deliberate, you know. Someone once again trying to scare or hurt me."

While he'd wondered the same thing, he shook his head. "We don't know that for sure."

"Really?" she challenged. "What else could it have been? Who shoots off fireworks out here in the middle of the ranch, so close to livestock?"

He said the first thing that came to mind. "Teenaged kids skipping school. That's one possibility. They don't always think before acting."

"True." She conceded the point with a slight dip of her shoulder, which made her wince. "If you don't mind, I'd like to get back to the house. I'll need your assistance to walk, just in case."

"I'll drive you," he said. "Much easier."

After helping her into his truck, his heart squeezing every time she winced, he drove slowly toward the house. At every bump, he heard her swift intake of breath, but she never complained.

Once there, he helped her down and offered her his arm. Leaning slightly on him, she limped into the house with her head held high. "I'd like to go straight to my room if possible. I don't want to worry Hal or Delilah."

Though privately he doubted they'd be able to do that, when they walked through the front door, Hal had fallen asleep in front of the TV. He didn't stir at all as they went past him. Delilah must have been busy in another part of the house, because they made it all the way to Scarlett's room without encountering her.

"Argh," Scarlett said, letting go of his arm and falling onto her bed. "My entire body aches. I'm going to run a nice hot bath and just soak in it."

His mouth went dry, though he managed to nod. "I'll leave you to it," he managed to say. When he left, he almost felt as if he were fleeing.

Back at the barn, he spent the next hour searching the area on foot. Judging from the loudness of the sound, whoever had set off the firecrackers had been pretty damn close. While no doubt they'd taken enough precautions to ensure they weren't seen, Travis figured they'd probably left behind some incriminating evidence. He planned to find it.

As he moved closer to the road, right past a small thicket of pine trees, he found the firecracker wrappers and detonator shafts. They'd been placed carefully in a drainage culvert, out of sight of both the road and the arena. Had the person who'd set them taken off on foot or left by vehicle? Either one would have been possible, considering the chaos caused by the stampeding cattle.

He picked up all the paper scraps he could find, looking for any other clues. Unfortunately, with the gravel road nearby, it seemed likely the culprit had simply gotten into a vehicle and had driven off.

Somehow, he doubted this had been a teenager playing a prank. First up, this person had to come onto ranch land with the firecrackers, drive to find an area close to livestock and the arena and place the firecrackers in a hidden location.

But if this had been intentional, all with the intention of causing bodily harm to him or to Scarlett, someone would have had to have pre-knowledge of both of their locations. As far as he could tell, the only people who knew were family. And none of them would have done anything as crazy-stupid as this.

Just to be safe, he drove downtown with his evidence and stopped at the sheriff's office. Even though he didn't have an appointment, the receptionist showed him right in.

One of the good things about living in a small town.

The sheriff looked up when he entered. "Travis Warren." He stood, offering his hand. "It's been a long time. What's up?"

Travis handed over the bag of firecracker scraps and outlined what had happened. "She's also had a truck try to run her off the road—nearly hit her, and took out a section of our fence. And before that, she got a weird note. All cut-out letters, telling her to leave."

"Cut-out letters?" The sheriff's gaze sharpened. "That's textbook and slightly concerning. Did you bring the letter with you?"

"No. Scarlett still has it."

"See if she'll let you make a copy and email it to me. Now tell me." Sheriff James leaned forward. "Why would anyone want her out of town?"

"I've thought about that myself. While I'll admit, at first I was a bit suspicious of her, showing up just when the oil company was increasing their pressure on us to allow them to start drilling, I have no reason to doubt her now. Not only does her being here make Hal happy, but she fits right in and everyone seems to like her, including my mother and sister."

"That's amazing." Even the sheriff knew how difficult Vivian could be sometimes. "But why don't I run a quick check on her, just to make sure."

Though Travis felt slightly guilty doing such a thing

without her permission, he nodded. Might as well find out the truth.

"Do you know her date of birth?"

Travis shook his head. "No. I'm guessing she is in her late twenties, early thirties. She used to live in Georgia, somewhere near Atlanta, if that helps. Her last name is Kistler."

The sheriff jotted that down. "Let me get to work on this. I'll call you if I find out anything."

"Thanks." Travis shook the other man's hand and left.

As he got into his pickup truck, his sister called. "I heard about what happened," she said.

"Already?" Astounded, he glanced at his watch. It had only been a couple of hours.

"Yeah, Delilah ran into Scarlett as she was running a bath."

He winced. "I hope they kept it from Hal."

"They did. But Delilah called Vivian, and you know how that goes. Though she did promise not to say anything to Hal."

"Good," he said, meaning it.

"It sounded scary as all get-out. Are you all right?"

Touched, he assured her he was. "Scarlett got the worst of it. Bob bucked her right off."

"Bob did?" Everyone who'd ever ridden knew Bob to be the most placid horse they had. "It must have been frightening if it scared Bob."

Quickly, he outlined what had happened and what he'd found. "I just left the sheriff's office. He's going to look into this."

"Wow." She sounded thoughtful. "Do you think it was deliberate?"

"Why else would someone come onto the ranch and shoot firecrackers off near a herd of cattle?"

"Do you think it was Kendra?" she asked.

The thought hadn't occurred to him. He swore. "That's one possibility. I need to mention that to the sheriff."

"But Scarlett's okay, right? From what Delilah said, she was pretty banged up."

"She had some cuts and bruises, but nothing broken. She was damn lucky." He sighed. "I don't know that she'll ever be willing to get back up on a horse, though."

"Of course she will." The certainty in Amber's voice surprised him. "I know you're busy, so I'll make a point of inviting her to go riding with me."

Touched—and slightly concerned, since he still didn't know if someone was targeting Scarlett—he swallowed. "That's kind of you."

"I really like her," Amber continued. "I think we can be friends. I've never realized how lonely this ranch could be for someone my age. Scarlett's only a few years older, and I'm going to invite her to go into town and eat, maybe see a movie or have a few drinks."

"I'm sure she'd appreciate that." More than ever, he hoped the sheriff didn't turn up anything on Scarlett. Not only Hal would be affected, but Amber too. Even Vivian acted as if she liked Hal's daughter. As for Travis...well, he liked her a little too much.

"Earth to Travis," Amber said. "Are you still there?"

He must have gotten lost in thought. "Yeah. I'm sorry. I've got a lot going on. What did you say?"

"I asked you if you two were dating?"

His heart actually skipped a beat, which annoyed him. “No. Why do you ask?”

“I don’t know,” she drawled. “Maybe because you seem really into her.”

Not sure how to respond to that, especially since she was right, he changed the subject. “Any more discussion over the costumes for the ball? It’ll be here before we know it and I don’t want to wait until the last minute.” Though personally, he had no problem with wearing his costume from last year, he knew the ball organizers would frown on that. Especially since they made the costumes the highlight of the entire night, with large prizes for the ones they deemed the best.

Amber laughed. “Deflecting much?”

“Not really,” he lied. “I actually do want to know about the costumes.”

Her loud sigh told him he wasn’t fooling her. “I think Mom is planning to talk to Scarlett about that. Whatever they decide is fine with me, as long as it’s not too froufrou.”

After years of choosing his own costume, Travis wasn’t sure he felt the same way. Though he still felt sort of bad about nixing the whole Camelot thing. As long as he didn’t end up having to wear tights, he supposed he’d be okay.

Chapter 11

Glad Delilah had rounded up some bubble bath, even if it belonged to Will and was in a bottle shaped like a holiday snowman, Scarlett sank into the bubbles up to her neck and willed her aches away.

After removing her torn jeans and shirt, which had been more painful than she'd expected, she'd grabbed a short robe to cover herself and bolted down the hallway toward the guest bathroom.

Her luck hadn't held. Scarlett had nearly collided with the other woman. Delilah had taken one look at her cuts and bruises and scratches and had taken over. Missing her own mother, Scarlett had let her clean the wounds. Delilah had brought a glass of water and two ibuprofen, which Scarlett swallowed.

"Now tell me what happened to you," Delilah ordered.

Scarlett did.

After hearing the explanation, a tight-lipped Delilah had agreed it would be best if Hal didn't find out. She'd extracted a promise that Scarlett would put antibiotic ointment and self-adhesive bandages on after her bath and left her alone to run her bath. She'd returned with the bottle of bath bubbles a moment later, laughing as she handed it over. "Better than nothing," she said. "Though I imagine I can round up some Epsom salts if you'd rather have those."

"Just the bubbles for now, thanks." Grateful, Scarlett had made the water as hot as she could stand. Locking the door, she'd winced and bit her lip as the hot water hit her wounds.

It could have been worse. If Travis hadn't been there, she might have been trampled by those spooked cows. Never mind the freaked-out horse.

For the first time, she wondered about Travis's ex-fiancée. Was it possible she might be behind all this? The letter, the truck almost running her down and now the fireworks causing a stampede? Somehow, Scarlett couldn't imagine what the other woman might have hoped to accomplish by scaring her off. It wasn't as if making Scarlett leave would send Travis back into Kendra's arms.

Then why? Were all these things, with the exception of the vaguely threatening note, mere accidents? Had the driver of the white pickup been drunk or an unskilled teenager out for a joyride? Because there hadn't been any way anyone could have known Scarlett would be walking down that road. Ditto for the horseback riding lesson. Only a few people had been aware Scarlett and Travis were meeting at the barn so she could learn to ride.

Circumstance and happenstance, maybe. If so, then

she might possibly be the unluckiest person on the planet. Since she hated feeling paranoid, she decided to keep her eyes open and try not to worry.

By the time she finally climbed out of the tub, the water had cooled. But she felt better, almost normal, though a bit shaky. After carefully drying herself off, she applied the antibiotic ointment and used the adhesive bandages. Then, robe back on, she hurried to her room.

She felt like she needed a nap.

Instead, barely five minutes after crawling beneath the covers, a soft tap sounded on her door. "Are you hungry?" Delilah asked softly. "I made tomato soup and grilled cheese sandwiches. I can bring you a tray if you'd like."

One of her favorites. If anything could entice her from bed, that combination would do it. "I'd love that," Scarlett answered. She propped her back up with a pillow, glad she'd put on an old T-shirt, and turned on the light.

A few minutes later, Delilah brought her a tray with a steaming bowl of tomato soup and a perfectly cooked grilled cheese sandwich. She'd also added a tall glass of cold milk and one of her signature chocolate chip cookies.

"This looks wonderful," Scarlett said. "Thank you so much. I don't know what any of us would do without you."

"You'd manage," Delilah responded, her tone dry. "Neither Vivian nor Amber work full-time. They'd just have to pitch in and help out more than they do."

About to spoon up the first mouthful of soup, Scarlett paused. "You sound like you've given that some thought. Should I be worried?"

"Oh honey, no. My son lives in Phoenix and I'm long overdue for a visit, but there's no way I'm leaving—even for a few days—with Mr. Hal doing as poorly as he is."

"Thank you." Digging in to the meal, Scarlett noticed how hungry she'd been. Delilah sat with her while she ate, telling her about the pie-making competition at the Halloween Harvest Fair.

"I always enter," Delilah said. "And I always come in second or third place. I've never won. Sarah Sepkie—she owns the bakery on Third—takes home the top prize every single year. This time, I'm bound and determined to best her. I've been perfecting a recipe for a decadent butterscotch pie." She leaned in close. "I've decided to put meringue on top of mine."

"That was my mama's favorite." Scarlett sighed. "If you need anyone to taste test between now and the contest, let me know."

Delilah laughed. "Oh, Travis has already claimed that job. He's brutally honest too, which is what I need."

"I can imagine." Scarlett looked down at the empty tray. Though she wasn't fond of milk, she'd managed to drink almost all of it. Again, milk made her think of her mother. "Delilah, why do you think someone is out to get me?"

"Are you certain that someone is?" Delilah's practical tone felt reassuring. "I mean, yes, you got a weird note. But the other two incidents were most likely not targeted at you."

"Travis said something similar." Scarlett sighed. "And you're both probably right. I just can't shake this feeling..." She swallowed back the rest, not wanting to appear foolish.

"It's all right." Delilah pushed to her feet and took up the tray. "You go ahead and have your nap. I'm sure you'll feel better after you rest." She left, closing the door quietly behind her.

Full and warm, Scarlett clicked off the lamp and snuggled down under the covers. Her body still ached, though the anti-inflammatory had helped dull some of the pain.

She must have slipped into sleep immediately, because when she came awake and opened her eyes, the nightstand clock showed she'd been asleep two hours. Still groggy, she stretched and turned on the light. Stumbling from her bed, she eyed herself in the mirror and grimaced. At least none of her cuts and bruises were on her face.

After pulling on a clean T-shirt—she could get used to wearing these all the time—and a comfy pair of yoga pants, she padded to the bathroom to wash her face and brush her teeth. While she was there, she put on some light makeup and brushed her hair.

She felt like a new person. Satisfied that she'd done the best she could, she pulled on a long-sleeved denim shirt to cover her arm bandages. Leaving this unbuttoned, she headed into the living room. Hal still sat where he'd been earlier, his wheelchair parked in front of the TV.

But this time, he wasn't asleep. As soon as he caught sight of her, he used the remote to turn the television off. "Hey there," he said, his voice rusty from either sleep or lack of use.

"Hey there, yourself." She perched on the edge of

the couch, eyeing him. "You spend an awful lot of time in front of that thing."

He frowned. "What else can I do? It's not like I can climb up on a horse and go riding."

"How about we go for a walk? I can push you down to the end of the driveway."

Though she could have sworn interest flickered in his eyes, he shook his head. "Not now. Maybe later. I've got a headache. How'd the riding lesson with Travis go?"

She debated for a second. "I fell off the horse."

"Seriously?" His mouth twitched, and she could tell he was trying not to laugh. "What horse did he put you on?"

"Bob." Bracing herself, she waited for his reaction.

He didn't disappoint. "You fell off Bob?"

Now she couldn't tell him the whole truth, that Bob had actually bucked her off, without filling him in on what had happened, so she simply nodded. "And yes, I'm embarrassed. And no, I don't want to talk about it anymore if that's all right with you."

He burst out laughing. Hearing the sound of pure joy coming from him made her happy. She smiled happily, soaking in the feeling. Delilah even poked her head out of the kitchen, no doubt drawn by the commotion. When she caught sight of Scarlett, she gave her a thumbs-up sign before returning to whatever she'd been doing.

Finally, Hal wound down. Wiping tears from his eyes, he shook his head. "Only you," he commented. "I'm so glad you came. You make long days much more interesting."

"Happy to be of service." Her light response hid

her concern. If anything, Hal looked as if he'd taken a turn for the worse over the past twenty-four hours. Her heart ached. So sad. So frustrating. She failed to understand how not a single doctor or hospital could figure out what kind of illness was making Hal waste away.

The front door banged open and Vivian swept in. "There you are," she said, heading straight for Scarlett.

"How are you?" Vivian trilled, enveloping Scarlett in a perfume-scented hug. "I heard about what happened," she murmured her Scarlett's ear. "But you look perfectly fine to me."

"I'm actually great," Scarlett said, raising her voice slightly for Hal's sake. He grunted and immediately turned the TV back on, barely glancing up to acknowledge his visitors. "I'm worried about him, though." She inclined her head toward Hal. "Maybe we should try to get him back to see another doctor."

"I won't go," Hal harrumphed, proving he had been listening. "There's no point. Bunch of damn fools that keep telling me there's nothing wrong. They don't know and they don't care."

Vivian shrugged. "He's kind of right, you know."

"I am right." Deliberately, he turned up the volume, making conversation impossible. "If you gals want to talk, do it in the kitchen," he shouted.

Left with no choice, Scarlett got to her feet and led the way. In the midst of making dinner preparations, Delilah looked up and, when she caught sight of Vivian, looked back down.

"I'm glad you're okay," Vivian continued, looking Scarlett up and down. "You seem like a strong-willed girl, so please don't wait too long to get back up on that horse."

It had been a long time since anyone had referred to her as a *girl*, but Scarlett knew Vivian didn't mean anything derogatory by that, so she let it slide. "I've heard that too," she admitted. "And I'm sure I'll try riding again, once everything heals." Maybe, though she kept her doubts to herself.

"I wanted to talk to you about the costume ball," Vivian said. "It's getting closer and we've got to decide on costumes. Since Travis has ruled out Camelot, we need to consider another option." She dropped a fresh stack of pages onto the table.

"Maybe we should wait until he's around to decide," Scarlett said, eyeing them. "I hate to get all excited about something and then have him say no."

Both Delilah and Vivian chuckled at that. "That's not how it works, darlin'." Delilah winked. "You just choose, get the costume and then give it to him. Don't give him a say."

"That hardly seems fair," Scarlett protested. "He's the one with the biggest stake in all this."

"Bull." Vivian pooh-poohed that notion. "For as long as I've been going to that ball, the women choose the costumes and the men go along. Men generally don't expect to have to make that type of clothing selection."

About to comment on what she thought of that remark, Scarlett closed her mouth. What did she know? She'd never been married and her last serious relationship had been a couple of years ago.

Vivian smiled sweetly and indicated the papers. "Let's go through these."

Maybe she was making too big of a deal out of this. Pulling out a chair, Scarlett sat. Vivian did the same. Delilah even came over to the table and sat, so she could be in on the discussion.

Vivian eyed her. "You are still going with us, right?"

"Definitely," Delilah answered. "Y'all are a lot more creative than my family. My husband will wear whatever I tell him to."

"See?" Vivian crowed. "That's how it works."

Deciding to let that topic go, Scarlett thought of her one ally. "Where's Amber?" she asked. She really valued the younger woman's input, especially since Vivian could be a bit overbearing.

"She's volunteering up at Will's school. Today is the kindergarten harvest party. They're also having a festival this weekend."

"Oh." Disappointed, Scarlett eyed the older woman. "Don't you think she should get a vote?"

"She doesn't care," Vivian answered emphatically. "If she got to choose, we'd all go as vampires and werewolves. Since we aren't, she'll go along with anything as long as she can have the opportunity to make it dark."

Right then and there, Scarlett decided to call Amber later that evening. She truly liked the other woman and would have welcomed her feedback in selecting a costume. Which meant she'd delay making any sort of decision until she talked to both brother and sister.

Slowly, Vivian flipped through pages. Roman nobles, Greek gods and goddesses, all clearly photocopied from a costuming magazine. Nothing caught Scarlett's eye until she saw a page of elves. “Wait,” she said. “Let me see that. It’s kind of interesting.”

But after she looked it over, she realized Travis wouldn’t appreciate any of the men’s costumes. “Never mind.” She slid the page back to Vivian.

The next one that caught her eye was 1920s style gangsters. Now that she could picture Travis wearing. “What about this?” she asked. “Has he done anything like this before?”

“Nope.” Vivian smiled. “He could be an Al Capone type. We could be flappers.”

The more she thought about it, the more Scarlett liked that idea. Especially when she thought of all the other choices she’d seen so far. “Those would be easy costumes to make or rent, wouldn’t they?”

“They would.” A gleam of interest shone in Vivian’s eyes. “Is that your choice? Or—” she indicated what had to be at least thirty more pages “—do you want to keep looking?”

Suddenly weary of the entire thing, Scarlett decided to make a quick decision. “I think this will work. Let’s go with it. I’ll let Travis know the next time I see him.”

In fact, she resolved to tell him as soon as possible. That way, if he had any issues with her choice, she’d tell him to talk to his mother and choose something on his own.

The next morning, Travis stopped by the main house before heading out into the fields. Though the sun had just begun to rise, the instant he pulled up and parked, Scarlett came out onto the front porch. Almost as if she’d been waiting for him.

The early autumn air carried a pleasant crispness, even though the leaves had barely begun to turn.

He walked up, pleasantly surprised when she handed him a steaming mug of coffee. "Thanks," he said. "But how'd you know I was coming by this morning?"

"I didn't. But I'd gone out onto the porch to get a bit of fresh air, and I saw your headlights coming down the road. Since I'd already started a pot of coffee brewing, I poured us both a cup. No big deal."

No big deal. Yet, the simple kindness touched him.

"We decided on costumes yesterday," she blurted out, her gaze flying to his. "We're going with Roaring Twenties era gangsters."

He kept his face expressionless, though he found her earnestness interesting. "You want me to be a gangster, huh?"

She nodded, lifting her chin while holding his gaze, almost as if daring him to say something about her choice. He thought about his conversation with Amber and realized his baby sister was right. Maybe he had been making a big deal out of nothing.

"That sounds good." He kept his tone mild.

Visibly relieved, she finally looked down and took a long drink of her cup. "I'm glad."

"I assume you've told my mother and she's working on it?"

"Yep. She stopped by yesterday. She and Amber and I are going to drive into Dallas to pick up the costumes. She's already reserved them at a costume shop." Excitement made her emerald eyes sparkle. Fascinated, he forced himself to look down and take a drink from his own coffee cup.

"Great. Have fun." He started to turn away. But she

caught his arm, holding him in place. The touch sent a jolt through him, making him freeze.

"Wait." She tugged to get his attention. "I just have one question. You had problems with being Lancelot or King Arthur, but a gangster is fine? I don't get it."

"A gangster is generic. The others were specific individuals, so their stories are known." While explaining this way made him feel slightly foolish, he also didn't want to mention that his ex had always wanted to be Guinevere.

"I see. You're a complicated man, Travis Warren."

One second more and he wouldn't be able to keep from kissing her. "Thanks. I'll take that as a compliment." Gently pulling his arm from her grasp, he headed toward the door to go inside. "I've got to grab some breakfast," he said. "I've got a long day ahead of me."

Though she made no comment, she followed him inside. Delilah had made an egg casserole the day before and all they had to do was spoon it onto their plates and then nuke it in the microwave.

They ate in companionable silence. In days past, Hal would have popped in to the kitchen. He'd always been an early riser. Clearly, not any longer. The mysterious illness continued to take its toll.

They both ate quickly and silently, each lost in their own thoughts. Travis finished eating, rinsed off his plate and drained his second cup of coffee. "Tell Hal I said hello," he told Scarlett. She promised that she would. Then he headed out to start his day.

Travis started to feel queasy before lunch. He put away his horse, brushing him down like usual, but the thought of trying to eat anything made him break out into a cold sweat.

Instead of stopping at the main house, he went home. If he was coming down with something, he didn't want to pass it on to Hal. Any additional illness could seriously incapacitate the older man.

The only one home when he arrived was Amber. She took one look at him and scrambled up from the couch. "You look like death," she said. "Don't come anywhere near me."

He still felt well enough to be able to tease her. "Nice try at being sympathetic, sis," he growled.

In response, she snorted. "Good thing Mom and Scarlett and I are heading to Dallas tomorrow. Not only are you probably contagious, but you're an absolute pain in the rear when you don't feel good."

Pretending to be wounded seemed like too much effort, so he shrugged. "I'm going to bed. I'll have my phone if anyone needs me, otherwise tell them to leave me alone."

Wide-eyed, Amber nodded. "Sounds good. I'll, uh, let Mom know. And warn Scarlett."

Ignoring that, he stumbled into his room. His head had started to ache almost as much as his body. Closing his blinds, he stripped down to his boxers and climbed into his bed.

About to leave for one of her walks, Scarlett smiled when her cell phone rang and Amber's number showed up on the screen. They were all looking forward to their road trip to Dallas in the morning. Girls' day, Amber had taken to calling it.

"Hey, what's up?"

"Pray for me," Amber replied. "Travis has come down with something—flu or virus, I'm not sure. He's an absolute bear when he's sick. I'm so glad we're getting out of the house all day tomorrow."

Scarlett blinked. "Someone's going to stay with him, right?"

"Um, no. He's a grown man. He can take care of himself."

While that might be true, Scarlett felt a twinge of concern. "How sick is he?"

"No idea." A tiny bit of impatience crept into Amber's voice. "I know you're soft on him, but don't be thinking of doing anything crazy, like canceling going with us so you can take care of him, you hear?"

The instant Amber finished speaking, Scarlett knew that was exactly what she wanted to do. If he was truly ill, that is.

"Maybe he'll feel better in the morning," Scarlett said. "It's possible he only needs to rest and drink lots of fluids."

"That's the way to look at it. Anyway, Mom will be home soon and she'll check on him. I've got to go get Will at school. I'll be keeping him away from Travis too. He doesn't need to get sick right before Halloween."

"Neither does Travis." Scarlett couldn't help worrying. "Please keep me posted."

"I'll give you a full update in the morning when we pick you up," Amber promised and ended the call.

Ridiculous to worry so much about Travis, who surely could take care of himself. Scarlett wished she could make herself stop.

Pacing, she glanced at Hal, slumped in his usual

place in front of the TV. She wouldn't have believed it possible, but he had less and less fight left in him with each passing day. And he now stubbornly refused to go to any more doctors, claiming they didn't know what they were doing. While he was right, she also wondered if he was worried about finances.

Since she didn't want to wake him to discuss her concerns about Travis, she headed into the kitchen to talk to Delilah.

As soon as she heard the words *Travis is sick*, Delilah's eyes widened and she shook her head. "You want to stay far, far away from that one. Travis is generally an easygoing sort of man, but when he feels poorly, it's like he has a personality transplant."

Fascinated, Scarlett asked her what she meant. "I mean, I've heard all my life that some men can be difficult when they're sick."

"Oh, *difficult* doesn't even begin to describe him. For as long as I've known him, I'd have to say that's Travis's major flaw. Everyone who knows him is well aware to keep their distance when he's ill."

Some of Scarlett's thoughts must have shown in her face. "Oh, no, no." Delilah wagged her index finger. "Don't even be thinking about trying to look after him. I promise, you'll regret it if you do."

Scarlett smiled. "Forgive me if I feel like you're exaggerating. I've gotten to know Travis. I find all this difficult to believe."

"You'll learn," Delilah said, her tone dark. "Believe me, you'll learn."

Later that evening, Scarlett called Amber. "How is he?" she asked.

"No idea," Amber said. "I'm not even home. Mom

checked on him, so you might call her. Or—" she paused "—give Travis a ring. If he even answers, you'll see what I was telling you about earlier."

Though she hated the idea of bothering a sick man, Scarlett decided to try. After all, if he felt too poorly to talk, then she figured he wouldn't answer. In that case, she'd simply call Vivian.

To her surprise, he answered on the second ring.

"What?" he mumbled. Since he sounded as if he'd just woken up, she felt fairly contrite.

"I'm sorry. I hope I didn't wake you. I just wanted to check and see how you were feeling and see if there's anything you need."

"I need to be left alone," he snarled. A fit of coughing took over. In the middle of that, he ended the call.

"Wow," she mumbled to herself. Maybe there was some truth after all to what everyone had said. Still, Travis had sounded as if he felt pretty horrible. She decided to call Vivian.

"Oh, hello, Scarlett," Vivian practically sang. "I'm so looking forward to our girls' day tomorrow."

"Me too. I'm calling to check on Travis," Scarlett said, feeling better. Things couldn't be that bad if Vivian sounded so positive and happy.

"I made him some chicken noodle soup and left it in the fridge for him," Vivian replied. "I made sure to let him know on my way out the door."

"You left him there alone?"

"He's a grown man, honey. This ain't my first rodeo. He just needs to sweat it out and he'll be fine. I couldn't take a chance of catching anything and ruining our trip tomorrow. Plus, I don't know if anyone has mentioned this, but Travis is a horrible patient when he's sick."

"So I've heard," Scarlett drawled. "Do you know what's wrong with him exactly?"

"Probably the flu. He most likely picked it up at that gym in town where he goes to work out."

A gym? Possibly a good place to catch something.

"The flu can be serious," she pointed out. "Don't you think someone should stay with him, just in case?"

Vivian snorted. "No. Unless you're volunteering?" And she laughed.

That laugh did it. "I am," Scarlett said, her voice firm. "You and Amber will have to go to Dallas without me. I'm going to stay here and look after Travis."

No amount of cajoling from Vivian changed her mind.

Even Amber called later that night to state a case why staying was a bad idea. "Have you even asked Travis?"

"I'm not going to. He's sick. I'm going to help him out. If he doesn't like it, that's tough." Scarlett lifted her chin. Her mother had always said that the Kistler women were stubborn as heck. As it turned out, she was right.

"It's your funeral," Amber sighed. "You really have no idea what you're letting yourself in for. And now you're letting my mother choose your costume. You'd better hope it's not too ugly."

"That's what I'm counting on you for," Scarlett pointed out. "You know I'd do the same for you."

"Fine. All I can say is, you must really have a thing for my brother. However, I'm betting that might change after you spend one day in sick Travis's company. We're leaving at nine, so you'll need to come by before we go so you're not locked out. And bring some sort of protective gear so you don't carry any germs back to Hal."

Chapter 12

For the first couple of hours, Travis guessed he must have slept like the dead. He woke up sometime in the middle of the night, twisted up in his sheets and burning up from the inside out. Cursing, he pushed himself up out of bed and stumbled to his bathroom. He located a bottle of ibuprofen and took two, choking them down dry. Damn, he hated being sick.

Splashing water on his overheated face, he peered at himself in the mirror and immediately wished he hadn't. The last time he'd looked like that, he'd been sick with the flu for a week. Since then, he'd made sure to get his flu shot, though he hadn't this year. Heck, it wasn't even flu season yet.

Whatever this was that ailed him, it made him feel like hell. Somehow, he made it back to his bed and dropped back into it.

For the rest of the night, he alternated between freezing and shivering and dying of heat. He tossed and turned, alternatively wishing for sleep and an ice bath. Finally, he managed to doze into a kind of catatonic state.

When he opened his eyes again, bright sunlight streamed in through the blinds, making him wince. Never had he been so glad to realize this was the day his mother and sister, along with Scarlett, were all driving into Dallas for the day. On the rare occasions he fell ill, they all knew there was nothing he wanted more than being left alone. It looked like this time, this wish would be granted.

The nightstand clock said it was after nine, which meant Will would be at school and the women most likely had left. The silence of the house attested to that fact.

Coughing and wheezing, he made it into the bathroom and brushed his teeth, hoping to rid his mouth of a horrible taste. He located a throat lozenge and popped that into his mouth. He needed fluids and since the thought of coffee made his stomach churn, he decided to see if they had any ginger ale.

Padding into the kitchen barefoot, wearing only his boxers, he saw indeed that Vivian had bought a couple of two-liter bottles just for him. Still dizzy, he managed to grab a glass and pour himself some, without ice.

The carbonated bubbles tickled his nose as he swallowed. Though he knew he should eat something, the idea of actually doing so made his stomach clench. For now, he'd settle for the drink.

He turned to make his way back to bed and stopped short. Scarlett sat at the kitchen table, silently watching him.

"Hey," she said, her voice soft. "How are you feeling?"

"Go home," he ordered, too ill to waste time on pleasantries. A bout of coughing broke up his words. Raspy, he continued. "You're supposed to be on your way to Dallas anyway."

"I canceled. Vivian and Amber went without me."

Damned if he was going to ask why.

But of course she told him anyway. "I decided to stay and look after you."

He nearly dropped his glass. "Go home," he croaked. Then added as a bonus. "I'm contagious. I don't want to get you sick." While he knew she didn't realize it, he was actually making an effort to be nice. Comparatively, that is.

Waving her toward the door with his one free hand, he staggered back to his bedroom. He managed to set the drink down on his nightstand, before a bout of coughing nearly brought him to his knees.

Unbelievably, Scarlett had followed him. "Here." She offered a brand-new box of tissues. "It looks like you might need these. What else would you like me to get you?"

"An empty house," he snarled, at the end of his miserable rope. He snatched the tissues and ripped them open. Turning his back to her, he blew his nose. "Really, Scarlett. I appreciate your concern, but I'd like to be left alone."

"I'll be out in the living room or kitchen if you need me," she replied, clearly determined to ignore him.

He tried one more time, aching for his bed. "Hal needs you more than me. You can't risk bringing germs home to him."

"I'm thinking it's already too late." She smiled, apparently unconcerned. "Delilah will look after Hal.

And Amber has already decided to stay over there with Will as she doesn't want him to catch this. Vivian is going to stay with Frank. I refuse to leave you alone when you're so sick."

Having said her piece, she marched quietly from his room, letting herself out and closing the door behind her.

He let himself fall back onto the bed, his head throbbing. He felt either touched or annoyed, he couldn't decide which. He fell asleep while trying to figure that out.

Sometime later—judging by his nightstand clock, shortly after noon—a soft tapping on his bedroom door woke him. He considered ignoring it, but he'd drained his glass of ginger ale and needed to get more.

"What?" he rasped, trying to sound fierce, an effort that was ruined by a fit of coughing. While he struggled to catch his breath, his door swung open. Blinking at the sudden influx of light, he realized Scarlett stood framed in the doorway.

"I made you some chicken broth," she said, her voice calm and soothing. "That, along with a few saltines, might help settle your stomach."

Right on cue, his stomach gurgled. "I don't know..."

She came closer and he realized she carried a tray. The scent of chicken broth reached him. To his surprise, it actually smelled good.

"At least try," she said. "Do you need help sitting up?"

He almost snapped at her that he wasn't an invalid, but managed to hold his tongue. Well aware that his foul mood while sick was legendary in his family, he suddenly realized he didn't want Scarlett to see him that way.

"Thank you, but I'm fine," he said instead, propping his pillow against the headboard and using it for a backrest. He leaned over and turned on his bedside lamp, even though so much brightness hurt his head. "It's very kind of you to make me lunch. I'm not sure I can eat, but I'll give it a shot."

The effort of making such a long speech exhausted him, but it was worth it to see the dazzling smile bloom over Scarlett's beautiful face. She set the tray down on his lap. When she did, he saw she'd brought him another glass of ginger ale, though she'd poured it over ice.

"I brought a smallish sized bowl," she told him. "Because I know you need to start off slow. And there's only about five saltines, so if you need more let me know." Still smiling, she started backing toward the door. "You can either call me and I'll come get the tray, or put it on the dresser. Holler if you need anything."

He almost asked her to stay, but didn't. Instead, he nodded and waited until she'd closed the door behind her before picking up the spoon.

To his surprise, the rich broth soothed his throat. It tasted good, though he waited after a few spoonfuls to see how his still-queasy stomach would take it. When a moment or two passed and nothing happened, he finished the bowl and ate all the crackers.

Even the act of eating such a small meal made him feel wiped out. He managed to get up and place the tray on the dresser, swapping out the now half-full glass with his empty one. A quick trip to his bathroom, then back to bed.

He woke next to the sound of a phone ringing, then Scarlett answering it. Wincing, he massaged his aching temples, surprised to realize it was a little after three.

Stretching, he realized he felt marginally better. As

if the worst had passed. His head still hurt, but he no longer felt as if he were burning up from the inside out.

A bout of coughing had him doubling over, making him question his earlier assessment of his condition. Past experience had taught him he might be thinking overly optimistically. He didn't get sick often, but when he did, he got really, really ill. Since he hated being even slightly incapacitated, he tended to take out his frustration on those around him. This had earned him a reputation of being a horrible patient, and rightly so.

He thought of Hal, enduring all he had over the past few months, without complaining much and certainly without turning into an absolute bear. Hal had been poked and prodded, tested and retested, all the while growing more and more ill without any definitive diagnosis.

While still flat on his back with the flu, Travis realized he wanted to be more like Hal.

Swinging his legs over the side of the bed, he waited while the room spun. He made it into the bathroom where he washed his face and brushed his teeth, hoping even that small effort might make him feel more human. His bright red nose felt sore, despite the box of super soft tissues he'd kept with him. Nothing he could do about that, especially since it was still stuffed up.

He'd been ill for only twenty-odd hours yet he wanted it over and done. He had too much work to do to be able to afford to waste time sleeping.

Next, he knew if he wanted to venture out into the rest of his house, he couldn't continue to do it in boxers. Rummaging in his dresser drawer, he located a barely used pair of flannel pajamas someone had given him last Christmas. He managed to pull on the pants, and then attempted to put on the matching shirt. It took him three tries—he finally had to sit down on the bed and work up to it, but he finally finished. He thought about looking for the pair of slippers someone had given him that same Christmas but decided that would be too much work.

Barefoot, he padded down the hall of his unusually quiet house, looking for Scarlett.

He found her on the couch, sound asleep. She hadn't turned on the television, just simply curled up on her side with her arm pillowing her head.

Looking down and watching her while she slept, he realized two things. One, she was the most beautiful woman he'd ever met and two, he loved her.

He loved her. Once, even thinking such a thing would have brought on denials, maybe even panic. After all, he'd thought he loved Kendra once. She'd taken his heart and wrung it dry, after twisting it up in knots. Clearly, she'd never loved him despite agreeing to marry him, because to this day Kendra didn't understand how he could have been so devastated.

He certainly hadn't planned on ever letting himself be that vulnerable again. Especially not opening his heart to a woman who most likely would always choose city over country, white-collar man over rancher. In other words, a woman who couldn't be more wrong for him if she tried.

Scarlett stirred, for a moment confused. As she sat up, she got that she'd fallen asleep on Travis's couch. To her surprise, she saw Travis dozing in his recliner, the chair back and a blanket tucked around him.

A rush of tenderness filled her as she gazed at him.

For such a big man, he could be surprisingly gentle. She thought of his kiss, of the way he held her and touched her, and remembered his passion too. Her feelings for him were complicated and intense. And real. More real than anything she'd ever felt for anyone.

Lost in thought, she jumped when her phone rang. Luckily, she'd turned the volume down earlier. Still, she answered it quickly, hoping the sound hadn't woken Travis.

"How are you holding up?" Judging from the thread of laughter in Amber's cheerful voice, she wasn't expecting a positive answer.

"I hate to disappoint you, but I'm fine." Scarlett eyed Travis again and smiled, her heart full.

"Really? Travis hasn't bitten your head off yet? Believe me, it will happen."

"Nope." Scarlett lowered her voice, not wanting to wake him. "He's had a few grumpy moments, but mostly he seems grateful for the attention."

"What?" Amber fairly shrieked into her ear. "Hold on, I've got to tell Mom this."

Though Amber covered the phone, Scarlett could still hear the majority of the conversation. Vivian expressed loud disbelief, while Amber said something that made Scarlett smile. *He must really like her.* She certainly hoped so. Because sick or no, she really liked him too.

When Amber uncovered the phone, Scarlett asked her about the trip and the costumes. According to Amber, they'd had a great time, eating in a downtown Dallas restaurant and paying Neiman Marcus a short visit. They hadn't purchased anything at the iconic store, but simply looking had been fun.

"When are you coming back to the main house?" Amber asked. "Delilah's cooking a huge meal since we're all here."

"Not tonight," Scarlett answered softly. "How's Hal?"

"He seems better. He's actually alert and making himself part of the conversation. He's also asked about Travis."

This made Scarlett happy. "Tell him I'm sorry that I can't be there tonight. And let him know Travis seems to be doing better."

"Maybe he just hasn't gotten to the worst part of his sickness yet," Amber pointed out. "When he starts feeling truly awful, that's when his snarky side comes out."

"I'll keep my eyes open for that," Scarlett promised. "Thanks for the warning."

Once she'd ended the call, she looked over at Travis and realized he'd been watching her.

"I'm guessing that was my sister," he said, his voice a little less raspy. "And that she warned you about me."

"She did," Scarlett answered cheerfully, meeting his gaze. "Again. So did everyone else. I was fully prepared for the horrible, mean side of you to come out. So far, I haven't seen that."

He ducked his head, appearing embarrassed. "Sorry. I really appreciate you sticking with me through this. Especially after receiving all those warnings."

"I take it you're feeling better?"

He inhaled deeply and considered. "Maybe? I don't ache all over like before." His effort at talking brought on another coughing spell, though even that didn't seem to last as long or sound as deep.

"You're on the mend!" Her grin invited him to celebrate. To her surprise, he smiled back.

"You know what, I think I am."

Her stomach growled, making her laugh. "Are you hungry?" she asked, jumping to her feet. "Because I am."

He considered her question for a moment. "You know what? I think I might be. I could eat."

Delighted, she started for the kitchen. Halfway there, she turned around. "Do you need something to drink in the meantime?"

He heaved himself up out of the chair and stretched. "I'm not an invalid, so I'll get it myself."

Once they'd reached the kitchen, he filled his glass with more ginger ale and took a seat at the table. His color seemed better and he definitely appeared to be feeling much better.

She opened the fridge and made a bit of a face. "Hot dogs, nope. Something that looks like leftover spaghetti—"

"My mother made that last week. I'll pass," Travis said. "As should you."

Hiding her smile, she continued to peruse the contents. "Oooh, ground turkey. And corn tortillas. How about some tacos? Or I can make enchiladas if you'd prefer those."

Since she'd read that no Texan worth his salt ever refused Mexican food, she felt pretty confident in his response. When he didn't comment, she turned to eye him. "What? You don't want tacos or enchiladas?"

"It's not that." He scratched the back of his neck. "I'm just wondering how someone who's from Georgia might make them."

Piqued, she glared. “We eat Mexican food there too, you know. And making tacos isn’t difficult, believe me.” She almost added that he could make his own now, and if he wasn’t still recovering from his illness, she would have.

One corner of his mouth twitched. Fascinated, she watched him. When he let loose with a laugh, the deep sound coaxed a reluctant smile from her.

The tacos were delicious and Travis managed to eat three. She covered the leftovers and placed them in the fridge.

To her surprise, Travis went back to the recliner in the den. She took the couch and they spent a companionable evening watching TV. When the evening news came on, she glanced over at Travis to find he’d fallen asleep.

Vulnerable would never have been a word she’d have chosen to describe such a big, capable man. But right now, with his breathing even and deep, his head pillowed on his hand, that’s how he looked. If they’d truly been a couple, she could have climbed up there with him and curled into his side. Instead, she left the television on for him though she lowered the volume, and retired to her makeshift bed on the couch.

In the morning, she got up to find Travis in the kitchen, already on his second cup of coffee. He’d made breakfast too, a pot of oatmeal along with brown sugar and raisins.

“I feel almost normal,” he declared, grinning at her disheveled appearance. “I’m really considering going to work. If I use the truck instead of going on horseback, I’m thinking I could still do my job.”

She waited until she'd made herself a cup of coffee before turning to face him. "I noticed you said *almost* normal. Define *almost*."

He shrugged. "I feel maybe a bit weak. And my head still hurts some, though nothing like before. I took my temperature and it's only slightly elevated. So almost back to normal."

"I think you should give it one more day," she said, sipping her coffee and watching him. "Especially since you still have a fever, which means you're most likely contagious."

"Well, it's not like I plan to go around hugging or kissing anyone." He grinned. "As long as I keep a reasonable distance, no one else should have to worry about getting infected. Except I'm not going anywhere near Hal yet. I don't want to take a chance with him."

"That's all well and good, but I'm more concerned about you." She watched as his smile became a frown. "If you don't give your body time to rest, you could relapse. Do you really want to take that chance?"

He muttered something under his breath, but in the end he grimaced and agreed with her. "One more day then," he said. "But on the condition that you go home. Not that your help was unappreciated, but I'm well enough to take care of myself."

Heaven help her, she felt a twinge of hurt at his words. But she lifted her chin, determined not to show it. "Fine. I'll go. I've been missing Hal anyway." After a brief pause, she brightened. "I think I'll send Vivian home just in case. Amber can stay another day since we can't take a chance of you infecting Will."

The way he snorted at her words let her know he knew she was bluffing. "My mother is a true germophobe. I promise you, she won't want to come anywhere near me until I'm fully recovered."

Giving up, she made herself a bowl of oatmeal and ate it silently. When she'd finished, she rinsed the bowl and put it in the dishwasher. "I'll be out of your hair in an hour," she promised, careful not to look at him.

True to her word, she showered and dressed, packed up her things and slipped out the door without seeing him or saying goodbye. Maybe she was being ridiculous to feel so hurt, but clearly she enjoyed his company more than he did hers. Again, clear proof that it took more than sizzling sex to make a relationship work.

When she reached the main house, all the cars in the driveway startled her at first. But then she saw one of them belonged to Vivian, one to Amber and, of course, Delilah's vehicle was there.

Grabbing her suitcase, she wrestled it into the house and down the hall to her room. Luckily, the old Victorian had more than enough bedrooms, so no one had stayed in hers.

It felt good to be back, she told herself, pushing away the crazy sense of loss. Being around Travis—even sick Travis—made even the air she breathed feel clearer and cleaner, the sky brighter and her heart happier. More proof she was a fool.

Judging from the sound of it, everyone had gathered in the kitchen. Glad she'd taken the time to clean up and make herself presentable, Scarlett sauntered into the room and headed for the coffeepot. "Mornin' everyone," she sang out.

"You're back," Hal exclaimed. Turning to face him, she saw that he did look a lot better.

She walked over and planted a soft kiss on one grizzled cheek. "You look amazing. You must be feeling pretty good."

"I am," He conceded. "How's Travis?"

"Yes," Vivian trilled. "Tell us how my son is doing."

Behind her, Amber smiled encouragingly. "We can't wait to hear. I take it since you're here, he must be feeling all better."

"He does feel better, though not 100 percent yet. He's hoping to go back to work tomorrow." Scarlett poured herself a mug of coffee, taking time to make it exactly the way she liked it. Behind her, everyone had gone oddly silent, as if they'd been discussing her and she'd walked in right in the middle of their talk.

She decided to simply take the bull by the horns. "In case you're wondering, he wasn't that bad. Oh, he was sick. High fever, chills, sweats, a horrible cough. But he's feeling so much better that I had to talk him out of going to work today."

"That's great news," Vivian exclaimed. "But if it's all the same to you, I'm not going back home until it's 100 percent certain he's not contagious."

"Mom hates germs," Amber clarified.

"It's a good thing whatever is ailing me isn't catching," Hal put in. "Or Vivian would stay as far away from me as she could."

"True." Vivian shrugged. "Now that you're here, do you want to see your costume?" Her brown eyes sparkled with anticipation while she waited for Scarlett's answer.

In all the upheaval since Travis had gotten sick, Scarlett had somehow managed to entirely forget about the costumes. "Sure," she answered, trying to summon up more anticipation. Clearly this ball and the costumes meant a lot to everyone here. She could only hope Vivian had picked something that was tasteful yet fun.

"We're flappers," Amber told her once Vivian went to retrieve the outfits. "You're actually going to be Bonnie, of Bonnie and Clyde fame. I wanted to be that, but they didn't have the costume in my size. So I'm a flapper instead." She winked. "No one will have ever seen a flapper like me."

To Scarlett's relief, when Vivian showed her the costume, it wasn't too risqué or, worse, tasteless. A black dress with white vertical pinstripes, a jaunty fedora hat with a small red feather and a plastic gun. "You do have a pair of black heels you could wear with this, right?" Vivian asked.

"I do." Scarlett smiled. "What does Travis's costume look like?"

Vivian and Amber exchanged glances. "It's a white shirt, black vest with a red tie, black pants and a hat. You two will look cute."

"Thanks."

"I'm a mobster moll," Vivian said proudly. "And Frank will be a gangster, just like Mike, Amber's date."

Scarlett nodded. "I can't wait to finally meet the elusive Frank," she said.

For a second, Vivian's mouth tightened, but then she made a face and laughed. "He has been rather busy lately," she said.

"Busy?" Amber's skeptical tone matched her expression. "Busy doing what?"

"Painting." Vivian looked at Amber. "Frank's an artist."

"I love artists," Scarlett said, choosing her words carefully. When she'd managed the gallery in Atlanta, it had seemed like everyone knew an artist of some sort, whether sculptor or painter, and wanted her to meet them so they could discuss a possible showing. At first, she hadn't minded. Unfortunately, she'd learned rather quickly that the majority of these people didn't have the right amount of talent or skill to become a professional artist.

"Then you'll love Frank," Vivian said, beaming. "He's amazing."

Judging by Amber's comical attempt to keep her expression neutral and Hal's sudden need to shuffle through the mail, Scarlett sort of doubted that.

"Hey, didn't you mention you'd once worked at an art gallery?" Vivian asked.

Scarlett wanted to groan. "Yes, in Atlanta."

"Then you must be knowledgeable about art. If I set up a time at Frank's studio, would you be willing to meet him and give him your opinion about his work?"

Searching for a polite way to decline, Scarlett settled on the ambiguous *we'll see.* She remembered what Hal had said about the other man's work. Even though art was always subjective, she'd rather not get involved.

But Vivian, being Vivian, pressed. "How about the week after the Halloween ball? I could check with him and then we can choose a day."

Still trying to not commit, Scarlett shrugged.

"Great!" Vivian said, choosing to take this as agreement. "You can meet him at the ball, and then see his art once you know him."

The face Amber made behind Vivian had Scarlett

struggling not to laugh. “Fine.” Giving in, she turned her attention to her costume. “I’m looking forward to this ball more than I thought I would.”

Chapter 13

After Scarlett left, Travis regretted sending her away. Yet he'd felt he had to, as the more the illness receded, the more being around her aroused his desire.

That morning when she'd walked into the kitchen, tousled and still half-asleep, he'd gotten instantly hard. He'd wanted her so badly he could scarcely think, never mind form coherent words.

Struggling to keep his body under control would have been difficult, never mind exhausting. And even as much as he knew he could arouse her passion to equal his, making love to her while he still might be contagious felt every sort of wrong.

So he'd made her go. He knew his abrupt dismissal had hurt her—she wasn't very good at hiding her feelings. He'd make sure and explain the truth later, once he could kiss her and hold her without fear of getting her sick too.

Even so, once he got past his libido, he missed her. He missed her laugh, the way they could discuss the plot of television shows, cooking together, eating together. The more time he spent with Scarlett, the more he felt himself falling.

And the more he knew he needed to resist her lure. He'd allowed himself to feel that way about Kendra, and when she'd accepted his proposal, he'd allowed himself to be swept up in dreams of a future with her. They'd made plans, even discussing children.

And then she'd called it off. He'd been decimated, destroyed and ruined. There was no way in hell he wanted to put himself through that again.

But he couldn't manage to silence that small part of him that thought Scarlett might be different. That tiny seed of stubborn hope refused to go away. Despite logic telling him otherwise.

He made it through the rest of the day, bored and out of sorts. Ready for his life to return to normal, he went to bed early.

The next morning, he rose early and showered. He felt like a new man. No more aches and pains, not even the slightest bit of a headache. Taking his temperature just as a precaution, when the thermometer showed 98.6 he breathed a loud sigh of relief.

Ready to go. Back to work, back to his normal life. He planned to throw himself into it with gusto. He needed some time away from Scarlett, time to get his head together.

The next two days passed in a blur. Travis rose early and worked late, often falling into bed after grabbing a quick meal. His mother, Amber and little Will were still staying up at the main house, which actually suited him fine. He didn't want to talk, he didn't want to even think, so he used the alone time to keep himself busy.

Unfortunately, next week was the big ball.

On the evening of the third day, he drove home with bleary eyes and debated heading into town for a quick beer. When he saw his mother's SUV and Amber's little economy car in the driveway, he knew his idyllic oasis of peace had come to an abrupt end.

He almost pulled a U-turn in his own driveway but knew with the way he'd been pushing himself, he'd be lucky to stay awake after having a beer and then driving back from town. Plus, he couldn't delay the inevitable forever.

At least when he walked in the door, the aroma of homemade fried chicken hit him. Mouth watering, he following the smell back to the kitchen. Vivian and Amber sat at the empty kitchen table, clearly having finished eating. Little Will had been playing with his toy cars on the floor. When he caught sight of his uncle Travis, Will jumped to his feet and launched himself forward, confident Travis would catch him.

Of course, Travis did, right under the armpits. He lifted Will up, swinging him around and smiling at the joyous sound of a young boy's laughter.

When he set Will back on his own two feet, he admired the toy cars before searching for the plate of leftover chicken. He found it, covered in tinfoil, on the counter.

"Help yourself, son," Vivian said. "It's great to see you all better."

"Yeah," Amber seconded. "You look totally normal."

"Thanks." His dry response made his sister grin.

He made himself a plate and grabbed a bottle of beer from the fridge. Sitting down, he dug in. He'd plowed his way through two pieces of chicken and started on a third when he realized the room had gone utterly silent. He looked up to find everyone staring at him.

"Hungry much?" Vivian drawled. "Would you like some of my homemade potato salad to go with the chicken?"

He stopped chewing long enough to nod. With the initial hunger pangs satisfied, he managed to wait while Vivian got out a bowl from the refrigerator and spooned two heaping mounds onto his plate.

Then he went back to eating, tackling his plate with a single-minded determination until he'd finished. When he finally sat back in his chair and took a long drink of his beer, he thanked Vivian for an awesome meal.

"You're welcome," she replied, clearly pleased. "It's good to be home."

She filled him in on Hal. "I'm delighted that he's feeling a bit better. I keep hoping he'll beat this thing, whatever it is."

"Me too," Travis said fervently. "Me too."

"I take it you weren't too hard on Scarlett," Amber teased. "Thanks for making us all sound crazy for warning her about you."

"You're welcome," he answered, stifling a yawn. Now that he'd eaten, all he wanted to do was go to sleep. While he tried to figure out a polite way to escape to his room, Vivian grabbed his plate, put the bones in the trash and rinsed the dish off before putting it in the dishwasher.

"I think I'll turn in," he began.

"Not yet." His mother wagged a finger at him. "Don't you want to see your costume?" Without waiting for an answer, Vivian went out to the hall closet and returned with something in a clear dry cleaning bag. "I've left Scarlett's with her."

Feeling as if he ought to brace himself, he tried to appear interested. Truthfully, as long as he wouldn't be wearing something weird, he really didn't care. In the past when choosing his costume, he'd simply gone with whatever would be easiest. Instead of making the two-hour drive into Dallas, he'd always ordered online. This would be the first year since he'd been a child that he hadn't chosen his own costume.

"Take a look at this," Vivian crowed. "It's fantastic." When she lifted up the plastic bag and showed him the gangster outfit, he breathed a sigh of relief. At least it wasn't anything too crazy. In fact, it looked like something he might have chosen himself.

"You and Scarlett will be quite the pair," Vivian continued, not giving him a chance to speak. "I think she really liked her costume. Luckily, it fits her perfectly. We would have been running out of time to get it altered."

He eyed her. "I'm guessing you're wanting me to try this on?"

"Please? With the ball less than a week away, you know the alterations shops will be booked. Especially since there are only two."

Grabbing the costume, he covered his mouth to mask another yawn, retreated to his room and tried it on. The pants fit fine, but the white shirt wouldn't even button over his chest. Which wouldn't be a problem, since he had a white dress shirt, still in the wrapper, that he'd purchased for the wedding. The red tie, while a bit loud, would be fine, and he had an old pair of dress shoes that he could shine up.

He opened his door and stuck his head out. "It mostly fits. I'll have to use my own white shirt."

"Great," Vivian called back. "I'm going to go take Frank his costume. I have some exciting news for him."

"Okay. And thanks for dinner and getting the costume."

When Travis emerged after changing back into his sweats, his mother had already left. Amber sat watching Will play. She looked up at Travis and shook her head.

"She's been going nonstop since we got back home. I'm getting the impression ole Frank has been making himself scarce, which makes Mom more intent on gaining his attention."

"What exciting news does she have for Frank?" he asked.

Amber sighed. "Mom conned poor Scarlett into agreeing to give Frank a professional opinion on his work." She grimaced. Frank was usually oddly secretive about allowing anyone to see his paintings or sculptures, but what little they'd been able to see had been terrible.

He shook his head. "Something tells me Scarlett can handle herself."

"I sure hope so, for her sake. And it's not Frank I'm worried about, it's Mom."

When Amber got up to make a protesting Will take a bath and get ready for bed, Travis excused himself and went to his room. He'd been up since 4:30 and though it was only a little after 8:00 p.m., he could scarcely keep his eyes open.

The next week passed in a blur. Travis continued to push himself at a breakneck pace, refusing to allow any time at all for introspective thoughts. Whenever one managed to creep in, he immediately refused to allow it.

Except in his dreams. Those, he could not control. While he slept, Scarlett filled his arms, his mind, his heart. He woke every morning feeling bereft.

Finally, the day before the ball arrived. He went to work as usual, though all the cattle had been either moved or sold, all the fences repaired and the horses brought in to closer pastures or, in some cases, the barn. All the hay had been baled and brought into the storage barn and, as the days had grown shorter, the ranch hands moved a little slower and took things easier.

Except Travis. He continued to push himself at nearly impossible speed. He worked on the tractor instead of calling a mechanic, did all the horse worming and shots himself rather than delegate to his crew.

Because tomorrow, he'd be putting on a costume and picking up Scarlett and taking her to the ball.

He hadn't talked to her at all since asking her to leave his house. Amber and Vivian had offhandedly kept him updated. While Travis felt guilty for not visiting Hal, he'd kept himself so busy that he'd actually had a legitimate excuse. Hal had called him a couple of times and they'd had long conversations. Travis suspected Hal knew why Travis kept himself absent, though the older man never asked.

While Travis had known he couldn't avoid Scarlett

forever, he hoped he'd managed to build up his armor enough so when he saw her again, he could remain impartial instead of aching to rip her clothes off and make love to her like he did in his dreams.

There had been no more threats, according to Amber. Scarlett, Hal and Delilah had fallen into a routine of sorts. Amber and Scarlett were still planning to go into town and have a girls' night, though they'd had to postpone it until after the ball because Vivian had kept insisting she go with them.

Since tomorrow was so important, Travis actually quit working at a normal hour and headed home. Vivian had said she'd be staying over at Frank's and riding to the ball with him, and Amber had taken Will for a playdate with one of his friends in town.

Which meant once again, Travis had his house to himself. Again, he thought of the couple of acres he'd asked Hal if he could buy, with plans of someday building his own house. He and Kendra had actually gone over plans, but when that relationship had fallen apart, Travis had scrapped the idea.

For the first time in a long time, he thought about revisiting the possibility. And not because of Scarlett, he told himself. But because the time had come for him to have his own space. Since he couldn't kick his mother and sister and nephew out, the only solution would be to move.

He resolved to discuss the idea with Hal after the ball.

The Halloween Harvest Fair and Costume Ball was the culmination of a season. Since the end of October signified the end of harvest, everyone turned their attention to the upcoming holidays. Life on the ranch slowed down a little.

Travis went into his room to double-check his costume. He couldn't shake the feeling that he'd forgotten something. And then he remembered. It had been so long since he'd taken a date to the ball, he'd forgotten about the wrist corsage he was supposed to buy Scarlett. The old tradition had started back in the 1950s.

Checking his watch, he figured he had time to drive into town and stop at June's Florist. While she took custom orders, she also kept lots of extras stocked.

He hopped back into his truck and headed to downtown Anniversary. Since he had to go right past the country club, he saw the decorators were already at the venue, getting set up for the festivities later.

When he pulled up to June's, he lucked into a parking spot two doors down. He got out and hurried inside, hoping he wasn't too late and that she hadn't sold out.

Only three corsages remained in the refrigerated case near the back counter. Two were sad little things, beginning to wilt. The third, a grouping of red-and-white flowers, seemed too large to decorate a wrist. But since beggars couldn't be choosers, he told the salesclerk he'd take that one. Waiting while she boxed it up, he waved to June working frantically in the back. Once he'd paid, he took his small box and headed out. He had plenty of time to drive home and get ready.

"Hey, Travis. Got a minute?" The voice belonged to Bubba Weber. His family owned a large sheep ranch and their land butted up against the HG. Wave Oil had been bugging him too, so much so that Bubba had finally resorted to posting No Trespassing signs with a note under that warning that violators would be shot. He'd also been instrumental in organizing a group of local farmers and ranchers who were against letting big oil take over their town.

"Sure." Travis turned around. "What's up?"

Bubba sauntered up, his dirty jeans and scuffed boots indicating he'd just gotten done working on his farm. A plug of chewing tobacco made one of his cheeks swell out. Before he spoke again, he spit on the sidewalk and then he looked Travis in the eye. "I'm a bit concerned over something I heard here recently, so I've got to ask. I'm wondering if you're still against letting anyone drill on your family's land or if you've changed your mind?"

Travis's heart sank. "I am. Don't tell me you've had a difference of opinion."

"No, not me." Bubba shuffled his feet, looking slightly uncomfortable as he tugged at the neck of his shirt. "But I have to ask, if you're still with us, why are you allowing an oil company employee to stay at Hal's place? We know he's been sick and it'd be just like those folks to take advantage of that fact and get him to sign something."

"An oil company employee?" Struggling to make sense of the other man's words, Travis frowned. "The only new person staying at Hal's is his daughter from Atlanta. She has nothing to do with the oil company."

"That's not what I hear." Bubba stuck his chin out stubbornly. "You need to make sure."

"I wouldn't pay too much attention to gossip," Travis pointed out. "I'd need more proof."

"You're sweet on her, aren't you?" The other man took a step back, as if Travis had suddenly developed a stench. "That's probably part of their plan too. Working on both Hal and you. They know how much pull you have with Hal."

Travis stared. "That's nonsense."

"Is it?" Bubba eyed the corsage box. "Because I heard you're bringing her to the ball tonight."

"That's true, but—"

"Save it," Bubba said, flipping his hand in dismissal. "You should know a bunch of us are planning to ask her to her face if what we've heard is true."

"You keep saying you've *heard.* Where exactly are you hearing these things?"

Bubba shrugged. "Around town," he said vaguely. "Here and there. You know how rumors spread."

"I do. Just like I know most of those same rumors are unfounded." Frustrated, he tried to find the right words. "Believe me, when Scarlett first got here, I was suspicious too. But as I've gotten to know her, I've realized that my suspicions were unfounded. There's no reason to confront her over such nonsense."

"Hmm." Bubba didn't appear convinced. "We'll see," he muttered, before he sauntered away.

Watching him go, Travis didn't know whether to be irritated or bemused. One thing he knew for certain, if he ever found out who was behind the gossip about Scarlett, he'd call them out on it. Because it most certainly wasn't true.

Or was it?

He thought about her story, which he'd checked out. Her mother had died and they'd lived in a suburb of Atlanta, true. But as far as her job, working in a small art gallery, that he'd never verified. What if she was working with Wave Oil, like Kendra?

The idea seemed too far-fetched. Kendra had been

completely up-front about her motives, so why would Scarlett lie? And quite honestly, she didn't seem like the type to work with a large oil company to try to convince a sick old man to go against his principles.

Yet as he got in his truck to drive home, the small seed of doubt Bubba's words had planted festered. He could imagine several scenarios, all of which someone wanting something might have engineered in order to get her way. Including making love to him.

Scarlett must have glanced at her watch thirty times as the afternoon crawled. She couldn't wait until it was time to start getting ready for the ball.

Her phone rang.

"Scarlett?" Amber said, sounding harried. "I forgot to mention the boutonniere."

"The what?" Scarlett asked, even though she knew what a boutonniere was."

"It's tradition," Amber rushed on. "Men get their date a wrist corsage, we get men a boutonniere for their lapel. June's Florist in town takes orders, but she always makes up a bunch extra for those who forget." Amber paused for breath. "And I forgot to get my date one too. I'm not going to have time, what with needing to get Will to the sitter. So I wanted to ask a huge favor… Would you go into town and grab one for me? I imagine you'll need to get one for Travis as well."

Scarlett checked her watch again. "Sure. I'm pretty sure I have enough time." She took a deep breath. "Actually, I'll welcome the distraction. I've been trying to figure out how to fill the afternoon until it's time to get ready. Do you want any particular color?"

"No." Amber laughed. "Beggars can't be choosers.

The floral shop is on Main Street. You can't miss it. Thank you so much. I'll pay you back when I see you tonight, okay?"

"No problem." Scarlett grabbed her car keys and headed out. Once she arrived in town, she drove slowly, looking for June's. She found a parking spot and went inside.

As Amber had mentioned, June had set up display cases with both wrist corsages and boutonnieres. She chose two and paid, waiting while the clerk boxed them up.

Once outside, she headed toward her car, pleased that she'd been able to find a red one for Travis.

"Ma'am?"

Scarlett turned. The young man wearing a tailored suit and tie looked as out of place on the Anniversary square as she'd felt the first time she'd worn her dress and heels. Today she had on jeans and boots, like almost everyone else.

"Were you talking to me?" Puzzled, she glanced around. The few other pedestrians out and about continued on past them.

"Yes, I'm sorry." The stranger held out his hand. "I'm John Mellon. I wonder if I could have a moment of your time."

Ah, now she got it. "Whatever you're selling, thank you but I'm not interested." She turned to walk away.

"I'm not selling anything," he protested. "Honestly. I work for Wave Oil Company. I wanted to discuss with you the possibility of drilling on your father's land."

She froze. "I'm sorry, but you have the wrong person. I have no authority over things like that. You'd need to talk to him personally, not me."

Adjusting his wire-rimmed glasses on his nose, he sighed. "Could I buy you a coffee so we can visit for a few minutes? I promise, no pressure."

Again she checked her watch. "I don't think so. You might not know, since you're not from around here, but it's a pretty big day here in town."

He smiled. "So I hear. A festival and costume dance. But I've been told it's going on all weekend."

"The festival is. But the ball is tonight. And I've got to go get ready."

"Please, I just need fifteen minutes of your time." He grimaced. "That way I can at least let my boss know I've tried."

She still had a couple of hours before she needed to start getting ready. Considering the prospect of trying to keep busy at home, she wavered.

Finally, she shrugged. "Sure, I guess. I don't see the harm. As long as you understand that you can talk to me until you're blue in the face, but nothing will change in that area. I have zero authority over what happens with the ranch."

With a smile and a nod, he gestured toward the coffee shop two doors down. When they reached it, he held the door open for her and asked her what she wanted. Once she'd told him, he placed the order for her cappuccino and his latte. "Pick a table," he said. "I'll bring the coffees as soon as they're ready."

Since there were only two available tables, Scarlett chose the one by the front window. Really, while a nice hot cappuccino sounded wonderful, she didn't understand why this John Mellon wanted to talk to her. She'd already made it clear that she couldn't help him. Apparently he didn't believe her.

A few minutes later he returned. After handing over her coffee, he took a seat across from her. "They have the best coffee in town," he said, still smiling.

She took a sip. He was right. It was great coffee.

"Please understand, I get where you're coming from," John began. "I know you're new here and also I've heard your father is very ill. I've been told he has tons of medical bills and no way to pay them."

Sitting a little straighter, she eyed him. "Even if that's true I fail to see how that's any of your business."

"Easy now." He held up a well-manicured hand in mock self-defense. "I'm not trying to pry. I'm just wanting to let you know if that truly is the case, and Hal needs money for his medical expenses, allowing us to place one or two small drilling wells would take care of everything. And more. It's something to consider, don't you think?"

Taking another sip of her coffee, she eyed him. "What I think is you need to discuss this with Hal. As I've told you."

"We've tried. But his ranch foreman won't even allow us to make an appointment."

"Travis?" Maybe she'd made a huge mistake in even talking to this guy, especially since Travis had already believed she was in cahoots with them. "Travis operates under Hal's authority. I'm sure if he won't allow you a meeting, that's at Hal's direction."

"Maybe. And then again, maybe not. All I'm asking is for you to talk to Hal about it. If you're right, and Travis is just doing what Hal says, then fine. It didn't hurt to try. But if Travis is taking it upon himself to make his own decisions…" He drank deeply, settling the cup down and gazing earnestly at her. "Don't you think you owe it to your father to at least find out?"

He had a point. Much as she might not like getting in the middle of Hal and Travis, she knew how much Travis despised big oil, as he called them. As for Hal, he'd said very little. And he had showed her his medical bills.

"I guess it won't hurt for me to ask him," she allowed, wondering why she felt as if she were doing something wrong. "No promises, no commitment to anything, you understand. But I will make sure my father truly doesn't want to meet with you."

"That's all I can ask," he said smoothly, draining his coffee and getting to his feet. "Thank you for your time."

He left her sitting there, wondering if she'd somehow just been played. But she comforted herself with the knowledge that the only thing she'd agreed to do was mention the meeting to Hal. She hadn't even said when, just that she would.

After arriving home, Scarlett put the meeting out of her mind. Right now, she had more important things to consider.

Chapter 14

Despite her efforts to stay cool, calm and collected, Scarlett couldn't help but feel a flutter of anticipation as the clock inched closer to the time when she'd need to get dressed for the costume ball.

Delilah had left early, since she too would be attending, and Hal spent the afternoon regaling Scarlett with outrageous stories from balls of years past.

Finally, she knew she needed to start getting ready. She took extra time with her makeup, then used a flat iron to make her thick hair perfectly straight. She put on the dress, adjusted the jaunty hat on her head and secured it with bobby pins, then stepped into her favorite pair of black stilettos, and eyed herself in the mirror.

The dress hugged her curves and made her legs appear a mile long. Since she wasn't fond of the machine-gun type prop that had come with the costume, she decided not to carry it.

When she emerged into the living room, Hal took one look at her and whistled. "Wow. You clean up well," he said.

She laughed. "Thanks. I think Vivian did an amazing job choosing this costume."

"She's good at that. But I guarantee you, whatever outfit she chose for herself will outshine you and Amber both. That's how she is, she can't help it. She always has to be the flashiest person in any gathering."

"That doesn't bother me," Scarlett told him. "Since I'm new here and don't really know anyone, I'd prefer to stay in the background."

"I doubt that's possible, since you're attending with Travis. I can't wait to see his face when he sees you."

She couldn't wait either, though she didn't admit this out loud since doing so would only give Hal reason to speculate on her feelings for his stepson.

And she most definitely wasn't ready to discuss them with anyone but Travis.

She heard the sound of tires on gravel and tensed. "I think he's here," she said, suddenly nervous. "Are you sure I look okay for this kind of thing?"

"You look perfect," Hal assured her, just as the front door opened and Travis walked in. "Doesn't she look perfect, Travis?"

Framed in the doorway, Travis studied her. She swore she could feel the heat of his gaze just like he'd caressed her. As for her, she allowed herself to drink in the sight of him. With his trousers and red suspenders, he looked like a jaunty actor about to play a rogue. In other words, sexy as hell. She wanted to rip his clothes off and jump him.

Instead, she looked down so he wouldn't see the heat in her gaze.

"You look amazing," Travis drawled. "Though I'm not sure how an outlaw would manage to run in those heels."

That got her attention. Raising her gaze to his, she frowned. "Do you think I should change? I'm sure I have a pair of black flats. It wouldn't take but a minute."

"Don't you dare." Though he laughed when he spoke, the intensity in his eyes told her he meant it. "Those shoes might not be authentic, but they're perfect." He reached into his jacket pocket and withdrew a small florist box. "Your corsage," he said.

Heart skipping a beat, she accepted the box and opened it. A perfect red-and-white wrist corsage lay inside. She laughed as she slipped it on. "Just a second. Let me go get yours." Hurrying to the fridge, she returned with an identical floral box. "Here you go. I can pin it to your lapel if you'd like."

When he opened his box, he grinned. "We have matching flowers." He held still while she pinned the boutonniere to his suit.

"All done," she said, butterflies in her stomach.

"Are you ready to go?" He gestured at the entry table. "Don't forget your mask."

Grabbing the mask and a small clutch purse, she nodded. "Ready when you are." To her dismay, she sounded as breathless as she felt. She didn't feel uncertain often, but for whatever reason, she did now.

He helped her up into his truck, the way his large hand lingered on the curve of her back sending a shiver up her spine. She noticed the way his gaze drifted to her legs as he settled into the driver's seat. The resulting rush of heat had her looking away until she got herself under control. She wasn't sure why, but something about being in costume and wearing a mask made every touch, every look, supercharged with sensuality.

Travis turned up the radio, and they sang along to George Strait and Keith Urban, which helped with her tension and brought a smile to her face. The road was clear until they reached the outskirts of town. When Travis exited on the feeder road, they were soon in bumper-to-bumper traffic.

"Look at the cars!" Amazed, she shook her head. "This reminds me of Atlanta. I don't think I've seen traffic like this since coming to Anniversary."

"They're all going to the ball," he told her, turning down the radio.

"Wow. When you said it was a big deal, you weren't kidding." Again, a bit of nerves made her swallow.

"What's wrong?" he asked, eyeing her as they crept forward. "Are you nervous?"

"Yes," she admitted. "And that's unusual for me. I tend to thrive in social settings. I have no idea why I'm worried." Maybe it was the fact that he'd asked her to pretend to be in love with him. What he didn't know was that she wouldn't have to pretend.

"You'll be fine." He squeezed her shoulder. "It's just the same people you see every time you go to town, except in costume. Even though the eye masks don't really give us anonymity, it's fun to pretend that they do."

"You enjoy it, don't you?" Slightly surprised, she studied him.

When he turned and flashed her a grin, she smiled back. "I do. It's a chance for all of us ranchers to relax and talk. The town comes together and celebrates. It's a lot of fun. You'll see."

Finally, they made their way into the packed parking lot. "Overflow parking is across the street," Travis said, as he took one of the last parking spaces, which was a good distance from the building. "Are you okay walking in those shoes?"

His question made her chuckle. "Yep. I've perfected the art of stilettos. I had lots of practice in my former job at the gallery."

Nodding, he got out and went around to her side to open the door for her. He offered his arm and she took it. Even in her heels, the top of her head barely reached his chin. They joined a crowd of people, all making their way toward the entrance.

"Don't forget to put your mask on," he said, leading her over to the side so they wouldn't hold anyone up. He reached into his pocket and put his on. The effect—mysterious and sexy—had her mouth going dry.

Luckily, she didn't have to speak. She got her mask out of her purse and slipped it over her upper face.

His gaze darkened, and he leaned in, but he didn't kiss her. Instead, he took her hand and led her into the crowded country club ballroom.

Elbow-to-elbow people was her first impression. But then, as someone called out Travis's name and walked up to greet them, she began checking out the costumes. As expected, she saw a wide variety, but nothing too daring. In fact, it appeared that everyone who'd attended the ball had given serious thought to their costumes. She saw cowboys and cowgirls, medieval kings and queens, and even several versions of fae. There were Southern belles in ornate gowns, and men in Civil War uniforms.

And Travis worked the crowd like a champ, introducing Scarlett to so many people she abandoned any attempt to remember names. He touched her often, the kind of constant, casual touches that said they were a real couple. A few times he even leaned in and kissed her neck or her cheek, making her dizzy with wanting him.

He got them drinks, a glass of white wine for her and a beer for him, and snagged them a couple of seats at one of the white-tableclothed, decorated tables. She sank into her chair with a grateful sigh, reflecting on how long it had actually been since she'd worn heels. Clearly, judging by her aching feet, it had been too long.

"They'll serve a meal and then, after we eat, a band will play and there will be dancing." Travis leaned over, his breath tickling her ear. The lilt of excitement in his voice made her smile.

Though she looked around, she couldn't see any signs to indicate where the restrooms were. When she asked Travis, he pointed. "Down that hall on the left. I'll stay here so we don't lose our seats."

"Good idea." Pushing to her feet, she gave in to temptation and brushed a quick kiss on his cheek. She enjoyed the stunned look he gave her, then made her way through the crowd.

She found the restrooms with no difficulty, and to her surprise, there wasn't a line. In fact, out of the three stalls, only one was occupied.

Once she'd finished, she washed her hands and assessed her appearance in the mirror. Her color seemed high, but she liked the way the black mask added a hint of mystery. In fact, she felt pretty and sexy—a lot more relaxed and confident.

As she exited the ladies' room, she went to turn left in the hall. Instead, someone stepped out of the shadows and wrapped a strong arm around her throat, put a large hand over her mouth and dragged her back into the restroom. Choking, she struggled, fighting to breathe, to break free. But her attacker—clearly a tall man despite the mask—was too strong.

"Listen to me," he rasped, his breath tickling her ear. "Hold still and listen."

Pushing down her panic, she froze. He loosened the pressure on her throat just enough for her to suck in a huge gasp of air, but kept his hand over her mouth to keep her from screaming. She nearly retched, but instead she worked on trying to continue to breathe.

"Listen," he repeated. "This is your last warning. Either you leave town immediately, or you die. Do you understand?"

Shocked, she could only nod. Would he kill her right now if she protested?

"Leave quietly, and tell no one why. If you do, I'll know." Releasing her, he shoved her hard, sending her flying into one of the stalls. A second later, the sound of the door closing told her he'd left.

Crying, gasping, choking, she struggled to get herself under control. Grateful for every breath, she touched her hurt throat, wondering if his hands had left marks. When she staggered to the mirror to see, sure enough red welts had already begun to form.

Despite the waterproof mascara, two identical black

smudges decorated under each eye and her ruby lipstick had been smeared all over her face.

The door opened again and she flinched. Two women wearing elaborate antebellum dresses came in, chattering happily. Scarlett recognized Kendra and tensed. Perfect, just perfect.

Kendra caught sight of Scarlett and gasped. "What happened to you? Are you all right?"

Scarlett started to nod but then shook her head instead. "Could one of you please find Travis for me? Tell him I'm in trouble and he needs to come get me."

The first woman nodded and went to grab Kendra's arm. Kendra resisted. "You go," she said. "I'll stay here with her."

Once her friend had gone, Kendra studied Scarlett. "You do have a penchant for drama, don't you," she drawled, looking her up and down. "Though I do have to owe you thanks for talking to my coworker, John Mellon. I really appreciate you being so open-minded about this. I promise we'll make sure you're well compensated for your trouble."

Staring at the other woman, Scarlett couldn't find any words. Wave Oil and their desire to drill on Hal's land was the last thing she wanted to worry about right now.

Instead, she closed her eyes and waited for Travis to show up and rescue her.

Waiting impatiently for Scarlett to return, Travis watched as a short, clearly rattled woman dressed like a belle from the antebellum South rushed toward him. As she drew closer, he recognized her as Sarah something, one of Kendra's friends.

When she reached him, she tugged at his arm and leaned down close. "Travis, something's happened to your date. Come quickly," she continued, slightly breathless. "She's in the ladies' room with Kendra..."

That was all he needed to hear. So help him, if Kendra had dared to do anything to hurt Scarlett, she'd be sorry. He'd press charges against her if he had to.

Fists clenched, he jumped to his feet and rushed down the hall. He pushed into the women's restroom with Sarah close on his heels. Scarlett looked up, her eyes wide and rimmed in mascara. As soon as he caught sight of her and the red welts around her throat, his heart stuttered. Fury and panic warred inside him.

"Come here." Pulling her into his arms, he smoothed the hair back from her face. "Are you all right?"

She jerked her head up and down in a silent nod. Behind her, Kendra cleared her throat, drawing his attention. She too wore an elaborate gown with some kind of hoop skirt.

"What happened?" he asked Kendra, clenching his teeth hard to keep from lashing out at her.

"I don't know," Kendra told him, lifting her chin and meeting his gaze. "Sarah and I were just entering and we found her like this. She asked us to come and get you, so we did."

Face against his chest, Scarlett nodded, giving confirmation of Kendra's words. He kept her close, wrapped up in his arms. He eyed Kendra, then jerked his head toward the door. "Leave," he ordered. "Both of you."

"But..." Kendra started to protest.

Her friend Sarah grabbed her and tried to drag her away. Kendra resisted for a few seconds, but finally nodded. She and Sarah pushed through the door and left.

Once they were alone, Travis lifted Scarlett's chin and made her look at him. "What happened?" he asked, keeping his voice soft. A closer look at the marks around her neck had his jaw tightening. "Who did this to you?"

"I don't know," she managed. "It was a tall man, wearing a black suit and a mask that covered half his face."

Since several men attending the ball had chosen a similar costume, that description didn't help at all.

"Hair color?" he asked. "Was he thin or stout? Any distinctive characteristics?"

Slowly, she shook her head. "He was thin, I think. Other than that, no. It all happened so fast."

"What did he want?" So help him, if he'd tried to sexually assault her, he'd go ballistic.

"He said I had to leave town immediately or he'd kill me." She swallowed hard. "I believe he meant it." Her voice wavered a little bit as she spoke. She used a wet paper towel to remove the mascara and then reached into her little purse and began working to repair her eyes.

He tamped down his rage and took a deep breath.

When she'd finished, she looked normal except for the angry red marks on her throat.

"Amazing," he told her. Again, he struggled to keep his voice level. "Come on," he said, gently guiding her toward the exit. "We need to file a police report." Since the sheriff and several of the deputies were in attendance, finding one who was on duty wouldn't be difficult. "If we have to, we'll take this ballroom completely apart until we find him."

"No." Scarlett dug in her heels. "I don't want to disrupt the ball."

"Why not?" Eyeing her in disbelief, he shook his head. "Someone physically assaulted you. We need to figure out who and if it's tied in to the other incidents."

"I'm pretty sure it is." Her dry tone sounded calm. "I'll make a police report, but that's it. Clearly, this ball is something everyone in town looks forward to all year. I refuse to ruin that."

Frustration warred with admiration as he gazed down at her stubborn expression. "You mean it, don't you?"

"Yes."

"Fine. But promise me you'll keep an eye on the crowd and if you see him again, discreetly let me know."

"I will."

As they wound their way through the throng of people, Travis caught sight of the sheriff talking to Vivian. As usual, instead of a costume, Sheriff James had chosen to wear his uniform.

Travis smiled at his mother and touched the other man's shoulder. "Do you mind if we have a word with you? Privately?"

"Of course not." The sheriff's gaze sharpened. "Is there a problem?"

Before Travis could respond, Vivian gasped. "Scarlett? What happened to your neck?" Her shrill tone had several people turning.

"Shh." Scarlett shook her head. "That's what we

want to talk to the sheriff about. Please, we don't want to make a scene."

"Come with me." Sheriff James led them down the same hallway that led to the restrooms. He tried several doors, finally finding an unlocked office.

Once they were all inside, he closed the door and crossed his arms. "What's going on?"

Scarlett repeated what she'd told Travis. While she spoke, Vivian clutched Travis's arm.

"Would you recognize this person if we corralled all the men matching that description so you could view them?" Sheriff James asked.

"I doubt it," Scarlett replied. "Plus, I've already told Travis that I don't want to disrupt the ball."

"And I told her that's nonsense," Travis interjected. "Though I have to admire her for thinking of our townspeople first."

Eyes narrowed, Vivian glanced from Scarlett to Travis. "I agree with her. Whoever assaulted her has probably already left."

"We don't know that," the sheriff put in. "Since there are a lot of men in attendance with similar costumes, the perpetrator might figure he'd blend in. That's why I suggested rounding up any likely suspects now, before anyone has a chance to leave. No one who's bought a ticket ever goes home before the meal."

But clearly, judging from her stubborn countenance, Scarlett had made up her mind. "I just would like to file a police report and request extra protection," she said. "Because this person threatened to kill me if I don't leave town. Since I have no plans to go anywhere, I'm going to need police protection."

"Fine." The sheriff sounded resigned. "I'll need to

tape a statement from you later, once I round up a recorder. And I'll assign an extra unit to drive the area around the ranch, though that's the extent of what I can do."

"Perfect." Scarlett smiled, an utterly false, achingly brilliant smile that shredded Travis's heart. "Then let's go back to the ball and pretend nothing happened. I wonder if we still have our seats."

When she took Travis's arm as if she expected him to lead her back into the crowd, he almost refused. But one glance at the pleading look in her eyes had him nodding. "Let's go find out."

With Vivian trailing along silently behind them, they stepped back into the crowd. Naturally, someone had snagged their table, but Vivian caught sight of Amber and Mark across the room.

"It looks like Amber saved us some seats," she pointed out.

"That's great. I picked up her date's boutonniere for her. I'm sure she needs it." Scarlett changed direction, slipping through clusters of people with graceful ease.

When they reached the table, empty except for Amber and her date, his friend Mark, Travis saw she'd put little placeholders with the word *Reserved* on them on every seat.

"Great thinking," Vivian said. "Where did you get those?"

"I brought them with me." Amber beamed. "I saw someone do it last year and decided it was a great idea."

"It is." Scarlett dropped into her chair, rummaging in her clutch for the last florist's box. It had gotten slightly crushed, but seemed intact. After handing it over, she exhaled, clearly trying to relax. Travis took the seat next to her, leaving the final two spots for Vivian and Frank.

"Where's Frank?" he asked, looking around the room.

"Who knows?" Apparently unconcerned, Vivian shrugged and arranged herself in one of the seats. For her costume, she'd chosen a silky fringed dress the exact same blue as her eyes. She'd tied some sort of long scarf in her hair and wore huge dangling earrings. "I'm sure he'll be along shortly," she said. "Frank's never been one to miss a meal."

After pinning the flower onto her date's lapel, Amber stood, smiling. "If you'll excuse me, I need to make a trip to the ladies' room. Scarlett, do you want to go with me?"

Wide-eyed, Scarlett only stared. Her mouth moved, but nothing came out. An awkward silence fell. Vivian broke it by jumping back to her feet. "I'll go with you," she said. "We need to talk anyway." And she hustled Amber away.

"I love her costume," Scarlett mused, as if nothing out of the ordinary had just happened. She leaned across the table and held out her hand to Mark. "Hi, I'm Scarlett."

Realizing he'd forgotten to introduce them, Travis spoke up. "Sorry. Scarlett, this is my friend Mark. Mark, this is Hal's daughter, Scarlett."

They shook hands, murmuring the usual pleasantries. Mark offered to fetch everyone a round of drinks and, since theirs from earlier had vanished, Travis let him.

Once Mark had gone to the bar, Travis turned to Scarlett. Her expression blank, she gazed off into the distance. The instant she realized Travis was looking at her, she blinked and focused.

"Are you sure you're going to be all right?"

For an instant, he thought she would lie. Her lips parted and then she shook her head. "Honestly, I don't know. I'm still in shock. I'm hoping once the festivities start, they'll distract me."

He covered her hand with his. "I'll do my best to help," he promised, hating the way she trembled under his fingers. "I hope you like to dance."

His words had the desired effect. She stared at him, one corner of her mouth curving. "A man who enjoys dancing. How rare is that? Yes, I love to dance."

"Good. I call first dance. They start all that after the meal."

Arriving back from the bar in time to hear Travis's comment, Mark snorted. "Since when do you like to dance, Travis? In all the years I've known you, I've only seen you do a drunken two-step once."

Travis looked his friend directly in the eye. "Ever since I got lucky enough to hold this woman in my arms."

Vivian and Amber arrived back at the table, cutting off any response Mark might have been about to make. Amber appeared pale, which considering her affinity for goth makeup, meant she'd received a shock. Heck, they all had. Finding out someone really did want to hurt Scarlett was sobering.

By the time the buffet had been set up and everyone started forming a line, Scarlett seemed to have returned to normal. Vivian started scanning the crowd for Frank, frowning impatiently. "Oh well," she said, pushing to her feet. "I'm just going to eat without him. Whenever he finally shows up, he can fix his own plate."

Just as they reached the end of the long line, Vivian's phone rang. She answered, her annoyed expression changing to one of concern. "I'll be right there," she began. Then after listening for a few seconds, she tried to argue. "But…no, I think… Are you sure?"

When she ended the call and dropped her phone back into her purse, she shook her head, her expression dazed. "That was Frank. He says he started feeling sick and went outside. He started throwing up, so he took himself home. I offered to go look after him, but he said he'd rather be alone in his misery."

Travis squeezed his mother's shoulder. "I can relate. Especially with nausea. Leave him be and try to enjoy yourself."

Though she made a face, Vivian continued to wait in the line. When her turn came, she began making herself a plate.

"She'll be fine," Travis told Scarlett. "I'm surprised she even offered to go, considering how deathly afraid she is of catching someone else's germs."

"I heard that," Vivian snapped, though she was smiling.

As they made their way back to their table with their loaded plates, Kendra and a man who must have been her date stopped by. "Do you mind if we join you?" she asked, indicating Amber's and Mark's empty seats.

About to say he did mind, Travis smiled when Vivian beat him to it. "Those seats are taken," she said. "Amber and Mark are still getting their food."

"No worries." Kendra flashed an easy smile. Travis looked past her to her date, who appeared fixated on Scarlett.

"Are you okay?" he asked her, balancing his plate in one hand while adjusting his eyeglasses with the other. "Kendra told me what happened to you."

"I'm fine, thank you," Scarlett said, suddenly preoccupied with arranging her silverware. "Thanks for asking."

"No problem." He flashed his easy smile at the entire table before returning his attention to Scarlett. "It was great seeing you again," he told Scarlett. "Remember our agreement." Then Kendra dragged him away, leaving everyone staring at Scarlett.

Chapter 15

Scarlett just knew her feelings of guilt showed on her face. Not that she'd actually done anything wrong, but still… She got out her fork and knife and began rearranging food on her plate. Avoiding eye contact with Travis, she looked up, relieved, when Amber and Mark sat down.

"Was that…?" Amber asked.

"Yep." Vivian grimly cut her chicken into bite-size pieces. "She had a lot of nerve asking to sit with us."

Travis had gone ominously silent. When she dared to glance his way, she found him as fixated on his food as she'd been earlier. Mark kept shooting him quizzical looks, but apparently knew better than to ask. He probably thought Travis's sudden quiet moodiness was due to Kendra's appearance, but Scarlett knew it wasn't. Travis was wondering how Kendra's date had known Scarlett.

"So," Vivian spoke up. "What did that man mean when he asked you to remember your agreement? What agreement?"

"I..." Fumbling for the right words, Scarlett was surprised when Travis spoke up before she could explain.

"That's something Scarlett and I need to discuss in private," he said, his no-nonsense tone letting everyone at the table know that would be the end of any discussion.

Grateful, Scarlett knew better than to thank him. Soon enough, he'd be demanding she answer Vivian's question.

And while she knew she could—and would—explain, she also knew Travis would feel like she'd deliberately kept something hidden from him. In a way, he'd be right. Though she hadn't had malicious intent. She just hadn't known the right way to bring the subject up.

The band started setting up while the tables were being cleared. "They'll push a lot of the tables out of the way to make the dance floor larger," Vivian explained. "Just about everyone dances." She eyed her daughter. "Since my date got sick, would you mind sharing your date some so I can dance too?" Vivian pouted.

Flushing, Amber shrugged. The set of her mouth indicated she did mind, but also knew there was no way she could decline without making a scene over nothing.

Scarlett finally abandoned any attempt to pretend to be eating and allowed them to take her plate. She'd mostly been pushing food around anyway. Between being attacked and knowing she'd have to discuss her conversation with John Mellon with Travis, her stomach felt tied up in knots. She'd be lucky not to get sick.

Everyone had eaten their desserts. Though Travis had been kind enough to bring Scarlett a piece of chocolate cake earlier, she knew there was no way she could eat it. Amber's date, Mark, kept eyeing it, so she finally slid it across the table to him. He devoured it in a few bites, flashing her a thumbs-up in the way of thanks.

Finally, the band began tuning up their instruments. A man stepped up to the microphone and introduced the group, explaining that they would be taking requests also.

A slow song came on. Travis touched her arm, inclining his head toward the dance floor. Swallowing, she nodded and pushed to her feet.

As they joined the other couples, he swung her into his arms. She tried—oh, how she tried—to let his strength calm her, but she only felt even more unsettled.

"Were you going to tell me?" he murmured, nuzzling her ear with his mouth and making her shiver.

"There really wasn't anything to tell," she replied. Immediately she knew it was the wrong answer. He stiffened, though they kept moving in response to the music.

"Maybe we could talk about this later?" she ventured to ask.

"Oh, we will." He held her gaze. "Though I'd really rather know now exactly what I'm dealing with."

"I promise you, it's not what you think. Please, let's try to enjoy this ball as best as we can and we'll discuss it on the way home."

Judging from the grim set of his jaw, he wasn't happy, but he finally nodded. They danced the remainder of that song, but he led her back to the table to sit out the next one, which was more up-tempo.

"Oh, to be so young," Vivian said wistfully, watching as Amber and Mark strutted around the dance floor. Travis eyed his friend, but didn't comment.

Head aching, stomach clenching, Scarlett felt as if she might be sick. Unfortunately, the thought of going to the restroom again terrified her, so she sat glued to her chair and wished the night would end.

Finally, after the costume contest winners had been announced, it did. Vivian had left earlier to, as she put it, find something more fun. Amber and Mark could barely keep their hands off each other and Scarlett suspected if Travis wasn't Amber's brother, they would have gotten even more demonstrative. They took off a few minutes after Vivian, leaving Travis and Scarlett alone at their table.

She could only hope Travis would soon put her out of her misery.

But he didn't. People continually dropped by the table on the way out, wanting to meet Scarlett. The men flirted with her and the women fawned over him. She smiled until her cheeks hurt, and called up every acting skill she hadn't used since high school to pretend she was having a good time. Inside, she kept telling herself that she hadn't done anything wrong and once she explained that to Travis, all would return to normal. He'd stop looking at her as if she'd betrayed him and they could go back to the burgeoning relationship for which she'd had such good vibes.

At least she fervently hoped that would be the case.

Finally, as the band played the last song of the evening, Travis once again led her back onto the dance floor. Though his gaze seemed shuttered and his face expressionless, he held her close as they swayed to the music. She let herself pretend that they were together, in love. Closing her eyes, she gave herself over to the sensation of being held in his strong arms, of his powerful body shielding her. How desperately she wished that they could leave here and go somewhere private and make love to reaffirm this thing they'd been building between them.

When the song ended, the remaining attendees gave the band a sincere ovation. Travis tucked Scarlett's arm into his and led her outside.

The parking lot had emptied and there were only maybe thirty vehicles remaining. They walked in silence to his truck and Travis once again opened the passenger side door and helped her get up into the cab.

He waited until they'd pulled out from the parking lot to speak. "Were you planning on telling me that you had a meeting with a guy from Wave Oil?"

The resentment in his voice made her bristle. "First off, I wouldn't exactly call it a meeting. This guy came up to me on the street when I was in town earlier today and asked to buy me a coffee."

She took a deep breath, aware of how that sounded. "I know I probably shouldn't have gone, but it was downtown Anniversary, two doors from the coffee shop. It seemed safe, so I went." She shrugged. "He really just wanted me to talk to Hal."

"Are you going to?"

"Yes." She saw no reason to lie. "Hal's already mentioned his medical bills to me once. The way he spoke, he was already considering other alternatives."

"Not drilling." The angry set of Travis's mouth

matched his tone. "He and I have discussed it many times. He'd have to be on the verge of losing the HG Ranch to bankruptcy before he'd allow drilling on our land."

Our land. She lifted her chin. "Then you shouldn't have anything to worry about. Yet you seem to be. Why?"

"Because you're the daughter he never knew he had. If you ask him to do something, he might just do it to please you."

"Maybe so," she allowed. "But why do you think I would ask him to allow drilling if he really didn't want to?"

When he didn't answer, she made a face. "Please tell me you're not back to thinking I'm somehow in cahoots with Wave Oil."

"I don't know what to think." The rawness in his voice spoke of his inner turmoil. "All of this nonsense with Wave Oil has been going on long before you came here. It's dividing our town. Some people think it's great, a sign of progress. Others, mostly the farmers and ranchers whose land Wave wants to drill on, don't want any part of it."

"I'm beginning to feel that way myself," she said, her tone dry. "I didn't ask for any of this. Now I'm wondering if the perception that I'm on Wave Oil's side might have something to do with the threats and attacks against me."

From the way Travis inhaled, she could tell he hadn't thought of that.

"And one more thing," she said, forcing herself to be brave. "This…thing you and I have started. If you can ever get over your distrust of me, I can see it actually going somewhere."

"Bad timing." Again, Travis's expression had shut down. "You bringing that up now feels forced, as if you're trying to get close to me in order to sway me to Wave Oil's point of view."

Hurt and sorrow filled her as the impact of his words sank in. "That's exactly what I'm talking about. If anything comes between us, it will be your absolute refusal to believe I have ulterior motives. I think you'd better take me home."

He gave a tight nod and did exactly that. They didn't speak again the entire drive back.

Luckily, Hal had gone to bed and she made it to her room without having to answer any questions about how the evening had gone.

She spent a restless night, tossing and turning, struggling with feeling guilty for something she'd had no control over. Worse than that was Travis's reaction. Somehow, he felt justified in continuing to believe she was working with Wave Oil despite knowing her.

Still, she resolved to discuss everything with Hal, including the fact that after this, she was bowing out of any talks about drilling or not drilling.

After showering and dressing, she felt a bit more like herself. When she went downstairs to grab a cup of coffee, Hal was already there. He looked better than she'd ever seen him. He sat up straight, his gray hair combed, wearing a nice button-down Western shirt. When he smiled at her, his green eyes sparkled.

She stared. "You seem chipper this morning."

"Thank you. I feel pretty darn good." He took a deep

drink from his coffee mug. "I'm even thinking about having Delilah give that physical therapist fella a call. I want to try standing and walking again. I know I'll have to build up to it, but I actually feel good enough to try."

"That's fantastic." She kissed his cheek and went to make her own coffee.

"Did you have a good time at the ball?" Hal asked.

She stiffened. Glad she had her back to him, she carefully considered her answer. She didn't want to upset him by letting him know she'd been attacked yet she didn't want to lie. She decided to focus on the things she'd enjoyed.

"The costumes were amazing," she said, turning to face him with her mug in hand. "And they had a good band."

"Did you and Travis dance?"

"We did." She took an appreciative sip. "I had no idea there'd be such a crowd. Amber seemed to really like her date, even if she did have to let Vivian dance with him."

"She did?" Hal shook his head. "Why? What's that woman up to now?"

"Oh, Frank got sick, so Vivian didn't have a date to dance with. It was fine. She only danced with Mark twice."

"That means you didn't get to meet Frank." He sounded disappointed. "I was hoping to hear what you thought of him."

Taking a deep breath, Scarlett decided to go ahead and bring up meeting John Mellon.

"Hal, something sort of strange happened to me

when I was in town yesterday," she began. "I wanted to ask you a question."

"You look so serious," he said, pressing the remote to mute the TV. "What's going on?"

"When I was in town yesterday, a man named John Mellon approached me. He wanted to talk to me about allowing Wave Oil to drill on the ranch."

Hal's expression darkened. "Isn't that just like them? Targeting my daughter. I'm sorry, sweetheart. What did you tell him?"

"That I was the wrong person to talk to about that. I told him he needed to get with you. And he said Travis wouldn't allow it." She swallowed. "He insinuated that Travis is making decisions without your consent."

Hal snorted. "Sneaky SOB. Those oil companies will do anything to get their way."

Relieved, she smiled. "I take that to mean you directed Travis to decline any meeting with Wave Oil."

"The topic never came up," he admitted. "But Travis knows how I feel."

This bothered her. "Hal, I'm not trying to be intrusive, but this John Mellon guy knew you had tons of medical bills."

He bristled. "I do. But that's none of his beeswax."

"That's what I told him," she hastened to reassure him. "But he also said allowing a drilling site would enable you to pay them."

"Did he now?" Hal squinted at her. "Are you advocating for Wave Oil these days?"

"Now you sound like Travis," she grumbled.

"You told Travis this?" Hal's eyes went wide.

Slowly, she nodded. "Kendra dragged John Mellon

over to our table and he made a point out of bringing up the fact that we'd met. I'm sure she did it on purpose."

"No doubt." Hal's quick response felt gratifying. "But why are you even talking to me about it?"

"Because I promised John Mellon I would, since I don't see the harm in having an open-minded discussion."

"Which makes it sound like you're in agreement with Wave Oil."

Again, his words echoed Travis's.

"I'm not in agreement with anyone. Actually, I'm neutral. After this talk, I hope to never have to discuss this again." She took a deep breath. "My entire point of bringing this up is to let you know you have alternatives. One other one is me. Mom left me financially well-off. I'd be more than happy to take a look at your medical bills and see what I can do to get them paid off. If you need money, that is. If you don't, then pretend we never spoke."

Hal shook his head and unmuted the TV, indicating the conversation was over. Then, as she turned to leave the room, he silenced it once more. "I'm going to talk to Travis."

Surprised, she eyed him. "Why?"

"Because it's ridiculous how he's letting this Wave Oil thing drive a wedge between the two of you."

"Too late," she said, not bothering to hide her misery. "After he found out about the meeting with John Mellon last night, we talked."

Scowling, Hal shook his head. "How did he take that?"

"Not well." She grimaced. "Not well at all. He actually seems to believe I want to coerce you into signing a lease with Wave Oil for some sort of personal gain."

Hal sighed. "I'll talk to him," he said. "And, Scarlett, as much as I love you and am overjoyed to have you in my life, I do what I want to do. Travis should know this. It's long past time I cleared the air around here."

The morning after the ball, Travis found himself at loose ends. Vivian left to check on Frank, and Amber and Mike had plans to attend the Harvest Fair. He'd originally planned to ask Scarlett if she wanted to go with him. Delilah always entered several of the baking competitions and he'd really wanted to show up and cheer her on.

Oddly enough, he found he didn't want to attend alone. Despite the fact that he'd done so the last couple of years, the notion held no appeal now. He'd actually been looking forward to showing Scarlett around, to seeing her reaction to the best and most heartwarming displays that Anniversary had to offer.

When Hal called and asked Travis to stop by, Travis jumped at the chance. Not, he told himself, because he wanted to see Scarlett again, but so he could get out of the house. Then, because he'd never been in the habit of lying to himself, he admitted it was so he could see Scarlett again.

Proof that he was a fool.

When he pulled up in front of the house, Scarlett's car was gone. Oddly disappointed, he went inside and made his way through the empty living room, into the kitchen where he found Hal at the table, eating a large sandwich.

"Do you mind getting me a glass of milk?" Hal

asked. "Vivian made my lunch and tried to get me to drink a new kind of smoothie, but I had her put it in the fridge. I'm tired of pretending to like those damn things."

Grinning, Travis grabbed a glass and poured milk into it.

"Just so you know, Scarlett and I have been discussing whether or not to allow Wave Oil to drill," Hal drawled.

Travis spun around so fast he nearly tripped over his own feet. Milk sloshed onto his hand. As he stared at his stepfather, his stomach flip-flopped at the knowledge that he'd been right about her all along. Despite her denials, despite the way their bodies fit together. Despite everything. "You did?" he managed to keep his tone casual. "You sound as if you might actually be considering it. Do you mind if I ask why?"

"The same reason everyone else wants us to drill. Money." Hal sighed. "No one considers what allowing such an operation will do to the land or our livestock."

Which meant he *wasn't* considering it.

"I agree." Relieved, Travis let out a breath he hadn't even been aware he'd been holding.

"But Scarlett did bring up a good point," Hal continued, scratching his head. "Those medical bills keep piling up and I don't have any way to pay them. One small drill site and I could take care of them all, at least according to the man Scarlett met with."

Travis stared. "She told you about meeting with that guy from Wave Oil?"

"She did. She also mentioned she discussed it with you." Hal frowned. "I'm guessing they knew who she was and targeted her."

Shaking his head, Travis tried to tamp down his feeling of betrayal. Even after vehemently denying any involvement with Wave, Scarlett had still gone ahead and talked to Hal and tried to convince him to cooperate with Wave Oil.

He should have known his gut instincts were right. But he'd allowed himself to be taken in by her beauty and her sweet nature. Right. He nearly snorted out loud.

Some of his thoughts must have shown on his face.

"Son, do you even know Scarlett at all?" Hal asked.

"What do you mean?"

"Even an old man like me can see what's been happening between the two of you."

Surprised, Travis wasn't sure how to respond.

"Don't be an idiot," Hal continued. "Open your eyes and your heart. Just because Kendra turned out to be rotten to the core, doesn't mean Scarlett is."

"You might be a little bit biased," Travis responded. "I'm just struggling with the fact that she's been cozying up to Wave Oil."

"Has she?" Tilting his head, Hal gave him a hard look. "It seems to me like you're in a rush to convict her for something without any evidence that she's done it."

Frustrated, Travis dragged his hand through his hair. "Hal, she admitted to meeting with a guy from Wave Oil. And she talked to you about considering drilling. Tell me that she wasn't for it."

"She wasn't for it," Hal immediately responded. "In fact, she seemed neutral. She pointed out the truth that if I did allow drilling, I could pay my medical bills. And then she offered to pay them herself."

Stunned, Travis stared. "She did?"

"Yes. Her mother apparently left her well-off. She

doesn't have a horse in this race, Travis." Hal took a deep breath. "I made a will out long ago. When I die, everything goes to you, Travis. I have no plans to change that. Stop looking for excuses and let yourself recognize a good thing when you see it."

Not sure what to think about this, Travis went to the fridge to get himself a bottled water. He couldn't help but notice the large brownish-green shake sitting on the top shelf. "Do you want me to pour this out? That way you won't have to explain to Vivian why you didn't drink it."

"Nah." Hal pushed his empty plate away and drained the last of his milk. "She means well, you know. Give it here. I'll try to choke some of it down now that I've got something in my stomach. If I can't, then I'll pour it out myself."

"Sounds good." Travis put the shake down on the table. "Speaking of Scarlett, where is she?"

"She said something about meeting Amber in town for the fair. You should know she seemed really upset last night."

"Maybe I'll just go into town myself and see if I can meet up with her," Travis ventured, feeling cautiously optimistic.

"I think that's a great idea." Grinning, Hal motioned him to get going.

The fairgrounds were predictably crowded. Travis circled for a good twenty minutes before finding a parking spot. The weather was perfect, sunny with a cloudless sky and not too hot. Judging from the line of people waiting to buy tickets, this year's Harvest Fair might very well break attendance records.

Once he'd made it through the gates, Travis headed toward the building where they held the baking competitions. Since Delilah always entered, he figured he'd stop by and support her and maybe he'd luck out and find Scarlett and Amber there as well.

But Delilah said they'd been by earlier and were out exploring. She kissed his cheek and told him she hoped he would do right by Scarlett. "She's special."

Not sure how to react to that, Travis eyed the older woman. "I could ask what you mean, but I suspect I already know."

"Honey, everyone could see it but you. Plain as the nose in front of your face too. I think you've got some apologizing to do. If you're lucky, she'll forgive you."

If he was lucky indeed. Thanking Delilah, he walked away. He tried Scarlett's number, but the call rang and then went to voice mail. He left a message. The exact same thing happened when he called Amber. He figured they were either on one of the amusement park rides or someplace where the noise level made hearing the phone ring impossible.

Fine. He'd search them out on foot.

Two hours later, he was forced to admit defeat. Checking his phone, he saw he had no return calls. He'd been to the livestock barn, the sheepdog show, the amusement rides and carnival games, plus the huge exhibition hall where people sold everything from homemade bread to belt buckles.

He ate a corn dog and washed it down with a cold beer. After tossing his trash in the nearest bin, he'd turned and headed for the exit when his phone rang.

Scarlett.

Smiling, he answered. "Where are you? I've been all over the fairgrounds trying to find you."

"I'm already home," she said, the anguish in her voice wiping the smile from his face. "Hal had some kind of seizure again. I found him unresponsive. I called 911 and they're transporting him to the hospital. I'm about to head that way too."

"I'll meet you there," he said, ending the call and sprinting for his pickup.

Chapter 16

"I don't get it," Scarlett said, pacing back and forth in the ER waiting area. "He seemed to be doing so much better."

"It's weird," Amber agreed, checking her watch. "Mom and Frank are on their way too. Will was spending the day with them, and they're bringing him." She drew a deep, shuddering breath. "I just hope everyone gets here before it's too late."

"Don't even talk like that." Scarlett ordered sharply. "He will pull through, just like he did last time he had a seizure."

"I sure hope so." But Amber didn't sound too certain.

The front doors whooshed open and Travis came barreling through. He went straight to Scarlett and pulled her into his arms. She allowed herself to sag against him, trying to draw comfort from his strength.

"How is he?" Travis asked.

"Not good," she admitted, reluctantly disengaging herself from his embrace.

"Can I see him?"

"No. No one can go back there now. They're trying to save him." She broke down as she said the words.

"Here's Mom, Frank and Will," Amber cautioned. Hurriedly, Scarlett wiped at her streaming eyes, not wanting Will to see how upset she felt.

Vivian rushed inside, Will trotting after her. A tall, thin man with gray hair followed at a more sedate pace.

"What happened?" Vivian demanded. "He seemed so much better."

"I don't know," Scarlett answered. At least her voice wavered only slightly. "I got home from the fair and found him unconscious."

"I saw him a couple of hours ago," Travis interjected. "He was fine."

Scarlett eyed the tall man who stood silently behind Vivian. Something about him seemed familiar.

Noticing her staring, Vivian made quick introductions. "Scarlett, this is Frank. Frank, Scarlett."

"Pleased to meet you," Frank said, holding out his hand. His elegant demeanor seemed at odds with his flinty gaze. "Though I'd rather it be under different circumstances."

She swayed, hoping her expression gave away none of her mounting horror. Forcing herself to shake his hand, she stepped back until she bumped into Travis.

"Steady there," Travis said, wrapping one arm around her shoulders. "Are you okay?"

Nodding a bit too fast, she turned so that she faced him. Desperately trying to figure out a way to talk to him privately, she went with the most obvious one. "I think I need some fresh air."

"Come on," he replied, keeping one arm around her shoulders. "Y'all holler at us if you hear any news."

"We will," Amber promised, distracted by her son tugging at her and asking what was wrong with Grandpa.

Heart pounding, Scarlett attempted to breathe normally. Having Travis so close helped.

"It's him," she said, keeping her back to the ER window. "Frank. He's the guy who attacked me in the bathroom at the ball."

"Frank?" Travis squinted down at her. "Are you sure? He always makes a big deal out of being a pacifist."

"Positive." She shivered. "I could never forget that voice. And even though he had a mask on, he's the same height and size. Frank's the one who threatened me."

Before Travis could respond, Amber stuck her head out the door. "Come back inside. The doctor wants to talk to us."

Travis took her hand. "Come on." They followed Amber to where the doctor waited.

"Please follow me into the family conference room," the doctor said. Scarlett tensed. That meant bad news. She'd been through this before with her mother.

One of the aides offered to keep Will busy so they could talk. Amber agreed, her eyes full of tears. After the aide led Will away to get a snack from the vending machine, they all silently filed into the small room. A wooden table and eight chairs were the only furniture. A large box of tissues sat in the middle of the table.

"Have a seat," the doctor said. "Mr. Gardner is in kidney failure. We've tested his electrolytes and found ethylene glycol—antifreeze or some other household poison. Over time, this will crystallize in the kidneys and can be fatal. We've begun treatment to help with this. He's in the ICU now and it will be touch and go for a while. Any questions?"

They all looked at one other in stunned disbelief.

"Have you run this test before?" Vivian asked, her expression bewildered. "Because Hal has visited multiple hospitals and seen many doctors. No one has ever mentioned anything like this."

"Mr. Gardner has never had this test before as it's not part of routine blood work. We decided to try it just in case and we're glad we did."

His pager went off and he checked it, before looking back at Vivian. "It's possible this is a recent development. I've got to go. I'll leave you alone to discuss." The doctor exited the room, closing the door behind him.

"Someone poisoned Hal?" Amber asked, sounding bewildered. "Who? And how?"

"You did it," Frank said, pointing a shaky finger at Scarlett. "I imagine you couldn't wait for your father to die so you could claim your inheritance."

Scarlett stared back, letting her expression mirror her disbelief and fury. "Such blatant hate from the man who'd physically assaulted me is the last straw."

"Physically assaulted?" Vivian looked from Scarlett to Frank and back again.

"Yes. At the ball. It was him." Scarlett pushed to her feet, facing Frank down. "You're the one who attacked me when I went to the restroom. I don't know why, but I'm willing to bet you also tried to run me off the road and used fireworks to stampede the cattle."

"But Frank wasn't even at the ball," Amber interjected.

"Oh, he was." Crossing her arms, Vivian glared at her boyfriend. "He supposedly wasn't feeling well, so he left. But he was there."

"I recognized his voice," Scarlett told the older woman. "He had a mask on, so I couldn't see his face, but I'll never forget the voice. And his build. He attacked me. I'm positive it was him."

"You know what? I believe you." Judging by the tight set of her mouth, Vivian was trying to tamp down her own shock and fury. "I don't know why he would do such a thing, but I know you wouldn't lie."

"Thank you," Scarlett said. "And I also think Frank was somehow poisoning Hal."

Frank opened and closed his mouth. Before he could even attempt to respond, Vivian grimaced, eyeing him with fresh horror. "It was you," she said, pointing at him with a shaking finger. "You poisoned him. Those shakes you made for Hal. You put antifreeze in them. What'd you do, double up the dose on the one I left him this morning?"

"That's why Hal was feeling better," Travis said. "He'd stopped drinking those smoothies. When I was there earlier, he had me give him that giant one that was in the fridge."

"What if someone else had drank that?" Amber demanded to know. "What if you'd poisoned me or Will? Or Travis or Scarlett? What kind of monster are you?"

Scrambling from his chair, Frank lunged toward the door. Travis jumped him, grabbing his arm and spinning him back around. "Sit." Travis ordered. "What my mother says makes sense. You poisoned Hal and tried to hurt Scarlett. Amber, call the police."

"I'm already on it," Amber replied, phone up against her ear.

"I demand an explanation." Arms crossed, Vivian glared at her boyfriend. "What did Scarlett or Hal ever do to you?"

Staring back at her, his mouth working, at first it seemed as if he wouldn't or couldn't answer. Finally, he sighed and shook his head. "You just don't understand. I didn't do any of this for me. I did it for you."

"That makes no sense." Clearly, Vivian wasn't buying that.

"Once Hal dies, the ranch will revert to you. You were his wife after all and he never remarried. Unless he changed his will to let his newfound daughter inherit it all. I wanted her to leave before he got the chance to do that." Frank spread his hands, his tone conciliatory. "You and I would have married and let Wave Oil put as many drills as they liked. We'd use the money to travel. I know you've always wanted to see the world as much as I do. Paris. Rome. The Greek Islands. Just imagine it."

Judging by Vivian's repulsed expression, she had no plans to imagine any of what he described. "I hope you rot in hell for what you've done," she cried. "How can you justify murdering someone just so you could travel? How could you?" She turned her tortured gaze to her son. "Plus, Hal changed his will years ago. The ranch will go to Travis when Hal passes." Blinking back tears, she shook her head. "I can't believe this."

"The police are here," Amber announced, holding

up her phone. "I stayed on the phone with dispatch, just in case. I'm going to go get them."

Frank thrashed about, trying to struggle, but Travis effortlessly kept him in place. Though they were of similar height, Travis easily outweighed the older man.

Amber returned, leading two uniform police officers. Travis quickly explained what was going on, including Frank's admission of guilt. "Everyone witnessed it," he said. "And in addition, Scarlett would like to file assault charges against him for attacking her at the ball. She'd already made a police report."

"Is that true, Frank?" one of the cops asked.

"I want an attorney," Frank replied. "I'm not saying another word until I speak with a lawyer."

They read him his rights and then cuffed his hands behind him before leading him away. Once they'd gone, Vivian sank down into a chair and put her hands over her face. "This is all my fault," she moaned. "I brought Hal those smoothies and encouraged him to drink them."

"Mom, it's not." Amber squeezed her mother's shoulder. "You didn't know. You thought you were helping him."

"She's right," Travis said. "Don't beat yourself up about this. What we need to do now is focus on getting Hal well."

"I wonder if they'll let us see him." Restless, Scarlett knew if she didn't get out of the little room, she'd lose it. Bad things happened in these consultation rooms. She'd had her fill of those. Time to move on to good.

"I'm going to go ask the nurse," she said, heading for the door. Everyone else filed out silently behind her, following her to the nurses' station.

"One family member at a time can visit in the ICU," the nurse said. "And we ask that you don't stay very long. We need to focus on monitoring and healing. He's in room four."

"Understood," Travis replied, when Scarlett found she couldn't speak past the sudden lump in her throat. "Scarlett, you go first."

Though she turned in the direction the nurse pointed, Scarlett stumbled. Travis took her hand, engulfing it with his much larger one. "Come on. I'll go with you but I'll wait outside the room."

More grateful than she could express, she drew on his strength and made her way down the hallway. Though he had no way of knowing, her past memories mingled with the present, filling her with sorrow and apprehension. It hadn't been very long since she'd found herself in a similar place in Georgia, walking toward the ICU to see her mother.

"Here we are." Travis pointed to the room number. "I'd go with you if I could, but I don't want to take a chance on us all getting thrown out for breaking the rules."

Gazing up at him, she managed a smile, though she still gripped his hand. "Thank you," she said. "It's been a crazy day."

And then she made herself let go of the man who was rapidly becoming her lifeline and opened the door.

Inside, Hal lay with his eyes closed, attached to several beeping machines. She went closer, her heart aching, still trying to fathom how someone could have deliberately hurt this man.

Dropping into the hard plastic chair next to the bed,

she leaned over and took his wrinkled hand. "I just found you, Dad. I refuse to let you leave me so soon."

She could have sworn his eyelids fluttered, but when nothing else happened, she figured she'd imagined it. "Get well," she ordered, planting a light kiss on his forehead. "I'll let the rest of your fan club take a peek at you now."

Though technically obeying the nurse's request of one visitor at a time, Travis watched through the side window where the ICU nurse observed and made notes as Scarlett talked to an unconscious Hal. When she leaned over and kissed her father's forehead, Travis's eyes stung. He'd been wrong about so many things, and nearly let his own stupidity completely ruin any chance he had at happiness.

He could only hope it wasn't too late.

Scarlett came out, wiping her eyes. "Your turn," she said. "I'll go get Vivian and Amber. I'm sure they'll want to see him too." She rushed off before he could comment.

In the hospital bed inside the room full of machines and screens and electronic sounds, Hal looked smaller somehow. And too damn vulnerable.

Throat aching, Travis approached his stepfather. While he'd known this day would eventually come, he wasn't ready for it to be now.

There were a hundred things he'd never said. If he got the chance, he vowed to say them, no matter how difficult doing so might be.

Glancing behind him, he saw Scarlett had returned with Vivian and Amber. He slipped quietly out of the room and put his arms around his weeping mother. "It's not your fault," he reassured her. "You didn't know."

While he comforted Vivian, Scarlett took Will's hand while Amber went into the room. A moment later, a nurse came along and shooed Amber out. "Just for a moment," she said. "I need to check a few things."

Amber's mouth worked and her eyes glistened with unshed tears. She retrieved her son and informed everyone that they'd be in the waiting room. Then she hustled Will off, her head down and her shoulders bowed.

Seeing this, Vivian straightened. "Is he conscious?" she asked. When Travis shook his head no, she nodded. "I will never forgive myself for this."

The nurse came out just then, leaving the door open so Vivian could go inside. With her shoulders back, Vivian lifted her chin and marched on inside, as if she intended to do battle with Hal's illness and physically yank him back from the brink of death.

Watching her, Scarlett sighed. "So much pain, all because of one man's greed."

"I know." He took her hand, tearing his gaze away from the room. "Wouldn't it be amazing if Vivian can somehow get Hal to regain consciousness?"

"It would." A half smile hovered on her lips. "That would be awesome."

But Hal didn't wake. A few minutes later, Vivian emerged, her expression sober. "Let's go," she said. "I know Amber needs to get Will home. I'd also like a shower and a nap. We can take turns sitting up here with him."

"You all go ahead." Travis kissed his mother's cheek. "I'm going to stay here for a bit."

"I'll stay with you," Scarlett said.

Vivian looked from one to the other. "Call me if anything changes, okay?"

Travis promised he would. Together, he and Scarlett watched as Vivian walked away.

"Why don't you two wait in the lounge?" the nurse suggested. "We have a few more things we need to do with Mr. Gardner. The cafeteria is closed since it's the weekend, but there are numerous vending machines. We also have free coffee in the lounge if you want that."

They thanked her and turned to head that way. Scarlett slipped her hand in his as they walked silently toward the waiting area.

At this moment, the room was mostly empty. A large coffee urn sat in one corner. Travis considered getting a cup, but he remembered seeing a coffee shop near the lobby.

"Sit for a minute," Scarlett urged. "I don't know about you, but I did a lot of walking today and need to rest."

"I'll be back," he told her. He wasn't sure why, but he knew he needed to keep moving.

Once he reached the lobby, he saw the coffee shop, but he kept going. Down long corridors, he reached the closed cafeteria, saw the entrance to the day surgery clinic, turned around there and made his way back to the main lobby. He purchased a couple of large coffees and doctored Scarlett's up the way she liked it.

When he returned to the ICU waiting lounge, he found Scarlett asleep, pillowing her head with her hands. Setting the coffee down carefully on the table next to her, he stood looking down at her, his heart both broken and full.

Hal had been right. Someone like Scarlett didn't come along very often. Travis had been a fool. And like Vivian, he felt his own measure of guilt over what had happened.

"All along, I thought I was taking care of everyone," he quietly told a still sleeping Scarlett. "Protecting everyone. Instead, I've let down two of the people I care about the most. You and Hal."

Scarlett opened her eyes, the vivid green a shock of color in her pale face. "You didn't let me down," she told him, sitting up and blinking. "Nor Hal. Please don't allow yourself to even think like that. None of this was your fault. Or Vivian's." Her gaze met his. "Must be a family trait," she quipped. "Blaming yourself for things that are completely out of your control."

He'd never loved her more. Wondering if she could see the emotion in his eyes, he realized he couldn't leave something so important to chance. He sat down next to her, leaning over her to place his coffee next to hers.

"I love you," he said. "More than I ever believed it was possible to love someone."

To his consternation, her beautiful eyes filled with tears. "Come here." Voice rough, he gathered her as close as the hard plastic chairs would allow. "Is it really so terrible, me telling you I love you?"

"Of course not." Her watery smile made him ache to kiss her. "I—"

A nurse poked her head in the waiting room, forestalling whatever else Scarlett might have been about to say. "He's awake. I'm not sure for how long, though. But if you want to see him, now would be a good time."

Together they pushed to their feet and walked side by side through the double doors after the nurse.

"You both can go in," she told them quietly. "Just don't tell anyone I said so."

Grateful, Travis nodded. Still holding on to Scarlett's hand, they entered the small room.

Sure enough, Hal's eyes were open. They'd propped up the back of his bed and he semireclined. He was still hooked up to multiple machines, but he turned his face toward them, clearly hearing them come in.

"Hey there," Scarlett said. "You scared us for a minute or two."

"Sorry." Hal eyed his daughter, clearly noting the way she and Travis held hands. When he met Travis's gaze, he managed a lopsided smile. "Glad to see you took my advice," he said.

"What advice?" Scarlett asked.

"He told me to stop being afraid to go after what I wanted," Travis replied, squeezing her hand. "He was right."

Another doctor came in. "I heard you were feeling better," he told Hal. "So I thought I'd come in and see for myself. We're flushing your kidneys out now, getting all the toxins out of your system."

Though Hal nodded, his eyes had started drifting closed. By the time the doctor finished his exam, Hal had gone to sleep.

The next couple of days passed in a blur of hospital and home. Travis tried not to allow himself to be bothered by the fact that Scarlett had not told him she loved him, or reacted in any way—positively or negatively—to his declaration of love.

They took shifts, sometimes going in small groups.

Vivian, Amber, Travis and Scarlett. Day by day, hour by hour, Hal continued to improve.

"No lasting damage," one of the doctors told Travis. "He's lucky."

Damn lucky. They all were.

And if Scarlett seemed different, more remote somehow, Travis tried to chalk it up to the constant trips to the hospital and the fact that he was trying to keep the ranch running without his active supervision. They barely had a moment alone together. He wondered if she felt as exhausted as he did.

Finally, four days after he'd been rushed to the ER, Hal was discharged and ready to go home. He still needed his wheelchair, though physical therapy had been scheduled so he could regain strength in his legs.

Travis went alone to pick Hal up. Scarlett, Vivian and Amber were at the main house, putting the finishing touches on a welcome home party.

"About time you showed up," Hal groused. "I can't wait to blow this Popsicle stand. I want my life back to normal."

"Me too." Travis grinned. "You have no idea how badly. I haven't been on horseback since this entire thing started."

"Are you serious?" Hal frowned. "Who's been looking after the ranch?"

"My team," Travis promptly replied. "They're well-trained and hardworking and I trust them. They've done a great job these past few days."

The nurse arrived, pushing a wheelchair. After handing Travis an envelope with all the signed paperwork in it, she turned to Hal. "Are you ready, young man?"

Hal grinned. "I am. It feels good to be wearing real clothes after so long in that awful hospital gown."

While the nurse wheeled him to the exit, Travis went and got his truck. Once Hal sat securely inside, they started for home.

"Delilah's been cooking since yesterday morning," Travis informed his stepfather. "She's forbidden any of us from even tasting anything, so it's been torture. The house smells like heaven."

Laughing, Hal rubbed his hands together in glee. "I can't wait. Food hasn't tasted right for a while. I'm guessing because of Frank's poison."

Travis refused to let anything darken this day. "He's in jail, you're getting better and you have family who love you who are putting on a hell of a party to welcome you home. Let's not even say his name today, okay?"

"Okay," Hal agreed. "I hope Delilah made fried chicken. She knows that's my favorite."

Not wanting to tire Hal, they'd kept the gathering small. Just family and a few close friends. Amber had invited Mark, letting Travis know they were a couple. And true to Hal's wish, fried chicken was on the menu, along with barbecue ribs, potato salad and fried okra. Two large pitchers filled with sweet tea and fresh lemonade sat alongside two pies and a huge coconut cake.

Hal gorged himself until he could barely keep his eyes open. Though Travis tried to get a private word with Scarlett, she kept herself busy helping serve food and then all of the women pitched in to clean up.

Life returned to normal, in a way. Travis had a hundred chores to check on, while Vivian, Amber and Will spent every free moment up at the main house with Hal and Scarlett. Travis didn't mind. He knew everyone would settle down after a while.

Despite all the hectic activity going on, Travis managed to take a minute to drive into Longview to buy a ring. While Anniversary had a decent jewelry store, he didn't want tongues to start wagging before he had a chance to propose.

Finally, after Hal had been home three days, when his physical therapist showed up to begin his first session, Vivian and Amber took off. Delilah had to run errands in town, and Travis got a chance to finally be alone with Scarlett.

He caught sight of her slipping from the house to go for a walk, something she hadn't been able to do in a while.

"Hey," he called out, stepping outside. "Do you mind if I join you?"

She shrugged, waiting for him to catch up. "Not at all. I just needed some fresh air to clear my head."

When he finally reached her, they fell into step together and started out down the long drive.

"How have you been?" he asked.

"Fine." She blinked, tilting her head as she gave him a sideways glance. "How about you?"

The casual mundaneness of the question had him struggling to suppress a smile. He felt giddy and nervous, his heart already pounding long before he figured out a way to ask her the big question. "I feel like you've been avoiding me."

She met his gaze and swallowed. "You're right. I have."

"Why?" His voice came out tight. He tried like hell to ignore the sudden knot in his stomach, but he couldn't shake the premonition she was about to tell him she didn't feel the same way.

"Because of Hal." She waved her hands, appearing to struggle to find the right words. "What you told me is big. Important. And life-changing. I didn't want us to make such major decisions while in the midst of a crisis. We deserve better." She swallowed again, drawing his gaze to the graceful lines of her throat. "Plus I didn't want this *thing*—whatever it is—to be because of Hal."

"Because of Hal?"

"Yes. Sometimes when people are faced with the possibility of great loss, they reach out for something, anything, to make them feel better."

Staring at her, he wasn't sure how to respond.

"What?" she asked, frowning slightly.

"That's nonsense," he said. "Take it from me, who apparently has become a master at making up excuses. Hal's part of our lives. Hopefully, he'll continue to be for a long, long time. What's between us has never been because of Hal, and you know that."

Eyes wide, she slowly nodded. "You're right," she whispered. "But I wanted you to be sure."

"I'm sure. But are you?" Finally, he decided he might as well just say it. "I don't know how you feel," he admitted. "About me, that is."

"You don't?" Her incredulous expression made him work to suppress a smile. "Seriously?"

The knots inside him had already begun to ease. "Yes, seriously."

She shook her head. "How could you honestly not know how much I love you? I've shown you in every way I possibly could."

"Maybe I just need to hear you say the words." He crossed his arms, no longer feeling as vulnerable. Instead, he just felt certain. Certain of what he wanted and needed and could not live without.

"Fine." Her smile lit up her eyes and his heart. She stepped closer, stopping just a foot away. "I. Love. You. Travis Warren. With every ounce of my heart."

Though he ached to kiss her, no way did he plan to quit until he'd heard everything he wanted to hear. "How would you feel about making the ranch your permanent home? Anniversary really could use an art gallery. And I really could use a wife."

"*That's* how you plan to propose?" she asked, clearly torn between laughter and incredulity.

Heart singing, he shook his head. "No. *This* is how I plan to propose." And he dropped to one knee, digging out a small velvet box from his pocket. "Scarlett Kistler, will you marry me?"

"Yes!" she all but shouted. "Of course I'll marry you."

Opening the box, he slipped the ring on her shaking finger. And then he did what he'd been aching to do all along. He kissed her.

* * * * *

Don't miss out on other great suspenseful reads from Karen Whiddon:

The Texas Soldier's Son
Wyoming Undercover
The Texan's Return
Rock-a-Bye Rescue

Available now wherever Harlequin Romantic Suspense books and ebooks are sold!

COMING NEXT MONTH FROM

HARLEQUIN®

ROMANTIC suspense

Available May 7, 2019

#2039 A COLTON TARGET

The Coltons of Roaring Springs

by Beverly Long

A secret child, dangerous storms and an outside threat no one saw coming. Can Blaine Colton and his high school sweetheart, Tilda Deeds, keep their son safe and rekindle the simmering connection from their youth?

#2040 CAVANAUGH COWBOY

Cavanaugh Justice

by Marie Ferrarella

Looking for a break from his sometimes bleak life as a homicide detective, Sully Cavanaugh heads to Forever, Texas. But his quiet vacation is turned upside down when a body turns up—and by the beautiful ranch foreman Rachel Mulcahy, who works her way into the investigation.

#2041 SPECIAL FORCES: THE RECRUIT

Mission Medusa

by Cindy Dees

Tessa Wilkes has trained to become a Special Forces operator for her entire adult life...that is until she's unceremoniously tossed out of the training pipeline. But the gorgeous Spec Ops trainer Beau Lambert offers her the chance of a lifetime: to become part of a highly classified, all-female Special Forces team called the Medusas.

#2042 SOLDIER PROTECTOR

Military Precision Heroes

by Kimberly Van Meter

Zak Ramsey, part of the Red Wolf Elite protection squad, has the fate of the world resting in his hands with his latest assignment—keeping Dr. Caitlin Willows alive. She is the lead scientist reverse engineering a cure for the world's most deadly bioweapon—and there are many who wish to see her fail!

Tessa Wilkes has trained to become a Special Forces operator for her entire adult life...that is until she's unceremoniously tossed out of the training pipeline. But the gorgeous spec ops trainer Beau Lambert offers her the chance of a lifetime: to become part of a highly classified, all-female Special Forces team called the Medusas.

Read on for a sneak preview of the first book in New York Times *bestselling author Cindy Dees's brand-new Mission Medusa miniseries,* Special Forces: The Recruit.

Hands gripped Tess's shoulders. Lifted her slowly to her feet. Her unwilling gaze traveled up Beau's body, taking in the washboard abs, the bulging pecs and broad shoulders. A finger touched her chin, tilting her face up, forcing her to look him in the eyes.

"We good?" Beau murmured.

Jeez. How to answer that? They would be great if he would just kiss her and forget about the whole "don't fall for me" thing. She ended up mumbling, "Um, yeah. Sure. Fine."

"I don't know much about women, but I do know one thing. When a woman says nothing's wrong, something's always wrong. And when she says she's fine like you just did, she's emphatically not fine. Talk to me. What's going on?"

She winced. If only he wasn't so direct all the time. She knew better than to try to lie to a special operator—they all had training that included knowing how to lie and how to spot a lie. She opted for partial truth. "I want you, Beau. Right now."

"Post-mission adrenaline got you jacked up again?"

Actually, she'd been shockingly calm out there earlier. Which she was secretly pretty darned proud of. Tonight was the first time she'd ever shot a real bullet at a real human being. At the time, she'd been so focused on protecting Beau that it hadn't dawned on her what she'd done.

But now that he mentioned it, adrenaline was, indeed, screaming through her. And it was demanding an outlet in no uncertain terms.

"I feel as if I could run a marathon right about now," she confessed. She risked a glance up at him. "Or have epic sex with you. Your choice."